KISSING STRANGERS

JUDY SAVINAR

ILLUMIFY
MEDIA.COM

Contents

Introduction

If the title has led you to believe you've opened a book of torrid romance stories, I'm sorry I misled you. But don't go away. Instead, I present you with stories filled with the torrid emotions of ten women, women of a certain age, each seeking to overcome their situational adversity.

If we can share a nod of understanding when I tell you those misfortunes include children leaving the nest, elder parent care, losing one's mind in divorce, sitting by a toxic person on a plane, then you'll find this book filled with cozy familiarities. The coziness, however, won't last long.

The settings and characters of these stories vary, and as ordinary as their situations appear, ordinary is left at the door as their stories unfold. Watch for the twists and turns these women take in their pursuit of finding equilibrium in their lives. Threaded throughout is the universal struggle for each character's emotional growth, dignity, and self-respect.

My inspiration for these stories came from women I know and have known. As baby boomers, our parents taught us to toe the line, keep your head down, and set a course. BUT and I read between the lines very well, better you should meet someone, get married, and have children, so toe until you accomplish that. Unfortunately, the cultural revolution of the 60s and 70s stirred the pot of how things were done and many of us boomers went off the rails.

We adapted and over time, we developed a toughness. We no longer lived within the gutter guards of a predictable life. Through divorce(s), death, birthing children, not birthing children, careered or not, women everywhere have persevered through the disappointments, hard work, and happiness of the path they've chosen. We weren't always prepared, sometimes totally unprepared, but consistently and determinedly we pushed through to move up the meter on the happiness scale.

Each of the ten stories is titled by a woman's name distinctive as her story. We begin with Lorna. Newly divorced and airplane bound for Omaha, Lorna's seatmate shares a remarkable tale that shatters her sedate world. How does she make peace with what she knows? Next, we're introduced to Bianca, Tootsie, Louise, and Stephanie, whose obsession with a Barbie doll staves off her depression, but is it sustainable?

Following them comes, Lourdes, Amy, Joy, and Meg. Meg, who killed her husband, is haunted by his presence, which threatens not only her mental health but her daughter's life. Millicent ends the collection. Her lifelong friendship with Dotty endures jobs, marriages, children, and divorce. But when one of them receives a deadly diagnosis, how will the friends cope?

Confronted at pivotal moments by personal showdowns, the women tap into their inner strength to rise above their situations. My intention is that you will cheer for these post-menopausal characters without judgement but with empathy and understanding. And, after reading, be left with bits that niggle you at night. Like a shadow passing in your peripheral vision, something to keep you questioning what you saw, or if you saw anything.

All my life I've been submerged in words. From a young kid making up stories for my little brother, through school writing programs, eventually graduating in creative writing from the University of Colorado.

After moving to San Francisco, I became a copywriter, writing ads from bras to Levi's pants, and publishing stories in magazines. Most recently, I've surrounded myself by books as a librarian in a middle school. Nothing makes me happier than writing, reading, or matching books to people.

Thank you for picking my book to read. I have lived with these characters for a long time, and they need to be read. The wait has made some of the women a little crazy; perhaps you'll notice.

Lorna

Lorna handed her boarding pass to the ticket agent. She needed to put distance between herself and her impossible marriage. Or was it distance from her divorce? Either way, that plane needed to fly her away.

After checking in, she wheeled her bag to a chair and sat down. For the hundredth time that day, she checked Omaha's weather on her phone. Snow followed by sunshine. *Perfect.* Overhead, a voice announced boarding for her flight. She felt heart-pumping giddy as she joined the queue waiting to shuffle onto the plane.

Lorna found her window seat and settled in. With her book and reading glasses on her lap, she studied the line of passengers boarding the plane, assessing each for who'd end up next to her. A middle-aged gentleman in an expensive suit, earbuds in his ears, and a diving board for a chin winked at her and walked past. *Oh, well, so be it*, Lorna thought, disappointed. Behind him, a doughnut-shaped, genderless teenager, eyes locked on an iPad, ricocheted off the seats as they moved up the aisle. On their heels, their maple-bar-shaped parent growled, "Pay attention." Up next, a tiny woman with a mop of too-black-for-her-age hair and red lipstick that bled beyond her lips halted in front of Lorna's row. A crow tattoo spanned her chest. Her low-cut black t-shirt left little to the imagination, and from the looks of things, the crow had nothing to perch on. As the diminutive woman compared her boarding pass to the numbers above the aisle seat, the frayed straps of her tattered bowling-ball bag cut into her arm. She stuffed the pass into her jeans pocket, brushed off the empty seat, and plopped down next to Lorna. A deep sigh blew from her smeared lips. She hefted the bag onto her lap, untangled her arm from its straps, and rested her arms on top. A sour stink wafted from her area. Lorna felt compelled to watch her the way you would a train wreck.

"Goodness!" the woman said, turning full-face toward Lorna. "Packed flight. I was afraid I was going to miss it. I get so worked up on travel days. I don't fly often and rarely by myself because I don't like to travel alone, but this trip, let's say, I had to. Need to get to Milwaukee tomorrow and coordinating layovers, what a pain in the butt. Oh dear, I'm blabbing, aren't I? My husband hated it when I blabbered, hated it. And where are my manners? Sandy," she said as she extended her bony hand, ribboned with blue veins, toward Lorna. Her red fingernails matched her lips. An onyx ring hung on the side of her left-hand index finger, too bulky to stay upright. "Sandy, Sandy Villman. Wait, not Villman. Ha! Where's my head? Villman was my husband's name. Now it's Sandy Vexlend. Sounds the same, but really, it's not."

Ignoring the outstretched hand, Lorna opened her book and smiled at Sandy, then stuck her nose in her book. *I'm not spending the next two-plus hours talking to you,* she thought. *Not feeling it—you're a hot mess—no thanks.* She relaxed her shoulders, wrinkled her brow, and tried to figure out where she'd left off.

Faster than Lorna could find her place, Sandy started up again. "Oh, I love to read. I read a book a week. Well, not now, with so much to do, but I used to. A book a week. Not all fiction either. No, I read books about all sorts of things. I do love a good mystery, don't you? Birds too, lots of bird books. Love books on astrology. Hey, I can do your chart. I love doing charts. Wait." Sandy leaned around to face Lorna, cupped her hands in front of Lorna's head and moved them back and forth. "Bet you're a Taurus." She dropped her hands and sat back. "OK, fiction or nonfiction? No wrong answer, I'm just saying I read both." Sandy scooted her bag higher on her lap. Her head, pressed into the headrest, rolled toward Lorna. "I just love to read." Her broad smile revealed enormous teeth, not necessarily yellow, but brownish near her gums. *Probably a smoker*, Lorna thought. Sandy persisted. "Which is it, fiction or non-fiction?"

Lorna reluctantly returned her smile. A longer gaze revealed Sandy's deep wrinkled face under a thick chalky foundation, topped with a slab of orange on each cheek. Black eyeliner and heavy mascara encircled her goopy green eyes. Not wanting to appear rude by gaping, Lorna refocused her eyes back on her book and answered, "Both." *She is one scary-looking gal,* she thought and adjusted her reading glasses on her nose. "And by the way, I'm an Aries, not a Taurus."

A flight attendant spoke over the loudspeaker, instructing everyone to stow bags under their seats or in the overhead compartments and prepare for takeoff. Another flight attendant, whose nametag read "Dawn," a pert blonde with enormous diamond earrings, leaned into Lorna and Sandy's row and instructed Sandy to tuck her tote in the space underneath the seat in front of her. However, if she wanted, Dawn would be happy to put it in the overhead compartment for her.

"No thank you, you'll not touch this bag. This is precious cargo; only I touch it, understand? Too precious." Sandy clutched the bag to her chest. "Hell no." Sandy shook her head back and forth with her eyes closed like a petulant child, toes kicked out in front of her. "Ho no, no, no."

"That's fine, ma'am. But you'll need to stash it under the seat. All bags must be stowed for takeoff and landing. Sorry." Dawn smiled with Chiclet-white teeth as she spoke. "For your safety."

"Under the seat then," Sandy said and cradled the satchel to the floor like it was a baby and gently slid it under the seat in front of her. She patted its top. Lorna noticed electrical tape held the bag's bottom together. *Hardly worth the trouble*, she thought. The thing looked and smelled nasty. Lorna checked on her oversized cocoa-colored leather carry-on positioned underneath the seat in front of her. A prized gift to herself for the trip. She opened her book and scanned the page.

Dawn thanked Sandy and disappeared. The voice of another flight attendant began the takeoff spiel as the plane motored to the runway. The plane's high-pitched whir competed for airtime.

"I tell you, I get so damned mad at airline rules and regulations. They think they own you just because you buy a seat on their plane. Well, not me, no sirree. Hell to the no," Sandy said and leaned into Lorna, so close that their arms touched. Lorna shirked hers away. Sandy was oblivious. "Aries, huh? Do you have a husband? Married?" She stretched to fiddle with the fan. The seatbelt restrained her from full upward mobility. With a frustrated grunt, she dropped down in her seat and gnawed at a cuticle.

"Pardon me?" Lorna had just found her place in her book. She marked the spot with her finger and made a point of exhaling hard. She turned her nose down at Sandy as she peered over her reading glasses. The airplane engines ramped up into an erupting volcano, shaking the plane. "Sorry, reading," she said quietly, hoping the airplane fracas would squash Sandy's interest.

"Do you have a husband? You know, like married with a husband?" Sandy said loudly over the plane's deafening take off. Her eyes dropped to the finger where Lorna's wedding ring would have been.

Lorna rubbed her ringless finger with her thumb; she was divorced now. But after twenty years, the indented, pale skin from wearing a wedding band told another tale from her not-too-distant past.

"Looks like a ring used to be there, though, so unless you're one of those types that occasionally goes without, maybe you like to have affairs, I don't know." Sandy nudged Lorna's arm and winked. "Or you don't like your husband much, or you've been married so long you don't care, or maybe you're divorced. Are you divorced?" Sandy's eyes narrowed as she twisted her whole body toward Lorna. Lorna pressed her head back against the headrest. "I don't mean to get personal, of course." Her eyes fixed on Lorna as she fidgeted with her large ring. The toes of Sandy's pointy shoes tipped toward her satchel. "Divorced, I'm guessing."

"I'm divorced," Lorna said, lifting the book in front of her face.

Lorna thought, *I must look like a lonely, sad, middle-aged woman. But that's who I am. Sad, lonely, and middle-aged.* Lorna touched her gray hair. *I need to color it again. I should've never stopped. All those married years, pretending not to age. But now I must look like a spinster. I'll make an appointment with June's girl when I get to Omaha.*

Sandy punctured her thought bubble.

"I wanted a divorce once. At first, I loved him. I really did. I tried hard, but he got surly. Mean surly. He drank, you see, a lot. A shit-ton, in fact. Not at first, but a couple years into it. Man, he could drink. After the incident—well, never mind about that. But he drank so much sometimes, I'd leave him on the floor in his own stink. Sometimes he'd smell so bad I'd leave the windows open and wake up to snow in my house. For real, I'm not shitting you. Snow on my kitchen floor. An inch, well, maybe not an inch, but a half an inch at least. Yep, half inch. So, I get the divorce thing. I really do. You may not think I do, but I do." Sandy narrowed her watery eyes at Lorna. "So, what's your story?" She picked at her nails.

"I'm actually trying to read one." Lorna cleared her throat. "If you don't mind," Lorna said. She held up her book in front of her face and looked out the window. The plane had taken off and a mass of dark clouds eclipsed the sun, looming as far as she could see. She needed to get away from Portland and couldn't wait for the change of perspective and scenery her sister, June, and Omaha would provide. But she didn't need a Sandy seat mate and positioned her book higher, a literary blockade, she hoped.

Sandy flicked her hand toward Lorna. "I get it—just call me nosey. My marriage, though, I wanted the split, but he wouldn't hear of it. Damn him anyway. Bastard would've been smarter to say yes and walk." She tapped a couple of fingers on her chest above the crow, then stuck a finger in her mouth and chomped on a nail. Lorna tried to ignore her peripheral view. Sandy continued, "We weren't good after our fourth or fifth year, maybe third." Sandy shifted her back into her seat. "No divorce, he said. Loved me and couldn't live without me. Fuck him. Live with him in a shit relationship forever? Hell no. One way or another, I needed to punch out." She removed her finger from her mouth, pulled on it and popped her knuckle. "It was hell, absolute hell."

Dawn appeared out of nowhere, drink cart in tow, and leaned in from the aisle. "A beverage, ladies?" She passed Sandy and Lorna packages of biscuits and a couple of napkins.

"I'd love a cup of coffee, thank you," Lorna said, and took a biscuit and napkin from Dawn's well-manicured fingers.

"Cream or sugar?" Dawn's smile sparkled as she poured coffee into a paper cup.

"Cream, please," Lorna said and took the steaming coffee and creamer packet from Dawn.

"I want tomato juice with a splash of soda, and extra biscuits, please." Sandy snatched biscuits and a napkin out of Dawn's hand. "If you've a lemon, I'd love a slice. Love me some lemon in my bevvy."

"Sorry, we don't. Half and half on the tomato juice and soda?" Dawn smiled at Sandy like she meant it.

"Damn—really—no lemon?" Sandy's bottom lip puffed out. "OK, like I said, heavy on the tomato juice, light on the soda." Sandy lowered her tray and put her biscuits on one side and napkin on the other. She folded and unfolded the napkin, then patted it flat. The seat was too deep for her legs to comfortably bend at the knees, so they remained awkwardly outstretched under the tray table. *She looks like a demented child*, Lorna thought as she tapped her own toes on the floor.

Dawn placed Sandy's drink on her tray. She threw another package of biscuits down, flashed a princess smile, and turned to the people across the aisle.

"Ah, so refreshing," Sandy said as she sipped her beverage. She dipped a piece of biscuit into her drink. "I used to drink coffee, but it gave me the jitters, like wearing a wool sweater without an undershirt, so I quit. Yep, all night I'd be up. Had to take a shot of something to get me to sleep. Not a lot, just a nip or two of brandy or bourbon, either helped, or both. I slept like a baby. Terrible to be tired. I get wonky on no sleep." Sandy sighed. "So, where was I?" Lorna, who'd returned to her book, noticed out of her side vision that Sandy was looking at her as she folded and unfolded her napkin.

"Oh, I know. We were talking marriage. Your divorce. How long has it been?" Sandy chewed a bite of her cookie and widened her goopy eyes in Lorna's direction. "Who wanted it? Bet you did." She put her cookie down and chewed at her cuticles again. "You did, didn't you?"

Lorna's heart pounded. Sandy hit a nerve. She'd thought about calling Nick so many times. How often had she questioned her decision to divorce? In the end, she always came up with the same answer: she had to divorce to live again. That said, she'd never share her story with the freakish troll seated next to her. She took a deep breath.

"We divorced less than a year ago. Look, I really want to read my book. I'm sorry, I'm not a talker." Lorna broke off a piece of her cookie and went back to her book. She thought, *See me reading my book? Now read my mind: I. Don't. Want. To. Talk. Simple airplane etiquette. Everyone understands you don't engage with someone reading. Simple. So, please don't talk to me.* She cleared her throat and adjusted her glasses.

"Sure, I get it. Nothing like a great read, absolutely," Sandy said, looking straight ahead. She took a slurp of her tomato drink. "I never did get the divorce. Things might have been different if I had, but I didn't. He might still be alive. I give you, the Theo thing probably shouldn't have happened, but things happen, don't they, and you know, once the ball gets rolling, the ball gets rolling." With her free hand, Sandy held up the tray just enough for her to bend down and adjust her bag without spilling her drink. She checked the zipper on it and patted the top before shoving it farther under the seat. "Yes, a divorce would've made a difference . . ." Sandy's voice trailed off. "But he was an idiot, a bastard. A first-class fucktard." Sandy swished her drink around and took another sip. She put down her cup and nibbled her fingernails.

The seatbelt sign flashed on as the rumble of thunder sounded its warning drums throughout the cabin. The pilot's dour voice followed: "Things could get bumpy. Everyone stay seated with their seatbelt fastened. No trips to the bathroom." The plane shook like a roller coaster clattering down the tracks. Lorna gripped her book tighter and inhaled deeply. She had never been a good flyer, even though she'd flown to see June dozens of times. Now, though, with Cruella De Vil sitting next to her, the two-hour flight felt endless. A series of lightning flashes lit up the cabin. Lorna dropped the book on her lap, closed her eyes for a second and dug her fingers into both armrests. She looked down at her coffee sloshing in its cup. She grabbed it with her left hand, afraid it would spill, and crushed the cup a little with her tight grip. People around her shut their window shades, and the cabin, like the sky, darkened.

"Looks like someone doesn't like to fly any more than I do. Hon, you look like a ghost! Relax, I hate it, too, but keep it together. We'll be fine." Sandy patted Lorna's hand, which white-knuckled the armrest between them. "Just nasty weather, that's all." Sandy took another swallow of her drink. She burped and giggled as the plane lurched up and down. "So, like I was saying, no one would argue that my husband had turned into a bona fide drunk dick. Why did I marry a dick? To get the fuck out of my house, that's why. Everything sucked for me growing up. My entire life. Let's start with my mother leaving me with a pedophile for a stepfather." Lorna, who gazed upward, caught Sandy glancing at her. "I kid you not. A goddamn pedophile. And she left me, took off in the middle of the night, never came back. Left me alone with him. At twelve. What a motherfucker. But I got out of that, too—you bet I did—no one's getting the best of me, hell no. Not then, not now." Sandy stretched her arm to dim her overhead light. Her fan needed adjustment, too. Lorna listened to her grunt, as her fingers barely reached the knobs. The plane bounced through the air.

One more deep dive down and back up, and the airplane steadied. Lorna blinked, loosened her grip on her coffee, and stared at the back of the chair in front of her. She held her breath until the calm lasted longer than a count to ten. Her fingers released the center armrest. She exhaled, placed her half-crushed cup on her tray and picked up her book from where she'd left it on her lap. Out the window, she could see the plane had climbed high above the storm clouds, where blue skies prevailed. She wondered if any empty seats were available. As soon as she safely could, she'd ask to be moved. Despite her open book, the monologue next to her continued. Lorna mouthed *Lord, help me* with fizzling patience. She ate another bite of her cookie.

"So, one day, I got fed up. Really fed up: the booze, the carousing, the lying, the whole deal." Sandy patted Lorna's arm. "I had to do something about it. That's when Theo and Jezebel, our neighbors, got involved. They knew my marriage sucked. Hell, my hubby smashed my grandmother's dishes, the only things left from my childhood, right in front of them. He smashed each plate, one by one, fucking threw them at me. The boozer couldn't aim his way out of an empty can of hair spray, though, too plastered, thank God. Ironic, 'cause he loved a good baseball game. Hell, he threw eighty miles per hour plus, as a kid. Wanted to play in the majors, but like I said, the poor sap couldn't throw straight while under the bottle's grip, and it seemed like it took hold of him and never let go. Well, anyway, that's when Theo and Jezzy tried to stop him. But he couldn't be stopped that night. Like a bull in a ring, that ornery. So, who'd you say wanted your divorce?"

Lorna imagined taking her coffee and dumping it over Sandy's head. For a second, she'd been sympathetic, but now, she'd had all she could stand. Sandy's relationship with her husband mortified her. TMI was an understatement. Maybe she could stuff her paper cup into Sandy's mouth. She smiled to herself, her paper cup, Sandy's plastic cup, and both of their cookie wrappers, shoved into her mouth. *That'd shut her up.* "Sorry. Didn't hear your question." She raised her book again and pushed her glasses up the bridge of her nose.

"Your divorce, who wanted it?" Sandy insisted, ice cubes clacking as she polished off the last of her drink. "I could really use another." She shook her cup in the air, as if signaling a bartender. "I can't see the stewardess. Probably on a break." Sandy craned her neck behind her. "Doesn't look like she works too hard, does it, not with those nails. Did you see her teeth? Shit, they must have cost a fortune." Sandy's toes wagged back and forth, barely grazing her parcel underneath the seat in front of her. Lorna couldn't help but notice that one of her fingers bled around the cuticle. "OK, the divorce, who wanted it?"

"We divorced amicably," Lorna said, gulped the rest of her coffee, and returned to her book. An image of Nick, her ex-husband, formed in her mind. Handsome Nick, polite Nick, easygoing Nick. Smart Nick, all good things Nick. Teflon Nick, Nick who could do no wrong Nick. Nick loved by all, known by few. Non-interested Nick, unemotional Nick, no pulse Nick, slap the paddles on his chest and shock him alive Nick. Smiling on the outside Nick, nothing on the inside Nick. Ah, Nick. She had screamed her bloody head off the last time, just to get a rise out of him. Did he love her, she'd asked. Of course, he did, he answered, but without an ounce of passion. He didn't possess it. He would never give her an opinion, an action or reaction to show he really cared about her, cared about anything for that matter. Honestly, who knew if he ever loved her. Sure, he was nice and steady and true, and yes, handsome. So, she stayed. Then, that last night, the pebble sank the canoe. Lounging in deck chairs on their brand-new enormous deck on a gorgeous summer night, everything looked perfect. Flowers in full bloom, a fire in the fire pit, even the music sounded perfect. The picture of happiness.

Lorna had handed Nick a gin and tonic. He reclined on the chaise with the latest *Economist* open on his lap. She stood above him with her drink, a Sidecar, Grey Goose with soda and lime. "Let's go somewhere new this weekend. Your turn to pick."

"Thanks, Lorn." Nick took a sip of his drink. "Yummy. You choose, you know how I hate planning things." He lifted the magazine and started reading.

"Nick, just once I'd love it if you'd pick a place." Lorna moved on to his chaise. He scooted over just enough so she wouldn't fall off. "Seriously, we've been married twenty years, and you've never once chosen a getaway—let alone a movie, even a restaurant. Anywhere, just name a place." She sipped her drink and put her right foot on the ground to secure her position.

"Honey, really, I don't want to pick. You care more than I do about where we go. Really, I don't care." He took a sip and turned a page. "You know that about me."

Lorna stood up, clattering ice in her glass. "For once, Nick Lockabee, you choose the destination. I want to see where you'd go, just this once." She put her free hand on her hip.

Nick smiled at Lorna and put down the magazine. "I'm not going to." He shrugged his shoulders, raised his magazine, and began to read again. "I just don't really care, darling."

"Nick, just name a goddamn place. The beach, the mountains, the desert, hell, pick downtown, just pick a place!" Lorna's heart beat faster, and she felt her face flush. She took another swallow and moved to the chair facing Nick. The sun had set, but the temperature remained warm. The twinkle lights had come on. She loved this time of night and didn't want to be so upset. Why she'd worked herself up into a tizzy, she didn't know. She could easily pick a spot, and he'd happily go along, but she persisted. "Come on, Nick, just once, you pick." Under her breath she said, "After twenty years, for goodness' sake, make a decision, just this once, please—you're killing me."

"Darling, I don't care, really I don't," Nick said, while leafing through his magazine. "You know me. I'm good whether we stay or go." His eyes remained on the page as he slowly brought his drink to his lips. After a dainty sip, he swung out his arm with his drink in hand and swished around the leftover ice in the glass. His legs stretched out, shapely for a man, crossed at the knees. His shorts perfectly creased.

"Maybe I'll just go without you," Lorna announced, not knowing where it came from. "Since you don't care, I'll go without you. Maybe I'm just sick of you not caring." Lorna's heart felt as though it would throb out of her chest. Then she snapped. She did something sacrilegious. She got up, slammed her drink on the end table, grabbed his *Economist* from his hands, ripped out a handful of pages and tore them into bits which she tossed over his shorts like a snow flurry. "There, now do you care?"

Nick looked up at her with his sea blue eyes. Both of his arms extended out as though someone had dropped a water balloon in his lap. His lips pursed together. "Well, that was uncalled for." He spoke in a low modulated tone. "Do you feel better?" He bent over to pick up the scattered pieces. "I guess I'm done with this issue."

"Scream at me or something," she yelled. "Scream at me, then take me into your arms and tell me you love me!" She threw the magazine on the deck.

"Darling, I haven't the faintest interest in screaming at you. I don't want to further upset you. I'm going into the house and look for something for dinner. Perhaps I'll make another drink." Nick stood up. His tall body towered over her. Lorna remained still, except for the internal hammering of her heart trying to punch its way out of her chest.

"I want a divorce!" she screamed.

Then, she heard a screechy voice, erasing Nick from her mind's eye.

"Poor thing is having a hard time dealing with her divorce. She's an Aries—very impetuous and an ego for days." Sandy turned from Dawn, who hovered over them with a couple of new napkins, to Lorna. "Hon, Dawn's asking if you want another coffee." She patted Lorna's arm. Her legs kicked like a swimmer motoring around the pool. A dead-rat smell kicked up toward Lorna.

"Hon?" Sandy repeated.

"What?" Lorna took a beat to absorb what her seatmate had just said. "Impetuous? Ego for days? What are you talking about? You don't even know me." She straightened her napkin on her tray. "Gin and tonic, please." Lorna fixed some loose hairs in her bun.

"Of course," Dawn said, and winked at Lorna. "And you? Another tomato juice and soda water?"

"Thought you'd never ask. And more cookies," Sandy said. She folded and unfolded her napkin. Blood seeped from her nailbed. Irritated and grossed out, Lorna restrained herself from yelling, "Wipe your goddamn finger with your napkin, you nut job!"

Dawn signaled the flight attendant manning the cart in front of her for a gin and tonic before making the tomato juice mocktail for Sandy.

"Cookies?" Sandy asked. She took a sip of her drink and smiled at Dawn. "Man, you've got some beautiful teeth, girl. How much did they run you? You don't get those from brushing, I know that much."

"Ha," Dawn said. She showcased all her pearly whites with a big smile and tossed a couple packages of biscuits on Sandy's tray. Then she disappeared with her cart down the aisle.

"Hey." Sandy pushed Lorna's arm. "Didn't mean to upset you, but boy, you were out, gone—like in la-la land." Sandy, beverage in hand, used her fingers to pull up her tray a little and bent down to stroke her tote, as if she were petting a dog. "Almost there," she whispered as she sat up. "So, let's see, Aries by nature are rash people. Not saying you are, just saying that's a trait, and being foolhardy. Not to say Aries aren't also spontaneous, hard-working, and frank—and honey, that's you, too." Sandy ripped a piece of skin from another fingernail with her teeth, flicked it off with her tongue, then wiped her finger on her napkin. She flattened the napkin and placed her drink on top. Her tray table shuddered from her bouncing leg.

A different flight attendant arrived with a gin and tonic for Lorna.

"Ten dollars, please." She waited while Lorna bent over to dig through her purse for her wallet. As she did, she gagged at the rancid odor emanating from Sandy's bag. *I have a good mind to complain about this the next time I see Dawn,* she thought as she moved her tote as far away from Sandy's as possible.

Lorna paid for her drink and took a quick sip before she placed it on her tray. She steadied herself by taking a deep breath of nonpolluted air and said, "I'm not sure what you have in there, but it smells like a dead animal." Lorna took another sip. "And I'm not really into discussing my divorce. I'm very tired and just want to enjoy my book and drink and not talk. OK?" Lorna swallowed more of her cocktail and found her spot in the book. Her teeth clenched; *Please don't say anything, don't respond, just keep your mouth shut.*

"I hear ya. My husband didn't like me to talk either—all gibberish, he'd say. I'd open my mouth, and he'd call everything I said gibberish. But I'm not all gibberish. No sirree. I can identify birds, lots of them. I love birds—did you see my crow?" She spread her raw fingers over her tattoo and lifted her chin. Then, Sandy leaned in toward Lorna's shoulder and faced her.

"I'm getting sidetracked. That drink looks good. Maybe I should've had a shot. Anyway, one day Theo and Jezebel, my neighbors I told you about, came over for a visit. My hubby took off for the bar in a fit. I must have ragged on him good. I tried not to rag too much, but he'd really pissed me off. He'd taken the grocery money. I wanted fried chicken from Homer's Chickee Delight, and he boozed away the money. You'd be steamed, too, if you had to eat SPAM every day. Although, I do like it fried with rice and beans, occasionally. Anyway, Jezzy goes home because she's sick of listening to me. She's no prize herself, not sensitive like you. Besides, she's completely addicted to game shows. Loved Trebek. Loved him, but in a creepy way. I think she stalked him. Anyway, Theo and I were left alone on the couch. Great couch, we'd bought on sale—Macy's, an incredible deal, 75 percent off. Well, I guess I cried and cried, so upset, you know. And one thing led to another and before you know it, we were, you know, all arms and legs tangled up on the couch. I started to get nervous my hubby would find us because Lord knows what he would do." Sandy's legs flicked and flitted in front of her, as though kicking away swarms of mosquitos.

Suddenly, her whole body turned off as if paralyzed. Lorna resisted the urge to look at her, but at the same time, her eyes wouldn't shift to the next word in her book. On the one hand, she wanted to hear what happened, on the other, she didn't want to encourage Sandy. Like when you feed a stray cat, and they never go away. She took a sip of her drink without moving her eyes from the book. But she couldn't get Sandy's drivel out of her head. *Ignore, ignore, ignore,* she thought.

Sandy cleared her throat and lurched forward.

"I was afraid of what he'd do if he found us, Theo and me, tangled up like that, so I moved us out back. Big as a bed, our porch couch. It used to be in the living room, until the cat shredded it. But what a perfect size for, you know." Sandy made a clicking sound with her tongue. "Anyway, me and Theo continued playing hide the hoobie, if you catch my drift, and wouldn't you know it, before we could figure out what's going on, my husband busts out the back door, spitting mad and just as juiced. Marie was cocked and ready to go." Sandy swallowed a big gulp of her drink. She opened a package of cookies and broke one into little pieces. "Named his twelve-gauge shotgun Marie, after his high school sweetheart. Slap in the face, if you ask me, but that's how he rolled. He carried Marie to keep people honest, he said. So, he picked up one of Theo's boots, threw it into the air and shot a hole in it. Then did the same to his other boot. Meanwhile, poor Theo could hardly get his pants up, but when he did, he grabbed his shot-up boots and ran. My husband told him, 'Next time, your feet will be in the boots when I shoot, if I ever see you around here again.'" Sandy sighed. "As for me, well, I saw my end. That son of a bitch was going to blast me to kingdom come, sure as shit."

Sandy's voice stopped again. Lorna waited. She peered at her out of the corners of her eyes, without moving her head. Her hands slowly lowered her book to rest it against the tray. *Damn it, Sandy, where is this story going?* Lorna took a drink. Waiting.

Sandy remained quiet.

Lorna slammed the book down on her tray. She lost her grip, and it fell to the floor. "For god's sake, what happened?" She glared at Sandy and bent to pick it up. The smell slapped her, a putrid stench hanging at their feet. She grabbed her book and studied the bag. She didn't know how it could hold anything. Vinyl flecked off the wrinkled sides, electrical tape held each end of the zipper in place and a red piece of ribbon tied the straps together. The whole thing looked like it could disintegrate right there. But the smell, unbearable. "Do you have rotten eggs in there?" Lorna pinched the end of her nose while she regained her composure in the seat.

Sandy squinted her eyes at Lorna. "Why would I carry rotten eggs?" She slid down in her seat so the toe of her shoe could push the bag farther under the seat. "OK, I'll finish. I got off that couch faster than you could say, 'shitajigger,' and ran upstairs. I stayed in my bedroom the rest of the day and night. I say 'my bedroom' because, well, that's another story. Anyway, he didn't follow me or nothing. Everything got real quiet. Scary quiet, like you-don't-know-where-he-is quiet, like slasher-movie quiet."

Sandy's voice lowered. "So, after a while, I gotta pee, like bad. Probably held it in for eight to ten hours by that time. Usually, I can go four hours, but that's tops, happiest at two hours, maybe three. Anyway, the night still hung around, but a little light peeked through the curtains. I thought about peeing out the window but didn't know how that'd work. So, I decided to open the door. He could shoot me on sight, I knew, but I had to go real bad. I opened the door, and boom. There he sat. Right outside my bedroom door on a chair he'd dragged upstairs from the kitchen, good old Marie laid out across his lap."

Sandy shook her head and popped a few cookie bits into her mouth. "I told him, 'I got to pee, bad.' He just looked at me like a crazy-ass bear. He's a hairy guy—big beard, growing up to his beady black eyeballs. He said, 'Sure, go pee. I'm not stopping you.' So, I ran into the bathroom, shut the door, and peed my heart out. I cried, I had to pee so bad. Then, I opened the door and tiptoed by him. I saw at least a case of empty beer cans around him. If he'd been up all night, drinking, I knew he'd pass out soon. His eyes drooped like they do, and he leaned back on the chair. His hands hung by his sides. Floppy drunk. His head bobbed up and down, and side to side. He didn't say a word to me as I passed, so I bolted into my room. I decided then to get the hell out. I grabbed a few things, stuffed them in my biggest purse, but then, while I was deciding which shoes to take, he slammed open the door. I stopped everything and stared at him. I asked him what he planned to do."

Sandy stopped and rubbed her fingers across her mouth. Sitting forward, she looked up and down the aisle. Lorna rolled her head on the headrest toward Sandy.

"Sandy, for god's sake, wrap it up, the story, please. What happened?" Lorna sounded like she was begging but couldn't help it. Sandy sat back in her seat. The crow gliding across her chest looked tired. Its wings seemed to be pulled down by string-like wrinkles tugging from under her shirt. Her lipstick had long ago lost its luster. The initial brightness of Sandy had disappeared, revealing the gray hardness of her life. The pilot issued a warning for all passengers to remain seated for the duration of the trip. Their descent would bring more turbulence. The flight attendants marched down the aisle, making sure all seatbelts were fastened, while collecting empty cups and other garbage. Lights flickered from above. "Perfect," Lorna whispered to herself. "When do the snakes start crawling out?"

Sandy reached up to mess with the overhead controls. Then she settled back down and rolled her head on her headrest toward Lorna. "Are you wigging out on me again? I can't finish my story if you wig out."

"Finish the goddamn story, Sandy." Lorna closed her book on her tray, swigged the last of her drink, and slammed down her cup with an unsatisfying clack of ice cubes in thin plastic meeting thick plastic. *OK, you psychotic whack-job,* Lorna thought, *Thanks for ruining the contemplative, restful, even boring, flight I'd hoped for. But now I need closure to this ghastly* Lifetime-*made-for-*TV *movie.*

"You're pushy, just like a ram. I know my astrology." Sandy nodded in affirmation toward the seat ahead of her. She rested a hand over her crow. One leg bounced up and down. "I sure do." Two fingers appeared to be bleeding now.

Lorna couldn't stop herself. "I'm an Aries, remember, not a Taurus. Now finish." She inhaled through her nose and avoided staring at Sandy's disgusting fingers. The plane started to lurch to the left, rattling as it did. "Sandy, please, distract me, finish." She couldn't believe she was encouraging this lunatic.

"OK, OK, don't freak out." Sandy cleared her throat. "Now where was I?" Sandy rolled her head back toward Lorna. "You know, you should really dye your hair, you'd look so much younger if you did. Have you thought of going red? And maybe get rid of the bun, it's aging. If you go catting around, well, just saying a gray bun ain't going to get you inside any pants but your own, if you know what I mean." Sandy nudged Lorna's upper arm with her hulking ring.

"Sandy, the story." The back of Lorna's neck felt clammy with sweat. "And for your information, I used to dye my hair, but I stopped after my divorce." She tucked more hairs up into her bun. "I like it." But she thought, *I never should've stopped.*

"You like it?" Sandy narrowed her eyes. "Why'd you make yourself look older after divorcing? Girl, that's backwards. When my marriage ended, I dyed my hair darker. I always covered the gray, but I wanted to go darker, back to my natural color. This is me at twenty, right here." Sandy grabbed the longer-than-shoulder-length hair spread over her shoulders, pulled it into a ponytail, and brought the tail closer to Lorna's face. Then she twisted it in her fingers and laid it over her crow tattoo. "Makes me feel alive."

Lorna studied Sandy's hair. "It's too black, you need to go a couple shades lighter. You'll look younger. And get it trimmed."

"Really?" Sandy said as the plane took a sudden dive. Lorna and Sandy both grabbed the middle armrest at the same time, hands overlapping. They hung on until the plane righted itself, then yanked back their arms. A collective murmur of relief swept over the interior of the plane. More bumps and twists, and Lorna grabbed the armrest again. The plane's engine seemed to downshift like a fast-moving truck on a freeway.

Lorna's empty gin and tonic cup slid down the tray; her balled up napkin followed in its wake. Sweat beads began to pop up on her forehead. "The story, Sandy, if there's a God in heaven, please finish the story," Lorna whispered, eyes locked on the headrest in front of her.

"You're losing it, aren't you? Sure, it's bumpy, but the guys that fly these things are kings," Sandy said. "They're gods, really. They can land these hunks of metal regardless of weather, traffic, terrorist attacks . . ." Her voice trailed off.

"Sandy, I don't know what happened to your husband, but I'm sure you drove him crazy." Lorna rolled her head and stared directly at Sandy. "You're out of your mind, you know."

Sandy let out a squeaky little laugh, like a cartoon mouse. "Oh, you and my husband. You might've been pals, although no one really liked him, no one, which should have been a tip off to me, but as a kid, I was headstrong, like a billy goat. And a looker, too, no kidding. Hubby lost most of his looks before we met, from boozing. Damn, he started early. Eight or nine years old, maybe. Eventually, it changed his brain. I think it pickled him, like a jar of my cucumbers on the shelf in my basement. At first, they're fresh and green, but if they stew too long in their juices, they turn gray and bitter. Just like that." Sandy snapped her spindly fingers.

Lorna closed her eyes and knotted her hands together over her roiling stomach. "Oh, my God," she said loudly. "Just kill me now, put me out of my misery, dear Lord."

Sandy sloshed the last of her beverage into her agape mouth, put her tray up and stuffed her empty cup in the seat pocket in front of her. "So, I asked him what he planned to do with the gun, Marie. I probably said, 'Marie, what are you going to do with Marie?' He looked at me with his black-bean eyes, followed me into the bedroom, and sat down on the bed. I thought maybe he'd pass out. His head bobbled like those, you know, bobble-head dolls. My friend, Darlene, once gave me a cute one with a floral scent. All the way from Hawaii. Anyway, I picked up some more things, slow and quiet. I wanted my hairbrush. My friend, Tiny, who owns the beauty supply store, gave it to me, very expensive and has a lifetime guarantee."

"I'm going to scream, Sandy," said Lorna, her eyes blinked open wide. The plane rumbled, and the lights blinked on and off.

"Boy, you're irritable." Sandy scowled at Lorna and continued, "Well, he did pass out. Right there, just leaned back with Marie by his side, he just passed out flat on my bed. Like I said earlier, we weren't sleeping together anymore, which made him easier to live with, and anyway, his pecker was as limp as a week-old string bean. All the juicing, I suppose. Talked big, though. All the stories he told at the Shooting Gallery, the bar down the street, about his conquests. Jesus, nobody spun a story like him." Sandy touched Lorna's arm. "Not a one of them true. I should know."

"Sandy!" Lorna screeched. The man in front of Lorna turned around and glared at her over his seat. She mouthed, "Sorry," and rubbed her forehead.

"Jesus, you're high strung. So, I went on packing this and that, going through my things. Takes time when you're leaving and never coming back. I stuffed the last blouse in my bag when he sprung upright, like a jack-in-the-box, you know, just sprang right up from the bed. I screamed. He scared the holy shit out of me. He lunged for my neck, grabbed me, and squeezed hard, like this." Sandy clutched her own neck to demonstrate how her husband had grabbed her. She stuck out her tongue to emphasize the pressure from the hold. Lorna's jaw went slack.

"Oh, my God! Then what?" Lorna forgot about the vibrating plane and ignored her book, which had toppled to the floor.

"Well . . ." Sandy released her hands from her neck and wiped off the remainder of her lipstick with a crumpled napkin she plucked from up her sleeve. She cleared her throat. "I somehow wrestled us back onto the bed, and I snatched up Marie. I pointed her, best I could, and shot the fucker—*bang!* Right in the head. Blood and brains splattered all over me, everywhere. Shit, what a mess. That man had so much blood, unbelievable how much. I'd always read the head bleeds most. You can't believe it until you see it—in front of you—on you. Blood everywhere. I mean everywhere, the light fixtures, Grandma's picture, everywhere." Sandy took a deep breath and stopped talking. Lorna's hands covered her gaping mouth. Then she slapped her hands down on her thighs, which seemed to push Sandy's play button.

"Obviously, I was all torn up and so goddamn bloody, I ran to Theo's house. Jezzy had run to the store, thank God, so Theo came back with me, and we cleaned up as best we could. He deserved a medal, I tell you, although he'd probably say he wanted something else from me. He never liked my husband, the way he treated me, and once he heard what I did, he helped me get rid of him, like he'd been given an assignment from God. After we did a pretty good job, we wrapped up the fucker and Marie in a dog blanket and drug them out back by the burn pile. Him and his gun, buried there, but not before I hacked off his pecker. Don't ask me why, but I wanted that little pecker of his. A keepsake or trophy, maybe? I suppose it's weird, but I wanted it. His most prized possession, you might say. Except for maybe Marie. But sure as I'm sitting here, I cut off that little motherfucker." Horrified, Lorna wanted to scream, *Why on God's green earth would you do such a thing, and what did you do with it?* But she stayed mute, compelled to listen to the end of the story.

"After we buried him, we finished tidying up the house. It took hours and lots of bourbon and bleach. The whole time, Theo talked about how I'd better leave town for a while, put some time between me and the fucker's disappearance. But hell, I don't think anyone but a couple of bartenders would miss him. I knew, though, Theo was probably right, so here I am, and that's how the story ends. Right here next to you." Lorna cradled her head in her hands. Sandy futzed with her seatbelt, then slumped down low in her seat and tapped her bag with the toe of her shoe.

Lorna took a deep breath. "You've got to be kidding, right?" She squinted her eyes at Sandy. "Do you know how crazy that sounds? Do you? The story, everything you just told me?" Lorna twisted her entire body toward Sandy. "Do you know how much trouble you're in? If it's true. Is it true? You can't just go and kill your husband, no matter how much of an asshole he is." Lorna strained to keep her voice at a whisper. "How do I even believe you?"

The smile plastered on Sandy's face contorted. Her smudged-off faintly red lips amped up her weirdness. She looked like a cross between the Joker and the Cheshire cat. Lorna blinked and did her best to stay focused. "Listen, Sandy, you can go to prison for this. You could be put away for years—if it's true."

Sandy turned away from Lorna. She closed her eyes and rolled her head back and forth on her headrest. Lorna sat back into her seat. "You're crazy if you think you can get away with it, murder, you understand that, right?" Lorna said, "A dog or something is going to find your husband buried in your backyard. You know that, Sandy. You need to go to the police and tell them it was self-defense. Sounds like anyone who knew him would believe you. But you're crazy if you think you can get away with killing your husband, chopping off his penis, and burying him in the backyard." Lorna looked at Sandy. "Bat-shit crazy."

Sandy stared wide-eyed at the seat in front of her. She chuckled. "Ha, girl, I was just pulling your leg." Then she laughed, a maniacal cackle. "Me, kill my husband, ha, ha." Sandy strained her toes and rested them on her bag. "I'd have to be out of my tree." Sandy laughed again, more like a wheeze from someone who'd smoked three packs a day their entire life.

"You know what, Sandy, I believe it. I believe you. I don't think you or anyone could have made that up." Lorna scoured Sandy's twisted face and then looked out the window. The plane hit the ground with a bump and another and another, until it fully landed. Lorna couldn't remember being so relieved in all her life. The flight attendants made announcements: "Stay seated until we reach the gate," and "We'll be happy to assist you with connecting flights." People rustled in their seats. The lights blinked on. Shades slid up, conversations buzzed, and outside light poured in.

"Look, hon, I played you. Don't be a fool." Sandy batted her eyelashes at Lorna. "Hey, I have to check on my flight to Milwaukee."

Sandy touched Lorna's arm with her veiny hand that looked like skin covering a bundle of colored power cords. "Watch my bag for me. Be right back." Sandy swung her little body into the aisle and stood and stretched.

"Wait," Lorna said, "you can't walk around yet; the plane hasn't reached the terminal. You can't go yet. Take your bag with you, I'm not watching it." Lorna started to stand. "I have to meet my sister." She banged her head on the overhead bin and sat back down.

Sandy smiled at Lorna and said, "Back in sec, promise. Such a worrywart." She moved down the aisle at a fast clip.

Lorna called after her, "Sandy, wait! What am I supposed to do? What about your husband, the story, wait!" The man in front of her looked back and glared. "Stop staring at me," she scolded.

The plane taxied to a complete stop and luggage gathering from the overhead compartments commenced. Stretching bodies and rolling suitcases filled the aisle. Sandy disappeared, as if she'd beamed off the plane. A couple of minutes passed before people started moving slowly forward. Lorna didn't see the man with the pronounced chin walk by or the doughy kid. She stayed seated in a silent panic.

After the passengers had emptied out of the plane, Lorna stood up. She looked at her watch. She'd been on the ground for nearly twenty minutes. How long was she supposed to wait? She looked up and down the empty plane and decided she'd waited long enough. She had to think about June. Sandy be damned. Lorna pulled up her leather tote from underneath the seat and tucked her book and glasses inside, then reached for Sandy's bag. The smell had intensified. She held the satchel away from her body, afraid it would disintegrate in her hand. Dangling it at arm's length, she walked up the aisle to the gaggle of flight attendants standing by the open door. Lorna didn't want to speculate about what she carried, but she had an idea.

"Here," Lorna said and handed Sandy's tote to Dawn. "The woman I sat next to left it. She told me she had to check on her connecting flight, but she never came back. I have to meet my sister, so I'm giving it to you." Dawn took the bag by its perilous handles and immediately wrinkled her nose.

"God, what an awful smell." Dawn set the bag down on the first-class seat in front of her. "I'm sorry. Whose is it?"

"Remember the woman I sat next to? The woman with the huge crow tattoo across her chest? It's hers," Lorna said and wiped her hands on her pants. "I need to go, so it's yours. Like I said, she never came back to collect it."

Dawn's dazzling smile dimmed as she pulled a paper and pen from her apron pocket. "I do remember her. She ordered the tomato juice and soda, extra cookies. She forgot it?"

"I don't know if she left it on purpose or what," Lorna said. "Her name is Sandy Vexman—or Villman; I swear she told so many weird stories, I've forgotten my own name." Lorna turned to exit the plane.

"OK, we'll send it to the lost and found. If you see her, let her know." Dawn called after Lorna, who stepped onto the covered bridge leading to the terminal.

"God willing, I won't," Lorna said as she walked into the bright morning sunlight of the Omaha airport terminal. With every step she took in the wide-open corridors toward the baggage claim, she felt lighter. Like she'd been trapped in a nightmare and spit out, back into the light of Normalsville. *What a trip*, she thought, *In so many ways.* Lorna tried not to think about Sandy, although she couldn't help but wonder about her story. The husband buried in her backyard, the cut-off penis, and the bag's rotten contents. That horrid smell. *Could it be? Well, no matter.* That ship had sailed, as they say, and who cared anyway? At the same time, acutely aware that Sandy could pop up at any minute, Lorna's eyes darted from one passing face to another.

She reached the luggage carrousel and waited for her bag to come through the black flaps at the end. Furtively, she scanned the passengers surrounding her. But fortunately, she didn't spot Sandy and her crow tattoo anywhere. Eventually, Lorna's kelly-green Lily Pulitzer suitcase spilled out onto the conveyor belt. As she reached to pick it up, she backed into something.

"Sorry, ma'am. You OK?" A man dressed in an airport uniform with milky brown eyes backed up his cart of suitcases. He held up his cell phone. "Bad driver," he added with a smile.

"No problem. I'm fine." Lorna brushed off her arm. A metal tag on the cart read, "Lost and Found." Almost immediately, the waft of a familiar stench smacked her in the face.

"You have a good day then." The man put his phone in his pocket and guided the cart away from the crowd. As he did, Lorna heard the man mutter, "Damn, smells like something died in one of these."

Lorna watched him as he wheeled the cart into the lost-and-found office, walled in by an enormous window. As she walked toward the exit doors, a commotion erupted behind the lost-and-found window and recaptured her attention. Center stage, a security guard unzipped Sandy's odious bag, while surrounding TSA agents covered their mouths and noses. Some doubled over as if gagging. Another security agent got on his walkie. Meanwhile, Lorna saw her sister waving for her attention outside the terminal window. Torn, Lorna turned to June. As she did, two police cars pulled up right behind her sister's SUV. She turned back to the scene in the lost and found. Should she tell the authorities what Sandy had told her? Should she get involved? Was it even true? Police officers climbed out of their cars and pushed past Lorna as they rushed inside. Lorna slowly walked out the door to her sister. As Lorna let herself be embraced by June, over her shoulder, she saw a petite woman with too-black hair climb into a taxi. Lorna's heart raced. *Sandy. She got away with it. Whatever she did, she got away with it.* Lorna's insides churned like wet towels in a dryer. She blurted out, "Wait, stop!"

"What?" June dropped her arms.

Lorna pointed to the cab pulling away from the curb. "She got away with it. I could've said something, but I didn't, and now it's too late. She's free. Just like that."

"What are you talking about?" June said.

For the next forty minutes, as her sister drove Lorna to her house, she recounted every sordid detail of Sandy's story, from her husband's drunkenness to the murder and dismemberment.

"That's outrageous," June said, peppering Lorna's tale with a proper mix of repulsion and outrage. "Do you believe it?"

"I don't know," Lorna said as she slumped down in her seat, Sandy's preposterous story reeling around in her brain. "But June, this whole thing got me thinking. Here I am, gray, divorced, miserable, but why? Yes, Nick over-creased his shorts and was as even as a tabletop. That was it. Not a goddamn thing more. Not one good fucking story after twenty years of marriage." She turned to her sister and said, "June, you know what? I didn't want Niagara Falls for a marriage, but I sure as hell wanted more than tepid bath water. For Christ's sake."

A couple of weeks and a revitalizing blonde hairdo later, Lorna returned home from visiting her sister, June. She lounged on the new floral cushions on her new deck chaise, watching the small TV she had mounted on the wall underneath the eaves. Something Nick would have never approved of, but God forbid he ever tell her he didn't. *Ha*, she thought and took a swig of her gin and tonic. *Not your deck anymore, Nicky boy. Sorry, not sorry.*

Suddenly, on the TV. *It couldn't be. Impossible.* Lorna bolted upright. But there she stood, Sandy and her horrible inky black hair and chest crow. She turned up the volume. The interviewer asked Sandy, and the man standing next to her, whom he referred to as "Theo," what she planned to do with her lottery winnings, the largest payout in Florida's history. Sandy replied, "Oh, you know, have lots of good old-fashioned fun." The announcer laughed and pressed: "Anything in particular, anything you want to add?"

Sandy leaned forward, her face flushed with a red lip-sticked grin and wagged her finger back and forth in front of the camera. She said, "Hey, Marie. Who's the winner now?" and winked with her goopy green eye.

Lorna's G and T spilled all over her new seat cushion.

Bianca

HAND OF FATE

Spontaneous combustion: without warning or probable cause, organic matter ignites when rapid oxidation rises and things get hot, baby, hot, hot, hot.

SHATTERED

The clock encased in a crocheted frame strikes 8:30 p.m. Your cell phone buzzes. An unrecognizable number pops up. You're at an open house, celebrating your friend's new home, distracted by who would call on a Saturday night. You take another sip of wine. Then you slide your finger on the phone to answer. A neighbor is frantic on the other line. "I'm so sorry, it's your house, it's on fire, you better get home fast," he chokes. Your ears ring and your stomach backflips. Scooter, your dog, is in your home. Without thinking, you shout her name into the phone and hang up. You and your husband race the fifteen-minute drive home faster than legally allowed. Each bringing the other to the precipice of hysteria by whispering Scooter's name with heaving breaths. You're pumped up with angst and fueled by more than a couple glasses of wine, and your husband, the driver, is also filled with dread, but just one beer, thankfully, an expression of gratitude you won't use again for a while.

You arrive at your street but must park a block away, as emergency vehicles and yards of yellow tape block your path. You both jump from the car and sprint to your house. You're consumed with the violent horror of witnessing your garage burn, fingers of flames escaping through its orifices, clawing at the night sky. Nearby fire trucks blast water from powerful hoses, attempting to tame the white-hot rage. Black cinders ravage your nose and cloud your vision, but still, you watch your new-last-summer outdoor cushions drip into goopy fireballs from the rafters, and your husband watches his motor-cycles melt into smoldering *Mad Max*-like movie props. Most fright-ening, though, is knowing your dog is trapped somewhere in the smoke-engulfed home. The house is not attached to the garage but tethered by a breezeway—and at this point remains free from flames. Firefighters dash in and out of the doors to your personal oasis, the only place where you can traipse around in your jammies and watch movies at noon, your proverbial castle now threatening to become an unrecognizable shell. You're barred from entering your home because of the ongoing danger. You shout at the firefighters, "Get our dog, get our dog!" They respond, soot-covered faces emotionless, "We're looking for her, can't find her, but we're looking," as they disappear back into the house. *But it's my garage, my house, and my dog,* desperate screams echo inside your head. You float somewhere above the scene, as if you're watching the drama unfold from on high. Every-thing imploding, melting in front of you, just out of reach.

COMPLICATED

I can't think of anything to write. I need marketing content by Friday —as a freelance writer, I've had to keep up with my schedule come hell or high water, lest I lose a client. Since the fire, the marbles in my head have scattered all over the floor. I search my brain for the nugget of gold, a spark, the string of words to unravel the next compelling campaign. Nothing comes. Not a goddamn thing. I move from room to room where things remain in disarray. The vistas from my windows have morphed: rubble carpets the deck, and ash blankets the grass. A laurel hedge stretches out clearly in sight, where once my garage obstructed its view, an odd yet lovely distortion. I stumble around boxes of objects salvaged from the garage. I feel flat. Depleted. My focus, shot to hell.

In the fire's aftermath, I'm only able to fixate on a couple of "BFFs" who have failed to sufficiently support me through this, my ordeal. One had long ago invited me to a concert, after she and her boyfriend broke up. The tickets had already been purchased, and when she offered me the available one, I readily accepted—after all, the band is my all-time favorite—the best rock-and-roll band in the world and she is my best friend. The concert is a week away, but now I feel so disconnected from her, I'm not sure if I'm still invited. My expectations of this person used to be so high, too high, apparently. After doing the perfunctory post-disaster good deeds—delivering me dinner and taking me out for lunch—she disappeared. What I thought was a friendship built on mutual support is all but up in smoke, and I'm feeling burned and insecure. Until now, my traumas have been minor compared to her divorce and subsequent break up with her boyfriend. I've never needed her as much as she needed me. But now I do. The opportunity for me to feel her support and love finally presents itself, and it's fizzling faster than a campfire doused with water.

COOL, CALM, AND COLLECTED

Noxious smoke from your burning garage envelopes the crowd—puffs of wind clear the air for fleeting moments and expose a growing number of personnel. You wonder at the surrealness of the scene. Just like a movie, but not. This is your life, and you are a star in this dumpster-fire film. A puffy-chested Doogie Howser of a policeman, "crowd controlling," sticks his finger in your frenzied husband's chest and shouts, "I'll Taser you if you don't stay back!" Your husband, whose feet are firmly planted on the grass across the street from your house, drops his flailing arms and explains in a restrained voice that it's his house on fire and his dog is inside—Scooter, your Labrador, is terrified and hiding. "Let me go find her. I can find her," he implores. The cop puffs up like an angry teen and yells, "I said, don't move, or I'll Taser you!" Doogie stands close enough to his face that even you, standing to your husband's side, can see spittle flying from his lips. "So help me God I will!" Doogie's jowls jiggle as he barks his demands. You think, *He's the posterchild of a short-fused, donut-chomping cop stereotype.*

You, small of stature, balk at the policeman yelling at your husband, shove yourself between the two and shake your finger in Doogie's face. "You need to check yourself! Our house is burning, and our dog is lost inside!" You point to your smoking house. The policeman stops exercising his bad-cop behavior and stares down at you. He shouts, "I was going to Taser him if he went any farther. For his safety! You know, smoke kills just like fire." He pauses, and then adds, "I have a dog, too." Like this is supposed to justify his behavior. He relaxes his stance and crosses his arms across his chest. Your body becomes rigid. You clench your fists, and your eyes fill with tears. "What difference does that make? Even more reason to get my dog," you screech. A leaden fog wraps around your shoulders like a ghostly blanket. Neighbors close in around you, watching, as though your unraveling is a secondary event of a three-ring circus.

He tightens his arms across his chest—a bulletproof vest thickening his bulky body. His beady eyes squint at you from underneath his cop baseball cap. He does an about-face, skulks off into the black hole of the busy street.

A loud crackle shifts everyone's attention back to the flaming garage. Through the inky soot, a fireman signals you and your husband to come into your smoke-filled house to look for your dog. Inside, people in gas masks tromp around in muddy boots on your newly refinished wood floors, dragging hoses behind them. You both find Scooter cowering behind the TV in the den—your den, your once cozy sanctum turned hazy cave. "Scooter!" You and your husband cry.

Your husband crouches down and whispers to her, "It's OK, Scooter girl, I'll get you out." Scooter, scared out of her wits, lets your husband pick her up and carry her shivering seventy-five-pound body to the neighbor's house, to safety, swerving to avoid neighbors as they reach out with well-intentioned pats along the way. He whispers, "It's OK, girl, it's OK, it's OK," as he passes through the crowd.

MIGHT AS WELL GET JUICED

Finally, painfully last minute, my friend calls and says, "Hey, you still up for going to the concert this weekend?"

"Heck yeah!" My fast response surprises me. It belies my reels of negative thoughts that begin with *Where the hell have you been*? I'm hurt and needy, grateful and pouty all at the same time. And I want to go.

"Great! I made reservations at a hotel near the venue." She continues to lay out our plans. All of it seems amazing, I must admit, and a couple days later, before I have time to second guess myself for going, we sit driving the three hours north in her car. Now, I wrestle with whether I'm being inauthentic if I don't share my feelings of frustration with her. I decide the timing is wrong for such a discussion, plus my brain can't handle any additional drama. An ever-present fire cloud attaches to me like a hot-air balloon roped to a basket below, with me inside. So, I tell myself to reconcile my feelings later. I might as well try to enjoy myself—and she's always fun. As we get closer, excitement slowly trickles into my system, drip by drip, mile by mile my body loosens into a grin. I look sideways at her; she seems to be worry-free, head bobbing to the music from the radio. Any floating smolderings I have for her, I stuff into a box in my brain. After all, we are going to see my favorite band, the best rock-and-roll band in the world. And truth be told, she has always been my best concert mate.

She's ten years younger than I, ironed blonde hair with perfect eyebrows that frame beautiful blue eyes. She is at least five inches taller than I am and wears heels. She's a presence wherever she goes, and again, she's fun.

We arrive, check in to our hotel and immediately drink wine—lots of wine—and eat cheese and crackers in the room. The hotel is a round highrise. Unlike me, she likes to stay on the highest floor possible whenever she travels. I've been afraid of building heights since 9/11, but I keep my fears to myself as I ingest our twenty-seventh-floor view. After we finish prefuncting, we change for the concert.

She hands me a shirt. "I got us each matching logo t-shirts and customized them. Here's yours, with the neck cut out a bit." I try it on.

"Fantastic. I couldn't have done better myself." Her gesture makes me happy. At the same time, a gnawing in my stomach burns up to my throat. How did this thoughtful, wonderful person become the disappointing person of the last month? I swallow hard.

Not missing a beat, she pulls on her version, with cut-off sleeves, and it looks great. Next, like a skilled artist, she applies makeup. When she finishes, she gleams. I wear mascara and lipstick applied earlier in the day and only add fresh lipstick to my puckered mouth. I'd be uncomfortable wearing anything more.

We laugh at the reflections of our different body shapes: me, short and dark featured, and she so tall and blonde. And our t-shirts look perfect. We gather our purses, and the heavy hotel door slams after us.

Absorbing the nightlife with her as we wait outside for the Uber, I lecture myself, *I can do this, be in the moment, forget about things.* But my mind plays tug of war: fire and disappointment on one end and being carefree, all jacked up and expectant, on the other. One side threatens to suffocate my thoughts like a toxic gas and the other combust me into uncontrollable giggles. We climb into our Uber driver's large car and talk to Nina, introduced as our ride-share partner.

"Hi, you going to the concert?" I ask, sitting next to Nina in the backseat.

"Yes, can't wait, I'm going with my dad. My sister doesn't like concerts, so my dad and I have this special concert-going thing, just the two of us." Nina is youngish—maybe eighteen or nineteen. She has long brown hair in braids, wears rolled up jean shorts with a white peasant top. "We're meeting up there."

"Cool," I say and think, *Why didn't Nina's dad pick her up instead of making her meet him at the concert where 68,000 people are converging?* "Do you have a good meet-up spot?" I try not to be too weirdly nervous for her.

Nina throws her arm up on the back of the seat. "We're going to text each other for a meet up when we get there. No worries. Yeah, he loves this band, we both do. They're divorced, my parents, and my mom hates them. So does my sister." She smells musty, like she isn't wearing deodorant. *Doesn't her mother tell her she should?* I wonder if she shaves her armpits—if she isn't going to wear deodorant, she should at least shave. I worry her dad will be offended by her odor and take it out on her mom. I'm irritated at both her dad and mom. Her phone rings, and I jump. Christ, I jump at everything now. The Uber driver stops in front of the sawhorses set up to prevent cars from parking closer to the stadium. Nina bolts out of the car without a goodbye. I wonder if she'll get lost looking for her father. Nina evaporates into the crowd. I'm afraid for her, for everyone.

(I CAN'T GET NO) SATISFACTION

There's a celebrity aspect to a fire. As if watching a parade, neighbors line the roadside to ogle fire trucks blasting water into your garage and house. While you and your husband run around like circus clowns, hands on your heads as your property dissolves, this neighbor or that stops you to share their stories.

"I looked out the window and told Norman, 'There's something strange about the lighting.' It was dusk but lighter than dusk. Then I realized your house was on fire!" Phyllis's voice is shrill. "So, I called 911 right away." Phyllis lives across the street and down a house. She stands in a flimsy bathrobe and slippers, her hands flapping with the fervor of the tale. I want to put a blanket around her against the night's chill. She adds, "I'm so glad you weren't out of town. Can you imagine?"

Trisha chimes in with a baby on her hip. She lives in the house on the other side of the hedge. "We were putting our kids to bed, and Chris called me to the window. 'My God,' he said, 'a fire next door. Please don't let their dogwood tree burn down.' It was the first thought we both had, your gorgeous dogwood tree. Then we called 911."

You receive offers of drinks, food, rooms to sleep, and lots of hugs. You're so grateful, so in shock, and so mesmerized; the flicking sun-bright flames reaching out of your garage dance off the faces of those surrounding you in the obsidian night.

Then, you learn, comes the fallout.

The recovery and restoration of your garage, your house, and your lives are painfully slow, but excruciatingly well-staffed. You'd have never guessed how many people are invested in the aftermath of a fire. People to inspect and determine cause; people to haul out the contents of your house into trucks, where they take everything to be cleaned and de-smoked by other people; people to determine the extent of the damage; more people to determine the value of every-thing destroyed; people to compile inventory lists, item by item, of those things removed from your house; people to help you attach value to or assess total loss of those items; people to supervise the people emptying your house; people to secure lodging when you've been booted from your house until the smoke damage is mitigated. Finally, people to clean your house of smoke damage, thoroughly, inch by inch.

"Your house will never be as clean; we promise you that," the pimply-faced young man, Shawn, assures us. "Seriously, we clean everything. Your house will sparkle."

A day later.

To Shawn: "There're muddy footprints all over the bathroom floor. The washer and dryer are covered in wood shavings from drilling above. And what about the garbage bags filled with food by the backdoor? It's rotting. You need to get rid of it," you say. "So much for sparkling."

"Whoops, so sorry. Of course, we'll take care of the footprints and shavings, but disposing of the food is on you." He smiles.

"Why? You cleaned out my refrigerator, my cupboards, you

junked it into bags, why can't you throw it out? We don't have garbage cans anymore. We can't throw it out."

"We're not allowed to toss out food, sorry. The footprints and shavings we can take care of." He grins as he talks, and the bun on top of his head glistens with grease. A tall woman with a shaved head and a large black hoop through her nose walks through the kitchen wiping down a bungee cord, an old frayed bungee cord. *That's important*, you think. *Heaven forbid I have a dirty bungee cord. Jesus!* For the most part, the cleaners do the best they can, but they're younger than most of the bags of food.

Then there are the people at the hotel who bring you extra towels, the people who make fresh cookies for the front desk, who don't say anything when you take a plate of six up to your room.

You argue with the people who took your clothes away to be cleaned. "I specifically bought a dress for a formal wedding next Saturday. You took it and my husband's suit to be cleaned. Where the hell are they?" You fight the urge to raise your voice. Nonetheless, you hear yourself scream into the phone. "Why are my belongings, with a promised two-week turnaround, now two months late? Where the hell are they?" An earful of excuses comes spilling through the phone, and your brain shuts down. You are transferred to more people, each more important than the one before, and realize you'll need to buy another dress and your husband another suit. That means weaseling more money out of your insurance agent, who's never around to weasel. You eat another cookie and dial a supervisor's number given to you by the person you just hung up on.

"Are you the supervisor? I need to talk to a supervisor about my clothes." You speak with authority.

"I'm Andrea, yes."

"Andrea, I am going to a formal wedding, and I bought this dress just for the occasion, and I'm going to be really upset if I can't wear it. Can you please find it and send it to the hotel as soon as possible. And my husband's suit, shoes, and tie. You promised two weeks, and it's been over two months!"

"I'm so sorry. I'll see what I can do. Can I call you back at this number?"

"Yes, thank you." And for good measure you add, "I'm already upset because of the fire, then you take my clothes. I just need something to go right. I'm not upset with you personally; the whole situation just sucks."

"I totally understand how you feel. I'll check on your clothes and call you back. Do you happen to have their item numbers? If you review the inventory list, each item has an item number. It'll help me to locate the dress and suit."

"Item number? Are you kidding? You took thousands of items from my home! It will take me till the wedding to figure out item numbers!"

Eventually, you find the item numbers. But by then, Andrea has returned some of your clothes, sans the dress and your husband's suit. She offers her regrets, that's all she can do.

For every Shawn and Andrea, three or more just like them spin in your aftermath orbit. You try to remember their names. Systematically, this becomes true for you: the workers have one-syllable names, like Sam, Brit, and Shawn; supervisors have two syllable names, like Colby, Curtis, and Matthew. Three syllable names like Anthony, Andrea, and Gabriel are reserved for those in charge of the one- and two-syllable-named people. Gabriel, however, is unceremoniously let go, and you don't know whether to feel sorry for him or say good riddance because he never cleaned up the soot from the deck like he said he would. Your husband eventually completes this task.

You try to write at your desk in your home office, which reeks of a bonfire on the beach, because there's no room for both you and your husband to work in the hotel room. The influx of insipid Walmart-greeter types wandering around your house distracts you. They appear out of nowhere with clipboards and sponges and just as quickly disappear. You wonder when they'll be back, if they'll be back, or whether they descended to the basement, and you just didn't notice. You think of things you don't want them to take, to clean, to see; your stuff becomes like your children, your loved ones. Unnaturally so.

RIP THIS JOINT

Music blasts from the stadium. The first act drums out a noisy cross between rock and country music. Energized by the acoustics and droves of people converging toward the venue, we skip into the massive crowd and arrive at the check-in station before entering the gates. A man in a red shirt with "security" written in block letters across the chest measures each of our purses with a tiny purse-size diagram on a laminated piece of paper. The man tells us our purses are over the size limit, and we can't bring them into the concert. However, we can check them into lockers in a nearby van. The man points to a white tent and a huge van across the crowded parking lot. Curling between the cars is a line of people waiting to stash their belongings in the van's lockers. We snatch up our purses from the table and say, "What a ripoff," as we sashay toward the van and to the back of the line.

After storing our purses, we return to the stadium and run up the stairs to find our section and a bar. The front band has quit playing and the lull between performances provides lit concert goers time to take care of business. Determined to get wine before we sit down, we hustle to the bar and are met with another long line. I'm nervous about missing the grand entrance of the main attraction. I'm nervous my fired-up mood will take a nosedive. My friend assures me there's plenty of time, so we line up, gawking at the outrageous outfits walking by. The younger ones have ratted hair, stiletto heels and feather boas wrapped high around their necks. Their pants fit so tightly, if they had underwear lines to be seen, you'd see them. Then, reflecting the ages of the main band, the older crowd is made up of silver-haired men in skinny jeans, sporting random band t-shirts dating from the sixties, seventies, and eighties. Middle-aged women, also poured into too-tight pants and very visible underwear, wear too-tall heels and shirts with shoulder cutouts. Mixed in are plenty of people dressed like us, t-shirts with the band's logo on them and jeans —not too tight, but not mom jeans either—comfortable, but cool. Up at the bar, the woman bartender clad in red fires off, "What'll it be?"

"Two glasses of red wine each please," I say. "Also, can we have beer cups to pour them into?" I sound desperate, like I'm asking her to donate a kidney, but I don't want to carry two full glasses of wine into the massive blackness of the stadium. I'd surely spill.

"Fifty-seven dollars," The bartender growls and reluctantly hands us our beer cups and wine.

An outrageous price, but it's going to be an outrageous night. We pour our wine into the cups and take off toward our seats.

SPARKS WILL FLY

Because 99 percent of your friends have not experienced a fire, life for them proceeds as if nothing has happened. You fight resentment. Friends continue to surprise and sadden you, people you thought you knew, but, as it turns out, you don't. One tells you how lucky you are. Lucky? Lucky for watching a fire devour your garage and render your house unfit for living? Another tells you when God closes a door, he opens a window. Yeah, because God knows smoke inhalation kills. Some say they will drop by, but they don't. Ever. Surprisingly, when rain threatens, a new acquaintance helps you lug in hundreds of boxes from your lawn, where the restoration team left them. You feel needy and mean and surly and unforgiving. You're judgmental, and your expectations are through the roof. It's like having an unwelcome disease you can't control. You're mad at your situation and expect everyone to understand how you feel and, by God, Step. It. Up. Your emotions run away from you like an unbridled stallion. You could really use your dear, sweet, coddling mother, but she's dead and your Ninety-four-year-old father says he feels bad that he can't help. You assuage his guilt by telling him he walks with a walker and can't drive but that you are glad that he wants to help anyway. Secretly, though, you're kind of mad that he can't do something.

You stop working because you must watch over the squad of people doing different things to your house. You're a mess and can't think straight. You try to convey the disaster that is your current situation to your clients, but they tolerate more than they care. A colleague goes to the hospital with pancreatic problems. For a moment you become humbled and grateful and give yourself a figurative slap across your face. Attitude adjustment, please. Still, you don't feel lucky.

As time goes by, and it does somehow progress, without any attention to specific days or hours, you think you're doing better. You and your husband say things like, "We're on the same team," and "We're in this together." You hug more. The hotel you move into becomes a bit of an adventure. Clean sheets every day, a clean bathroom, and who doesn't like a free breakfast?

At first.

Then, more weeks blow by, and you tumble into a pit of insurance hell. You're sick of the hotel's rubbery eggs and gummy oatmeal, and your husband dismisses the cleaning people because he's working out of the hotel room and can't be bothered. Undetectable at first, like a momentary tweak in your back when you stand, all is OK. Spousal requests sound kind and gentle.

"Hon, remember to call whatshisname about adding the kayak to the insurance claim," you purr.

"Sure thing. And next time you're at the store, will you please buy dog food. I think we're out. And pick up some Fritos while you're there. You're the best, babe."

Then the heat turns up. "Why'd you buy this kind of dog food?" he says. "Where're the Fritos? These are Kroger brand not real Fritos; I want real Fritos."

"Oh, for God's sake, who can tell the difference? And the dog can't tell the difference between dog foods, either." The strain pulls from all sides.

You sit on the edge of the bed that isn't your own, attempting to regroup and get centered. The hotel room grows smaller with each passing hour, and even though you trek back and forth to your house during the day to orchestrate all the people employed by your fire, the hotel room is really your home now. It's where you hang out.

"I was watching HGTV, why'd you turn it?"

"I'm sick of that show—the woman's mean, and the guy is whiny."

"I want to see if they love it or list it."

"Who cares, it's an ugly house; they should leave it."

"I love the house; they should stay."

You both continue snapping after you move out of the hotel and back into your house. That's when a trickle of cleaned contents starts to return. Your frustration with the world worsens because your home still isn't right. Conversations reflect the collective mood.

"Have you seen my flip phone?"

"It's probably in some box, do you need it?"

"Yes, I get messages on it sometimes, you know."

"No, I didn't. Check the trash pile. Maybe I thought it was trash."

"Trash? Why would you think it's trash?"

"A flip phone, in my world, is trash."

"Well, it's not trash, I use it, a lot. Not trash at all. Trash. Jesus."

"Here, I found it. In the trash." And under your breath, "Because it is trash."

Never-cared-for items suddenly become paramount to staying alive. Grandma's blanket, which had lived a long life in a box with other unpopular items in the basement, becomes the Maltese Falcon your husband is feverish to find. Earlier, you had a few friends over to help pack up Goodwill boxes. You realize now, mistakes were made.

"Where's my grandmother's blanket? The gold and green one. I haven't seen it."

"I might have given it to Goodwill. It was itchy, and I purged."

"What? Before she died, she gave it to me. Actually, her neighbor finished it for her and gave it to me. It was the only thing I had to remember her by."

"Itchy and ugly. I'm sorry. Get over it."

The deterioration of your relationship continues after the demolition of the kitchen. You had planned its remodel before the fire, but since the stove stored in the garage had to be replaced and the kitchen repainted, you jointly decide to remodel while the house is torn apart. Part of that process means making coffee in the bathroom, where the light switch must be turned on for the outlet, and thus the electric coffeemaker, to work. You remind your husband of how things function before you go to bed because he makes the coffee for the following day.

The next morning.

"I made you coffee this morning."

"Thank you, but you turned off the light after you made it. The coffee is cold. It doesn't count as making it for me if it's cold."

"Oh, sorry, have some of mine—it's still warm. And it counts."

"It doesn't count. I want hot coffee, plus you drank out of it. I want my own. I'm going to Starbucks."

"It counts. Don't be such a snob. Oh, and while you're out, you might want to pick up another one of those scrubby things you use in the shower."

"You mean my Swedish loofah puff? Why?"

"I couldn't find the dish scrubber, so I used it to wash the egg pan. You're going to laugh, but it worked well."

"You're dead to me."

BLINDED BY LOVE

Tumblers in hand, my friend and I maneuver our way down the narrow aisle in search of our seats, inching past fans standing in front of their flipped-up chairs. Avoiding their toes, we shuffle by, captivated by the dark stadium, high strung with anticipation. Suddenly, the band rushes on stage and the crowd erupts into a firestorm of deafening cheers. They pump their instruments in the air above their lithe bodies. Bolts of multi-color lights flash across the stage; reflective smoke billows up from unseen fissures in the floor. I can't help but flash back to my just-as-impressive personal light show—my not-for-entertainment house fire. I swallow hard.

Flanking the stage, enormous screens stream close-ups of the band in a continuum of pictures beginning forty years prior. Like teenagers, we are spellbound and raise our fists toward the ceiling, as we continue our way down the aisle, bordered by shoes, stomachs and clapping hands. Eventually, we stop in front of two empty seats. My friend checks our tickets. She tries to get the attention of the guy next to us. He, like everyone else in our row, is mesmerized by the band's magical entrance. She uses her cell phone to light up the ticket numbers and checks them with the seats—one ticket seems to correspond to where the man is already sitting, or rather standing and applauding, oblivious to us. My friend nudges the guy and holds her ticket up to his face. He pulls out his ticket from his shirt pocket and they compare. The man points to his number and then to the number on the seat. Evidently, we are in the wrong section. With encouragement from him and others surrounding the two empty chairs, we decide to claim the seats as our own. After swallowing huge gulps of wine, we stuff our cups into the holders in front of us, and clap and sing. *Oh my god,* I say to myself. *This is unfrickingbelievable!* The band bursts into their first number-one hit, turbocharging everyone into a torrid frenzy.

We sit to the far left of the stage and four sections above its center. The gigantic screens continue to flash close-ups of band members as they morph from collagen-ripe kids to stringy-faced adults. As time catches up to the present, they look old—they are old—but they're still insanely fantastic. On stage, smiles plaster across their iconic battle-scarred faces, all except for the drummer, who seems to be in a world by himself. Straight-faced with a furrowed brow, he's not bored, but not into the fervor like the others. He's in a zone all to himself. He's that cool.

We sing along to the songs. I know all the words, my friend knows most of them—after all, it isn't her favorite band. She has a much better voice than I do, so it doesn't matter. The good thing is she's as giddy as I am to be here. Then, out of nowhere, I want to tug her sleeve and ask, "Where the fuck have you been?" I take a deep breath, will away my nasty thoughts and inhale wafts of pot smoke, bad aftershave, and hops. I let concert nirvana absorb me. The deafening din of the audience and acoustics boom yet remain tonally on point and clear. The lead singer belts out one famous song after another, blasting the audience to levels of other-worldly excitement, as if everyone won the mega million-dollar lottery and were universally doing adrenalin-infused tequila shots.

I slug back a mouthful of wine. My favorite song comes on. I scream, and we hug. Tears run down my face as I sing along. My friend dances in place besides me. Bliss permeates my pores. Minutes dissolve into hours and in a flash, never-never land morphs back into reality; the show is over. The band effusively says their goodbyes. They bow as deeply as ballerinas, as the lead singer struts around the stage, gives thanks, and shouts individual band members' names; a huge round of applause punctuates each one. They sprint off stage seemingly with the same fever they started with, only sweatier. They're gone in a flash. The crowd is out of their collective gourd. Lighters and cell phones ignite the stadium like millions of fireflies. The band rushes back on stage for their encore.

I have a moment and take a deep breath. They play one of their most famous songs. I must decide to go down in front to see my all-time favorite band for the last time in my life close up or stay where I am, safe and sound next to my friend. *Fuck it.* I slug another gulp of wine and say, "I'm going down." My friend waves goodbye to me and sits down in her seat for the first time since the concert began. I'm shocked she opted out. But no harm, no foul. After all, they aren't her all-time favorite band. I grab the center railing that follows the steps down to the front. As soon as I start walking, I realize how tipsy I am. I don't want to be the old drunk lady that face-plants down the stairs, so I hold on to the railing like it's my lifeline out of a deep well. My feet don't fall into a normal walking pattern, but somehow, I make it down to a row of seats just above the floor. All the chairs are empty. Remarkable. I sit down quickly so I won't draw attention to myself and get bounced from the concert at this late stage. The band pounds out another chorus of the final song to the delight and delirium of the audience.

A man sits down next to me, and I shout, "Wonder why these seats are empty."

"They're for the handicapped," The man mouths and claps to the music. "And they left."

"Oh," I say. Elated, I take multiple pictures of the band from my newfound perch. I'm in heaven now. I can't wait to show my friend my photos.

The song ends, much to the anguish of the teeming mass. The band prances around once more, blowing kisses and finally, they dash off stage. Lights from phones, lighters, and who knows what illuminate the stadium. Cheers from the rafters down to the floor pulsate against the walls and reverberate around me like I'm standing two feet away from the flammable end of a rocketship. My ability to shout suctions out of me. Known as the loudest stadium in the United States, I could have never imagined just how loud until now. I've never heard anything so deafening.

Suddenly, the lights burn from above, swallowing the darkness. The world is different, rocked on its axis, but appears normal. I stand and start making my way back up to my friend. I grab the center rail as before, my legs still struggling to follow my brain's instructions to put one foot in front of the other. My ears ring and the world seems muted. Waves of people push me along and prevent me from falling. I make it back to my friend, who sits patiently in her seat. Not smiling, she reeks of someone who has something on her mind. My brain is buzzing and filled with cotton, and I feel a little nervous beneath the lingering high of the show.

CRACKIN' UP

Months pass. Your house resembles a hoarder dwelling. Brown butcher paper covers your floors, a thin carpeting with rips, scuffs, and dozens of footprints. Strips of blue tape attempt to secure its edges, but it tears under use. A small path between the mountains of boxes, filled with your cleaned household goods, leads you from the front door through the living room to the dining room, which now houses your food. However, your refrigerator remains on your back deck. A neighbor gives you purple dahlias that brighten your dining table, but they are crowded in by your microwave, toaster oven, dog treats, food cartons, various utensils, an open bottle of wine, tape measure, pens, receipts, and a flip phone. In a small bowl, popcorn from the night before waits to be finished.

The simplest of tasks are complicated and throw you into a dark age of survival. Because the windows must be replaced and the walls on the side of the house closest to the now non-existent, burned-down garage must be re-sided and painted, you can't use rooms on that side of your home. You must walk outside and around the house to cook and eat on the back deck, so God forbid you forget something inside needed for cooking outside. As much as you try to tell yourself to buck up, your ability to sport a stiff upper lip is as likely as getting a buzz off a cup of tepid decaf.

Your husband can't find the peanut butter and jelly to make a sandwich. In your efforts to organize the relentless chaos, you've moved them from the dining table to a wire shoe rack that has been emptied of footwear and now serves as a pantry in your living room. The bread is buried under a wad of loose napkins, and the whereabouts of your knives is anyone's guess. For dinner, you dig through boxes of pots, pans and aprons to find a colander and saucepan to boil pasta—on the Coleman stove outside. A chicken thaws in the main floor bathroom and pulling it from the sink to wash your hands is at best awkward. You're grateful for a sunny spring and decent weather, but rain looms on the horizon. Nothing is easy. Nothing is intuitive. You bicker about who moved the egg frying pan outside when you're inside, and when you're in the backyard, you snipe about who moved it in. Nothing is right. Nothing stays in the same place for more than one use.

Your sense of order flamed out months ago. You no longer care if you stack dirty plates in the plastic tub you put in the bathroom to keep things neat and tidy. Now, everything spreads out over the vanity. You put a plastic cup near the hand-soap bottle to hold the dish scrubber to keep it out of the sink and avoid losing it. But your husband hasn't picked up on the practice, so it ends up in the sink or lost.

You vacuum the bathroom floor before you mop. Your instincts tell you to vacuum the other rooms covered with paper carpeting, but when you do, the paper gets caught up in the vacuum, mutilating the blue tape, so you stop. You learn to ignore the dirt, dog hair, and crumbs covering the floor, the sediment of life that reinforces your home's abandoned-shack-in-the-woods look. Debris piles up at the wall and floor intersections. Admirably, your husband sweeps the paper floor covering but leaves the dustpan and broom in a different spot each time. You discover their whereabouts only after tripping over them. Brimming with frustration, you return to the food table, unscrew a bottle of wine, pour it into a plastic cup and rip open a bag of pretzels marked "total loss" by the cleaning company. You clear a spot on the couch in the TV room and sit down to watch a British murder mystery. When you moved into the hotel, you cancelled cable, and now you're left with only one streaming channel, Acorn, the British TV channel. You sit on your couch, happy to be transported to a beautiful country village, even though there's a murderer on the loose.

And it isn't even lunch time.

Who cares, you think. You douse your efforts to maintain a good attitude with mediocre wine and a misting from the perpetual cloud hovering above your head. You're that gloomy sap who can't even muster the small step from "OK, I guess" to "fine" after being asked how you're doing. Pretending chronic stress doesn't alter your personality is not sustainable, and you feel yourself descending into a subterranean world of sour self-doubt and distrust. You feel a few football fields away from what you vaguely recall your former self to be.

EMOTIONAL RESCUE

"I lost my ticket stub. I have to find it," your friend says when you return. "I have to find it, it's my only souvenir."

I clear my throat. "Well, I got up close, really close," I say as she gets out of her seat and bends over to scour the floor. "It was amazing."

"That's great, I am so glad you went." Her head stays down. She sorts through debris as carefully as I picked through the ashes of my burned garage.

I join her for a minute, then stand up and watch people stream by. Still simmering from my close-up experience, the wine and standing up too quickly, I feel dizzy. A woman and a man wearing a starkly bleached hat pause in the row in front of me, stopped by the bottle-necked crowd.

I ask the guy, "What's your favorite song?" He is smallish with a dark complexion, exceptionally white teeth, and big brown eyes.

"'Dead Flowers,'" he answers. His black t-shirt underneath a jean jacket reminds me of what I would wear if I wasn't sporting my custom t-shirt.

"That's my favorite song, too. But the song is not 'Dead Flowers,' it's 'Sweet Virginia.' 'Dead flowers' are lyrics in 'Sweet Virginia,'" I say with 100 percent certainty. He's cute. In an alternative universe, he would be my type, just as my husband at home is my type in this universe.

"No, it's not. I ought to know. I've been to every concert since 1966." He smiles at me. It's clear he knows that's a hard gauntlet to challenge.

"1966? How old are you?"

"Sixty-three."

"So am I," I say. *Wow, we have so much in common,* I think. My head and heart float somewhere above the crowd. For the time being, the concert has completely wiped away the black soot clogging my brain.

We talk about where to get drinks in the area and how the woman he's with is not his wife, as I assume, but his sister-in-law. His brother had died, and they decided to go to the concert together in his honor. The woman doesn't look me in the eyes.

"Why don't you meet us at the bar around the corner?" he asks. Without thinking, I leave my unaware-ticket-searching friend and walk toward the exit doors with him and the sister-in-law. I make him tell me exactly where the bar is in relation to the stadium, even though I know I'm not going, let alone sober enough to remember any directions.

I try to reiterate our impending rendezvous to him, when he takes my cheeks in his hands, gentle hands, and draws my face to his and sears my lips with a kiss. Just like that. On the lips. He lets go and says, "That's for Mick Jagger and the Rolling Stones." Then he says, pulling away, "Come to the bar!" and he and his sister-in-law disappear into the dimly lit, crowded hallway of the stadium.

I stand still. I'm like a character from a Disney cartoon. My jaw unhinges from its sockets, and the bottom part hits the floor. Involuntarily, my face grows five feet wide to accommodate my smile. I touch my cheeks and rest my hands there for a few seconds. I breathe in. Like Ann Margaret in *Bye Bye Birdie* after Birdie kisses her. I glide back to my seat where my friend is still looking for a stub.

"No luck," she says, "we can go if you want. Hey, what's with you —did you just smoke pot?"

I replay the last few minutes for her. She's elated. I spare no detail. Not only was he cute—even adorable—he was my age and super nice. If the concert was cherry pie, that guy's kiss was whipped cream and a chocolate-covered almond on top. I'll never see him again, wouldn't recognize him if I did. But the spontaneity, the being in the moment, his adorableness, and that he saw me as kissable—in that moment we sparked some flames of our own. I love that my friend gets why I'm so happy—how out of nowhere and unexpectedly some sizzle can happen, amazing sizzle, that ignites you into a transitory state of bliss. Both of us feel jubilant, even if she didn't find a ticket stub to take home. And I get to take home something much more memorable than any souvenir. For a few minutes my feet don't touch the floor. Hot, hot, hot.

DIRTY WORK

Next week, the contractor says, he will install your kitchen cabinets. Then the flooring will go in. After the flooring is in, you can put away the boxes of stuff that belong in your basement because the dust will stop falling from above. Sometime after that, the appliances go in. At the same time, the cement foundation will be poured for your new garage and the walls will follow. Painting the house will come last. By October—six months after the fire—you assume your house will be back to being your house, only better, you hope. During this time, you'll expect to fight more with your husband, return to writing, and make better choices about sorting through boxes. You'll decide on hardware for the kitchen and new front and back doors to replace the ones kicked in by well-meaning firemen. You'll pick out paint colors. You'll decide if you're going to forgive the friends who disappointed you but realize obsessing about them must stop. You'll drive yourself crazy—crazier than you already feel. And you'll find some friends have circled back. Maybe they really do care, they just didn't know how to act—like when your mom got Alzheimer's, and some of her friends vanished—even though their disappearance still lingers in your gut.

Some people just aren't good when life blows up. Your emotions, their blistering exposed ends, have tempered, but the smoldering continues.

Your house forces you to live in the present, as it desperately tries to be the home it once was. The living room chairs are cleared for sitting, yet the paper carpeting remains. Boxes of velvet hangers wait to be exchanged for the cleaning company's wire hangers. A forty-pound bag of dog food is stowed in the hallway, and your old refrigerator continues to hum like a freight train outside. Pictures rest on the floor, waiting for repainted walls to dry. The peanut butter hasn't been seen in days.

No, the groundhog hasn't shown its face yet, declaring springtime in your house. The cloud of smoke refuses to be rushed.

YOU CAN'T ALWAYS GET WHAT YOU WANT

Santa Claus dolls line the shelves at Target. Bins of wreaths greet you at Costco. Wool coats come out and rows of boots crowd out open-toed flats. It's almost Halloween, and your house still looks like a scary movie. You open and sort through your boxes, sometimes systematically, sometimes randomly, like they're recycled Christmas presents. One box holds all your mother's cashmere sweaters. Your mother has been dead eleven years, and you've been hanging on to them ever since. You don't want to get rid of them because they're your mother's. But you determine now is a good time because you're purging your house of unused objects and because of the fire, the cleaning company has boxed most of your belongings. The sweaters look like new, cleaned, pressed, tissue paper inside the folds. You call the consignment place, and they say, yes, bring them in. You deliver them, and the thirtyish-year-old woman sitting on a stool says hello. Her eyelashes are so long they practically brush your face. You blink back at her and return her greeting.

"These are my mother's cashmere sweaters, twenty-two of them." You place the professionally folded lush sweaters on the counter. She bats her eyelashes at the pile and paws through them.

"They need to be on hangers, or we can't take them."

"They're in perfect condition, folded WITH TISSUE!" You

unfold one to demonstrate the care with which they've been packaged.

"Yes, I can see that. But they should be on hangers; we only take items on hangers." She sighs heavily. "Leave them here, and I'll take a look." She's too young to sigh like that.

You leave her to assess your mother's sweaters and walk around looking for something you can't live without. Eventually, you return to the woman on the stool, now studying her long pointy, mulberry-painted fingernails.

"I pulled two." She says and shoves the rest toward you on the counter. "Next time bring them in on hangers."

"That's all, just two?" *Incredible, an insult to my mother*, you think.

"That's all," she says as she grins and stands up. "Thanks for coming in," she adds, splaying her witchy fingernails on one of the kept sweaters. You pick up your dead mother's rejected sweaters and leave. You don't say thank you or good-bye. You're dumbfounded. They're perfectly good, clean cashmere sweaters.

It's raining now. You get in your car, shove the sweaters in the back and cry. You can't remember if you have cried at all since the fire. You're sure you haven't, and the tears stream from your eyes harder than the rain on your windshield. How fitting. You're angry at the stupid clerk, and sad for your mother, and mad at the fire, and sorry for your broken friendships, tired of being so constantly depressed, and exhausted from living like a displaced disaster victim in your own home and really, deep down, sick of yourself. You have no patience, no humor, nothing positive comes out of your mouth; you're Eeyore on a bad day. Your phone buzzes. It's your friend who took you to the concert.

"Hi, are you busy? Thought if you had time, we could meet for a drink." She is chipper as always.

"I'm not in a very good place right now, to tell you the truth." I wipe my eyes. I glance into the rear-view mirror. I'm a mess.

"You probably need a drink; do you have time for a glass of wine?" she says. "Just a quick one?"

"Well, OK. I'm in the parking lot below The Wine and Growl.

Let's meet there." I take a deep breath. This isn't going to go well, I can tell.

"Great, give me ten minutes, and I'll see you there." She hangs up the phone.

Another deep breath, and I wipe my eyes with a tissue from my purse. I can't imagine why I'm meeting her in my state of mind. I think, *I feel like a low-lit fire, waiting for someone to stir me up, then boom, I'll explode.*

I drive around the buildings and park in front of the bar. At a back table in the mostly empty place, I wait for her. When she arrives, we hug as we do when we see each other. We both sit. After exchanging pleasantries, she asks, "You seem upset, honey, what's going on with you?"

I blurt, "Sisters 'n' Style wouldn't take my mother's sweaters. They're like new, wrapped, clean, and folded." I take a deep breath and oxygen hits the cinders, "And I'm upset with you—you haven't been there for me, this whole time." Tears drop from my eyes onto a coaster. She grabs my hand from across the table and grips it.

"I know, honey, you were gone, then I was gone . . . then Buddy died."

I interrupt her. "The fire was in May, this is October. We each took short trips in July, your dog died in September. Six months have passed for you to be there, and you still haven't been there for me— except for the concert, the concert was the best thing ever." Our hands remain clasped on the table. The waitress drops off our drinks and leaves quickly. With our free hands we both take a sip of wine.

She puts down her glass and purses her lips. She seems to be holding back what she wants to say—*A protest*, I think, as she looks at me intently. Suddenly, her face relaxes. "You're right, I haven't been there for you. I'm so sorry. And you've always been there for me— before the divorce, Todd, the dog, everything," She looks directly at me, our eyes watering. "I am so sorry." She squeezes my hand. I feel her heart. At this moment, she's given me everything she has and everything I need. My hand warms inside hers. I can't ask for anything more.

The next hour goes by quickly—hashing out the drama of the

past months, lowlighted by the fire and its fallout, highlighted by a concert and a kiss, and punctuated with sips of wine. Our hands never loosen their grip. When we do leave, we hug and sniffle our love for each other in the parking lot. The rain falls heavy on our heads and shortens what might have been a prolonged goodbye. We rush to our respective cars. I sit in mine and take a few deep breaths. I feel like a burden has been lifted. My disaster has had cleansing properties for sure: it has given all my relationships clarity. This one was well worth the fight to salvage, even though I feel a shift has occurred. *Time will tell*, I think.

I look back at my mother's sweaters. I drive them to the thrift shop where Tanya is welcoming—even if a little churchy. She accepts everything and anything, and all sale proceeds go directly to veterans. That, and knowing my mother's sweaters will be worn by women who love them, gives me great comfort. And just like that, I feel lighter, better about everything. As my writing coach would say, the light at the end of the tunnel doesn't always have to be the beam of an oncoming train.

YOU BETTER MOVE ON

You return to your house, having left the sweaters with young, energetic Tanya. Shoving junk mail, rugs wrapped in plastic, and hangers off the couch, you clear a space to sit. Next to you, the small urn filled with your mother's ashes rests on the table. Before the fire, you kept her on your dresser in your office. When you left for the hotel, you took her with you. You pulled her out of your purse when you returned home, but then lost her for a couple months. Remarkably, one day she appeared out of the mess on the side table—you noticed her sitting there amongst books, safety pins, and plastic spoons and forks. Thrilled to see her, you thought you'd lost her forever, again. You realize there are ashes and then there are ashes, not all leave you violated and emotionally charred. You imagine your mom has been waiting to appear at the right time, when your head cleared, and you could appreciate her return.

While an unpredictable and ruinous fire can change the course of your life, not everything is destroyed and, in some cases, singed relationships can be dusted off, restored, and improved. You realize, too, after almost eight months, that it might be time to let go of the firewall you built, a self-protectiveness that has become so much of your identity. Just to see how you do on your own again. To lean into being whole—never to be the person you were before, but perhaps regenerating into someone better. To feel fine again. Really that's more than you've hoped for a long, long time.

Tootsie

"Why does Mr. Samson want to see me?" Tootsie muttered to herself as she swiveled side to side in her desk chair. Jason trotted away from her cubicle before she could ask him. One minute he was there, telling her to report to Mr. Samson in HR immediately and the next, he was gone, zip. No manners, like most people under forty. Normally, she would have told him he had something green in his braces, but he didn't leave her time for that, did he?

The fact that she'd been called to meet with Samson, the head of human resources, annoyed her more than it made her nervous. The days she took off to have her carpet cleaned most likely sent up a red flag. If he refused to pay her, she'd give him a piece of her mind.

Afterall, she had loads of comp time.

Standing up, she fluffed her tight black curls. *Better rattle Jennifer's cage before I go.* Jennifer worked on the other side of her cubicle, an entitled Gen Y-er, Gen X-er, or millennial, whatever the current term was for the all-about-me generation. Tootsie needed to enter a report generated by Jennifer into Excel before EOD. She stood on her tiptoes to see over the wall. Not surprisingly, the phone stuck to her ear, Jennifer yammered on a personal call. The report was nowhere in sight. Tootsie cleared her throat. Jennifer looked up at her with raccoon-like eyes, blinked, and waved a dismissive hand, before staring at her pointed, painted nails.

Ignoring Jennifer's disrespectful behavior, Tootsie said, "Mr. Samson has asked to see me immediately, and I'd like to input the financial analysis report when I return. June in sales is hosting a Tupperware party after work and prizes are given out promptly at 5:30, so I don't want to be late." She overlooked Jennifer's eyeroll, what eyeballs she could see through her forest of fake eyelashes, and turned away from the wall. After locking her tote into her bottom desk drawer—she didn't trust anyone—Tootsie headed for the elevators through a maze of cubicles.

Corey from Logistics stood waiting at the third-floor east elevator when Tootsie arrived. She reached across his path and pushed the already-lit button. Using the chrome doors as a mirror, Tootsie mashed her red lips together and scrunched her curls. *Time to get root spray*, she thought as she turned her head one direction and then another. She was sure the top of her head was resplendent with gray grow-out, a real reveal for anyone taller than her, which was most people. Her curls concealed her skunk stripe when her dye job was overdue, but she'd let it go too long this time.

Straightening her posture and positioning the curls on her head, she turned to Corey and said, "Good morning, how are Lynette and the new baby?" She smiled at Corey, who covered a yawn with the back of his hand. The dark circles under his eyes made them look bruised. He appeared Jennifer's age, but without her attitude, and had a worn-out movie star mystique about him. Like a James Bond with his stubbled chin, razor sharp parted hair, and black turtleneck. Like Sean Connery, not the others.

"Fine, Tootsie, she's keeping us busy." Corey returned Tootsie's smile, but it struck her as half-hearted and weary. *Understandable*, she thought. His teeth were as white as her pearl necklace. She'd want her daughter to marry a guy like him, if she had one.

"Well, I guess that's babies for you, busy, busy. Did you set up the musical mobile yet?" She'd given the mobile as a baby-shower gift. She checked her watch while she waited for his reply: 10:00 a.m. *Mr. Samson better not keep me long. If Jennifer had finished her damn report on time, I wouldn't be so under the gun.* Tootsie wanted to tattle on her to Mr. Samson, not that it mattered. They appeared overnight, everyone working at Consolidated was half her age and adhered solely to their own agendas. Unlike her generation, who did their work on time and whose good word meant something. She noticed Corey had closed his eyes. "The mobile? Did you set it up yet?"

Corey's eyes blinked open. "Yep, put it over her crib," he said in a gravelly voice. The elevator opened. "After you." He motioned and followed Tootsie.

What a gentleman—an anomaly around here. She pulled at her curls. "Twelve, please. I've been summoned to Mr. Samson's office."

Corey pushed twelve for her and then pushed eight. "Samson? Really." Corey folded his arms across his chest and leaned against the wall, head tipped up, eyes shut.

"I haven't the slightest idea why, but I hope it's not about those days I took off last month while I had my carpet cleaned. I took off two days, probably could have taken one, but I wanted to get every-thing back in place before returning to work. You know how irritating it is, not having everything in place." She glanced at Corey. A long couple of seconds passed before his eyes opened. Her fingers combed through her curls.

"Well, honestly, Tootsie, nothing in our house is in the right place now, except maybe the dog dish." The elevator doors opened. Corey yawned into his hand. "Good luck with Samson," he murmured as he left.

"Thanks," Tootsie said and yelled after him, "I'd love to see baby pictures!" But the doors closed before she finished her sentence.

He's exhausted. And yet, perfectly polite. He could sure teach his peers a thing or two. Like Jennifer, rusty red hair, pasty skin, gooped-on eye makeup, arm tattoos, nose ring, basically, a walking Halloween costume. And as lazy as a sloth. She checked her watch again. The doors opened on twelve, and after a good fluffing of her hair, Tootsie exited toward Mr. Samson's office.

"Morning, Tootsie," Doreen, Mr. Samson's secretary, said as Tootsie approached her desk. "Have a seat, and I'll tell Mr. Samson you're here."

"Thank you, Doreen, lovely scarf, good color on you." Tootsie smiled and thought, *She's lost weight, not so puffy, but that hair.* Doreen had a buzz cut, and what little hair she had left was dyed platinum blonde.

"You think so? My daughter gave it to me. Green is my color, I think." Doreen lifted one of the scarf's ends and adjusted it over the other. She patted her handiwork and smiled, then resumed typing. Doreen had worked at Consolidated almost as long as Tootsie—Samson was her fifth or sixth HR director. She was one of the few remaining employees who was Tootsie's age, although Doreen seemed determined to appear otherwise. *Like a haircut can turn back time. Dream on, Doreen.*

Tootsie sat down on the hard, armless white leather couch. The black iron-rimmed glass table was pushed a little too close, so she had to keep her legs uncomfortably to the side and because her feet couldn't quite touch the ground, they dangled at an awkward angle. She tried to shift the table away, but it stuck in the shag rug. *Such impractical and uncomfortable furniture. Give me a nice wingback chair over this any day.* Cemented in her lopsidedness, she picked up a *Town and Country* magazine and leafed through it. *Who are these people, so young, rich, and beautiful?*

Finally, after she had nearly finished an article on Tara, the famous "twenty six year old heiress equestrian entrepreneur artistic" phenom and completely unknown to Tootsie, Doreen announced that Mr. Samson was available. Relieved to stand, Tootsie slowly straightened herself. Her knees wanted to buckle, but she resisted and wobbled through Mr. Samson's open door, fingers lifting curls from the top of her head.

"Hello, Tootsie, sit down, nice to see you," Mr. Samson said, brandishing his horse-like teeth. He stood up behind his desk and opened his hand, inviting her to sit in one of the low-back purple and red polka-dot club chairs facing him. As soon as she sat, he perched on the edge of his desk, hands clasped in his lap. His large frame strained against his fitted suit like an overstuffed sausage, its casing nearly bursting. His purple tie matched the handkerchief in his breast pocket and the polka dots of the chair. He smoothed back his gelled, too-long hair, then pulled Chapstick out of his jacket pocket and rubbed it over his flakey almost non-existent lips. As he returned his Chapstick to his pocket, his watch lit up, which triggered a light to blink on his phone. He punched a button on the phone, which lay next to him on the desk. Whatever he saw prompted him to display his teeth again. Then suddenly, as if he remembered some bit of sad news, his brow wrinkled, and his lower lip jutted. *Land the plane, Samson. I don't have time to watch you preen and do a Dick Tracy impersonation with your gadgets. I have a report to deliver by 5:00 and a Tupperware party to attend at 5:30, so for God's sake, out with it.*

"Well, Tootsie," Samson cleared his throat, "this is hard for me. Very hard. But Consolidated finds itself in a financial pickle, so to speak, that requires necessary staff reductions. Unfortunately, your position is one we have to cut. This was, of course, neither my idea or my choice, but . . ." His voice petered out. He pulled at his cuffs with his arms outstretched. Simultaneously, his phone and watch lit up. Glancing at one and then the other, he smiled again, this time with a chuckle.

Blood boiled to Tootsie's brain, causing her to flush. She didn't hear anything else after the word "cut." She sprang up. "What?" Her arms rigid at her sides. "Cut?" Tootsie shook her head vigorously. "Listen, you—I have been here over thirty-five years, and I'll be damned if you're going to cut my ass!" Her voice boomed bigger than the room. Her cheeks burned, as if ignited by a high voltage plug. No way was she taking this from a stupid, greasy-haired, dry-lipped, thirty-years-younger-than-her excuse for an HR director.

Mr. Samson patted his hands downward as though to quiet Tootsie. "Please, I know this is hard, you've worked here a long time, I'm well aware, but we have to downsize by thirty people. You're one of the lucky ones, you'll have a small pension to go along with your severance package, three months' pay plus any vacation you have coming. Personally, I think it's very generous—maybe better than what you would have gotten if you waited to retire down the line." Mr. Samson shifted his weight on the desk and read a message that popped up on his watch. He snickered.

"Lucky? Generous? Are you crazy?" Tootsie's eyes devolved into slits. "Hell no, Mr. Samson, I worked very hard for what I have. I live alone, I have no family in this city and can't afford to retire for three more years because unlike yourself, I make a piddly little salary, have always made a piddly little salary!" Tootsie crossed her arms. After all her hard work and loyalty, to be laid off, fired by this meathead, and why? *Because they're downsizing? Well, they can downsize someone else!*

Mr. Samson stuck a meaty finger between his neck and his shirt and wiggled it back and forth. Then he reached around, grabbed a nearby envelope off his desk and handed it to Tootsie. "Here, Tootsie, it's the best I can do. Please take it and don't make this any more difficult than it already is. Go buy yourself new shoes or something. Treat yourself." Mr. Samson continued to hold out the envelope, but Tootsie remained immobile. Awkwardly, he balanced it on top of her crossed arms. "Take it. You have till 1:00 p.m. to clean out your desk and leave the building. Thank you for your service here at Consolidated." Floundering like a fish out of water, he held out his hand for Tootsie to shake. Sweat was beginning to pool under his nose. Tootsie's arms remained firmly pressed across her chest with the check teetering on top.

Mr. Samson stood up; his sheer size invaded her personal space. She fought back her gag reflex after inhaling a waft of his musky aftershave. Then, like an autumn leaf falling from a tree, the envelope fluttered to the ground. Simultaneously, Tootsie and Mr. Samson bent to retrieve it from the floor. Their heads touched. Tootsie snatched the envelope as they both bounced up. She plucked at her hair and straightened her blouse. She glared at his beady brown eyes.

"Tootsie, there's nothing else to say. I've other business to attend to and wish you the best of luck." He gave her a thin smile with his moistened lips. She remained stoic, unmoved, even as his phone started to vibrate on the desk. The veins bulged on either side of his head as he restrained from looking at it. He inhaled long and loud. "Look. Take the money. Go shopping. Hell, my wife always says shopping makes her feel good, and I guarantee you, she won't live long enough to wear everything she has in her closet." He chuckled nervously and checked his watch. "Tootsie, go, goodbye—celebrate your early retirement for goodness' sake. Buy shoes, a watch, some earrings, something special, anything."

"Special? Ha! You know what's special? Staying in a job you've had forever and retiring like you've planned, that's special." She turned and stomped out the door, yelling, "And I love my shoes, Mr. Samson! I worked hard for these shoes and unlike this company, these shoes have never let me down! Never!"

On her way out, Tootsie shouted at Doreen, "Green has never been your color!" Wide-eyed, the executive assistant clutched at her scarf. "Never! Stick with the primaries."

Tootsie race-walked to the elevator, the envelope clutched in her hand. She pushed the down button. Her eyes welled with tears. She begged herself not to cry, *Not here, not in front of these degenerates.* At last, a *ding* and the doors slid open, producing Jeanette and Jason. Jeanette worked in IT and kept her head down. She worked like a beaver, looked a little like one, too. Jason, the hatchet man's messenger, and his child-bearing hips edged out Jeanette as they left the elevator, bumping into Tootsie as she entered.

Tootsie snarled, "Jeanette, watch out. Heads are rollin', yours's next!" She pushed three on the panel and shook her finger at a wide-eyed Jason. "Blood is on your hands, too, babyface, yessiree Bob!" The doors closed. "Idiots," she said and ripped open the envelope. Severance pay plus vacation pay looked like a tidy lump sum, but she was savvy enough to know, spread over several months, it wasn't much at all. She didn't want to draw Social Security yet either, too soon. And her pension amount? How would she live? Pay bills? Get her hair done? Her heart pounded like it wanted out of her chest. *Who's going to hire a sixty-seven-year-old washed-up old woman?* Her lips pursed pencil straight.

Tootsie stuffed the letter back into its envelope, folded it, and shoved it into her pants pocket. She mumbled as she exited the elevator, "I worked nights. I ate at my desk. I washed dishes in the break room. Criminy. I had an earthquake preparedness kit and never wore white past Labor Day. I did everything right."

Her head down like a charging bull as she tromped to her cubicle, the new deep blue and green carpet slapped her in the face. The contrast between it and her worn out shoes depressed her. But they were old friends, her shoes, shabby or not. Besides, who noticed? *Hmph, Mr. Samson did. Money for flooring, but not for me. Bastard.*

A nauseous feeling crept over her. Like the time years ago when she drank a bottle of wine by herself while waiting for that idiot, Phil, to call. After some stupid introduction by her friend, Leon, in acquisitions, the three of them lunched, Leon's idea, and she'd been strong-armed into giving Phil her number. He said he'd call her that night. She waited and drank, and waited and drank, but he didn't call. What a fool she'd been. For two days her body suffered. This felt worse, though.

By the time Tootsie arrived back at her cube, Jennifer had disappeared, and the report was stuck under her computer keyboard. A sticky note attached bore Jennifer's handwriting, small and scratchy. She'd drawn a heart followed by a few x's and o's scribbled after it. Classic Jennifer sarcasm. Tootsie sat down in her chair and swiveled back and forth. Then she tossed the report over the wall and listened to the papers flutter to the floor.

Tootsie scrunched her curls and surveyed her cubical area. A postcard from her niece and husband in Maui, another postcard from her high school friend, Norma, sent from Spain, birthday cards from the girls in legal, a thank you note from Corey and Lynette for the baby mobile, and of course, her award from the CEO for thirty-five years of exemplary service to Consolidated. *What a joke!* She'd received it just months ago. *Meaningless.* She stuffed the postcards, the thank you and the birthday cards into the tote she retrieved from her desk drawer. She spied the red stapler she'd purchased with her own money at Office Depot's 50 percent off Christmas sale. She'd take that. She opened another drawer, grabbed her lipstick, mirror, and assorted meal coupons from restaurants in the area. She loaded into her wallet the loose change she'd kept for special treats from the vending machines. A couple of random buttons to who-knows-what she stuffed into an envelope. She had three pairs of glasses, various strengths, she wanted those. *Ah, yes,* she grabbed the business card from her hairdresser, why, she didn't know, and one for a tarot card reader she promised to see, *Timing might be perfect,* and of course, her nail polish remover. And the Wite-Out. Wite-Out was hard to find now.

She scanned her cubicle one last time. *How dismal.* Thirty-five years reduced to a handbag full of nothing. She heard Taylor from down the hall yell to Alistair about grabbing Chinese food for lunch. Soon people would begin leaving for their noon break. She didn't want to run into anyone. She didn't want pity, or worse, sorrowful looks. Slinging her bag over her shoulder, she took a deep breath and walked toward the elevator. Several people were waiting in front of the doors when she arrived. She wormed her way to the front of the crowd and reached for the lit down button. *Please, no one talk to me,* she thought and adjusted her bag on her shoulder.

"Excuse me!" some guy from marketing said, as her tote bumped his arm.

"Sorry." Tootsie looked up at him. She fluffed her hair a bit with her free hand. He looked down at her. She didn't know him by name and prayed he didn't know her either. "No problem," he said and turned away. She faced forward. *Of course, he doesn't know me. No one does anymore.* A tension headache tapped at her frontal lobes. *Stay focused,* she thought and stared at the back of the woman who had wiggled in front of her. She wore a too-tight stretchy white shirt with a visible black bra underneath. *Since when was that OK?*

Someone said, "Hurry up, elevator. I got a date with my trainer. Can't be late." Glancing sideways, she saw two marketing guys. Artsy, untucked shirts, cowboy boots, and jeans, half-shaved, *The new uniform for men.*

Then someone from the back said, "Hey, did you hear, big layoffs today."

The guy next to her said, "What the 'f'? Please not me. Shit, my car loan by itself would bury me without a paycheck."

His friend added his two cents, "I know, right? I just took out a year's lease on a loft. Heard it all happened before lunch. Tess, the girl with the massive Obi-Wan Kenobi tattoo on her arm, works for HR? She told me. Hey, Max, you need to see my new place. Come by some-time, have some beers. I've got a great city view."

Tootsie held her breath. She wanted to scream, "It's me! They canned me! This is what downsizing looks like, kiddies!" But instead, she stuffed the words down her throat. She felt her cheeks turn bright red. She hoped no one noticed. She turned to the left, then to the right. *Ha, the invisibility of being old, of course no one noticed.* Exercise, car loans, lofts with city views, that's what they cared about—*What about bread and water, people? What about health insurance, a new roof and—and—*she looked down at her feet *and what about new shoes?* The elevator opened, and she darted toward the back. Conversations between twenty-, thirty-, and forty-somethings wafted around her throbbing head. She mashed her lips together. She told herself, *Just get out of here, get the "f" out. Don't even try to find out who's wearing that awful patchouli oil.* After what seemed like years, the elevator doors opened, and through crammed bodies, she tucked down and bulleted out.

She wove through the lobby to the stairs that led out, down to the sidewalk. Water pooled in her eyes. Her stomach churned. She scrunched her hair hard. "You go, girl, you're done with this hellhole." Swear words stacked up in her head. Then, like bombs dropping from an airplane, they fell from her mouth. Words she had never breathed now freely spewed. She felt wonderfully out of control as she flew down the twenty-seven steps that led to the building, a swear word for each step. And she didn't need a Fitbit to count her steps. She'd counted them every day IN HER HEAD. A surprising fresh energy surged inside of her. She felt like the wind, unbridled and free. Then suddenly, as she landed on the sidewalk, boom: heavy doubt stopped her cold.

She clutched her neck and squeezed back the panic rising in her throat. She ignored her body that rattled like a hull sinking into the sea. *OK, get a grip,* she thought. Not particularly religious, she thought of God. "If you're there, dear God," she said and closed her eyes, "give me direction." She stood still as people forked around her. Tootsie dropped her tote to her side. She opened her eyes. She patted her curls. Nothing. *Well, shit,* she thought to herself, then said it out loud. Saying it gave her goose bumps. "Shit, shit, shit." Felt better than praying to God, she had to admit. But she needed a plan. Plans were her life blood. Her mother had taught her, "Armed with a plan, you're never lost." Then, she spotted Jennifer puffing toward her in her ridiculous platforms. Not exactly the answer she was looking for. Tootsie braced herself.

"Hey, Tootsie!" Jennifer shouted, her phone in hand as she screamed, "Did you get my report? Like, I can't believe you'd leave your desk—like, you had so much work to do . . . hey, what's up? Like, what's with all your stuff?" The red arm of the stapler hung over the edge of Tootsie's tote, which leaned against her leg. Jennifer's hand fell to her side, phone in tow. A voice continued to chatter into her thigh.

"Never mind, Jennifer, you don't have to put up with me anymore," Tootsie said and pointed to Jennifer's leg. "Your phone is still talking." Tootsie stared at her through narrowed eyes, fluffed her hair, and pivoted away.

Jennifer screamed after her, "Tootsie! Like, what happened?" She reattached her phone to her ear and yelled, "OMG! Remember Tootsie, that older lady I work with? I think she got fired. Yeah, like fired!"

Tootsie, still within earshot, yelled back, "And you can shove that report where the sun don't shine!" She lifted her bag to her chest and stomped down the street.

A couple blocks later her pace slowed. "Oh, hell," Tootsie said and stopped. *Where the frick am I going?* Her hands were clammy and the sweat under her breasts seeped through her blouse. She picked at her dampish curls. Up the street, a bundle of store signs vied for her attention. The sign for Imelda's Shoe Store—a bright red boot—extended out from the storefront and caught her eye. Tootsie smiled—an omen. She had never noticed that shoe store before, and there it was right in front of her. *Well, Mr. Samson, you're on. Maybe I'll buy, or maybe I'll just look.* She stroked her curls as she strode toward the door.

Before entering, she peered through the floor-to-ceiling windows. *Crap, it's crowded.* Women milled around shoe racks; salespeople clad in black buzzed between them. She grimaced. *Well, nothing ventured, nothing gained.*

A bell tinkled above her as she entered. Inside, a sweet leathery smell and the sound of New Age music drifted around her. The sunlight glazed everything in sparkles. Chatty patrons babbled.

Tootsie closed her eyes and inhaled the pervasive cheeriness, pulling at a hair twist or two. Her shoulders relaxed. Some of the heaviness of the day evaporated. She readjusted her tote on her shoulder.

Tootsie recalled her mother taking her to buy new school shoes. Year after year, she left with the same saddles, but Tootsie didn't care. Being with her mother was all that mattered—even if her decisiveness about the saddles made for a short, predictable trip. One time, to extend their togetherness, Tootsie entered a drawing at the store for a new transistor radio. She begged her mom to wait for the winner announcement before leaving. She'd pulled her mom around, showing her all the different shoes she wanted but knew she'd never own. Her mother, a consummate scheduler, who never dallied, indulged her, but only for a brief time. A disappointed Tootsie and her mother left before the winner was announced. When they arrived home, the phone was ringing. Tootsie ran to answer it and discovered she'd won the radio. Her mother hugged her, one of the few times Tootsie experienced her mother spontaneously showing her affection. Tootsie smiled—she hadn't thought of that for a long, long time.

"May I help you?" said a young willowy woman with large, deep-set charcoal eyes. Draped from head to toe in a black caftan, her feet glittered in five-inch-heeled silver sandals. "Are you looking for anything in particular?" Her soft voice calmed Tootsie, who noticed the woman's hands were clasped in a prayer position. Lips red and full, her copper-colored skin and stately presence reminded her of royalty.

"Just looking, thank you," Tootsie said. The woman's inviting and exotic manner was mesmerizing. Polar opposite from her coworkers at Consolidated. *Former coworkers.* She felt very drab in comparison and gave her hair a good scrunch.

"May I show you some of our new styles? Some are on sale." She outstretched a long, graceful arm and pointed toward a table topped with a bouquet of colorful shoes.

"Oh," Tootsie said, chuckling. She shook her head. "I don't do colors. Basic black only. It goes with everything."

"Won't you have a look? You might surprise yourself." The woman gently touched Tootsie's elbow with her elegant hand. The tiniest leopard print Tootsie had ever seen dotted her painted coral fingernails.

Going limp under the woman's touch, Tootsie let herself be guided to the table.

Tootsie had never seen such a shoe display. Then again, she hadn't been in a shoe store for years. Her black shoes had been purchased at a medical-specific shoe store. When Tootsie had started her job, her mother, a nurse, had said, "Spend a little more for nurses' shoes—they're built to last and are comfortable for those of us on our feet all day." Her mother had been right. They were not fashion-prize winners, but they had been comfortable for a long time, even if she sat at a desk most of the day.

Tootsie shook her head at the rainbow of hues and styles artfully arranged. She clucked her tongue. Lovely, but not for her. She'd feel like Joan Collins from *Dallas* in any one of them. Tootsie twisted a top curl.

A group of women walked up to the display and surrounded Tootsie like a swarm of bees. A woman in a lime-green coat and yellow boots reached for a pair of blue suede flats in front of Tootsie. "Oh. My. God. I love these. Tiff, did you see these? Do I need these?"

"You don't NEED anything, Alli, but if you love them, get them. They're super cute, they look like you."

"Do you have these in an eight?" Alli asked the saleswoman. "I love them, don't you? Aren't they gorgeous?"

"Yes, love them, fabulous—you have great taste. I'll be right back." To Tootsie, she said, "You keep looking. I'll be right back." Her flowing black robe, or whatever it was, billowed behind her as she glided to the stock room.

The hive of women buzzed around to the other side of the table, alternatively holding up a shoe and gushing with emotion over its magnificence. The saleswoman brought out a size eight for Alli. The passel moved on to the seating area, oohing and ahhhing along the way.

"See anything you like?" The saleswoman said to Tootsie, whose gaze followed the women. "Here, look. These shoes match your shirt."

She held up a pair of bright cherry Mary Janes to a red rose on Toot-sie's blouse. "Come on, just to try?"

"Oh, God, no. Black, remember? A low pump to replace these." Tootsie pointed to her shoes and tittered. "Red shoes, puh-leaze, not in a million years."

Unrelenting, the salesclerk waved the Mary Janes under Tootsie's nose. Tootsie couldn't help but inhale the new leather smell. She felt mildly intoxicated.

"They won't look good on me," Tootsie said and snickered. "Trust me."

"What size?" Two dimples presented themselves as a grin grew across the saleswoman's face. "Come on, at least try them."

"Sevens, but I'm telling you, they're just not me." Tootsie looked up at the mobiles of colorful cardboard shoes floating around the ceiling. "Maybe seven and a half. My feet have gotten wider with age. How did you get those up there?"

"I'll bring both. You'll love them, trust me," the saleswoman said and added, "with a very tall ladder." And disappeared into the backroom.

"Cripes, what am I doing?" Tootsie said to no one in particular. She sat down in the nearest chrome chair and dropped her tote to her side. With a quick fluff of her hair, she casually scanned the store to see if anyone was looking at her. Groups of gushy women dawdled around the displays, oblivious to Tootsie and her sensible shoes. *Old and invisible,* thought Tootsie. The group from earlier now stood in line at the checkout counter. They shoved their shoeboxes in front of one another, each ogling the others' purchases. *Ha. By now Mother would have whisked me away. Nothing for us here, she would've said. But she did have a fun side. I saw it.*

As a young girl, Tootsie would spy on her mother after she put Tootsie to bed. Her mother would spend hours applying makeup, then comb out her hair and flirt with herself, as if a man lived in the mirror. She looked beautiful, like a movie star. Then she'd wash it off. No trace the next day. Back to "keep your head down and nose to the grindstone." That's the mother she wanted Tootsie to see. "Take care of business, stay close to the plan, and all will be fine." For the most part, it worked, and the two of them were fine. Until she died, too early—not in the plan—and before she had a chance to be self-indulgent. Dropped dead at the hospital, ten minutes before her shift ended. Just like that. Tootsie had been on her own ever since.

Tootsie held up the flaming Mary Jane from the display. *I bet I'll get noticed with these on my feet. God, they're bright.* She set down the shoe and removed her ten-year-old black shoes. Peering through her nude stockings, her painted red toenails looked dull and tired. As usual, she penny pinched, waited too long to get a pedicure, just like her haircut and color. *Personal stuff gets put off, always the fricking job came first.* Her stomach knotted.

"Look what we found for you." A sing-song voice behind two hot pink shoeboxes walked toward her. Tootsie appreciated the saleswoman's efforts, but there was no way in hell she was buying those shoes. A quick try-on, and they'd be off her feet. They were the pinnacle of impractical. Tootsie glanced at her old shoes. *Pitiful old things,* she thought.

"I'm so excited," The saleswoman said as she helped Tootsie slip into the shoes, so intensely scarlet, Tootsie was sure the color would rub off on her stockings. "Love them! What do you think?" The woman clapped her hands, and her eyes glistened with anticipation. "They look fabulous!"

Tootsie studied her feet encased in ruby shoes. "Goodness. Bright, aren't they?" The toe was pointier than she was used to and the heel higher, but they were surprisingly comfortable. "Goodness."

"Aren't they fabulous? Come on. Don't you love them?" The saleswoman clapped her hands again. "Tell me, tell me what you think?"

Tootsie rotated her feet at the ankles. "Goodness—crap. You really like them? Be honest. I think I'm too old." She had to admit she liked them, but they made her nervous. She stretched out her legs and pointed her toes. "Wouldn't lose me in a crowd, would you?" She chuckled and glanced around. Shoe displays still held court with cliques of women, with no one breaking formation to look at her.

"Old? Not at all! They look fabulous on you! And guess what? I checked and they're 30 percent off—today. Isn't that fabulous?" Then she leaned forward and wagged her gorgeous long finger in Tootsie's face and said, "I don't know you, but seems to me you don't let loose very often. Maybe you need a pick-me-up. An indulgence, something special for yourself." Her vanilla-tinged perfume tickled Tootsie's nose and made her light-headed. "Today's the day." She clapped again.

"Well, criminy, I don't know," Tootsie said. "Son of a gun." She ran her fingers over the brilliant leather of the shoes. They did fit perfectly, and they were beautiful. Just gorgeous, she had to admit. She shook her head and stomped her feet on the floor. She slapped her hands on her thighs and said, "OK, darn it all, I'll take them." *Mother is spinning in her grave now, rotating like a chicken on a spit.*

"Fabulous!" The saleswoman stood and threw her hands up, as if declaring a touchdown. "Don't take them off. You need to wear them right now—out of the store." She picked up the empty shoebox, dropped in Tootsie's old shoes and said, "Wearing those is going to rock your world."

"Well, I don't know about that." Tootsie let out a snort and did a quick fluff of her hair. "You'd better ring them up fast, before I change my damn mind." Then she traipsed over to the full-length mirror and pointed one toe and then the other toward her reflection. She giggled at her silliness, but had to agree, the shoes did make her look good. The saleswoman put both thumbs up in Tootsie's direction and headed to the counter with Tootsie's old black shoes in a fluorescent pink box.

At the counter, the saleswoman rang up the sale and took Tootsie's credit card. She said, "You did it—I'm proud of you! Enjoy them." She winked at her.

"Thank you. You're very kind. I do appreciate it," Tootsie said and thought, *It's silly, but I could cry. No job, no money, but I got fancy shoes. Goodness Lord.*

"Stop looking so worried. Fun is just around the corner; I just know it. Promise me you'll wear them all day." The young woman came from behind the counter and gave Tootsie the shopping bag with her old shoes inside. She reached out her hand for Tootsie to shake. "I predict they'll bring you good luck." She winked again.

"Ha, too late for that today, I'm afraid, but thanks for the thought." Tootsie shook the woman's extended hand. Stunning and young, yes, and Tootsie hoped a little clairvoyant, too. She took a deep breath, pulled up the tote on her shoulder, swung her shopping bag in her hand and exited, the jingle following her out onto the bustling street.

Outside the store's door, she assessed her shoes again. *Jeez Louise, they are very red. Lord, God. Jennifer would get a kick out of these. And Mr. Samson, I bet his wife never had shoes like these. Chutes and ladders.* Tootsie adjusted her bags and didn't try to control the grin that had formed on her face. *Goodness me, fuck.*

Trails of people pushed past her. Their bodies nudged one side of her then the other. Without really thinking where she was going, Tootsie joined the jostle of bodies. Plucking at her hair with her free hand, she noted the cushiness of her new shoes. Almost as much as her old shoes, but much more sophisticated. As she trotted down the street, her elation subdued and like the first drops of a rain shower, the slow drip of her disastrous morning began tapping on her consciousness. Her heartbeat sped up. She walked faster. Remarkably, her shoes kept up. *So plush,* she thought. *So comfortable, so pretty.* The tapping dissipated.

Now hunger knocked on her shoulder. Tootsie checked her watch: 12:30. Lunch. Normally, she ate no later than noon and only a little dinner. Her metabolism had slowed so much over the past couple of years—yes, she'd put on some weight but certainly without increasing her intake. Every night she'd eat her usual bowl of popcorn. *OK, with oil and butter,* she thought, and admittedly, the bowl was large. But she loved the bowl. Her neighbor Maureen had given it to her filled with fruit after Tootsie had foot surgery. She didn't want it back, even though Tootsie had tried to return it. Maureen was a wonderful neighbor. *Never enough time to visit, though.* Ever since Maureen took the job at Home Goods after her divorce, Tootsie stopped running into her at the mailbox on weekends. That could change now, she supposed. Her weeks were suddenly free.

Tootsie kept walking until she saw the Flanagan's Diner sign. She'd stopped there once or twice to get a sandwich to go, but had never dined in. *Hell, this is a day for firsts*, she thought and pushed open the door.

A voice from somewhere yelled, "Seat yourself, ma'am!" The place buzzed. The red vinyl-topped counter stools were nearly all taken. Booths in matching Naugahyde were filled, except one at the very end of the diner. From where Tootsie stood, she could see empty water glasses and a couple of crumpled napkins on the table. She liked a booth, so she made her way there, bumping a couple of arms with her tote and shopping bag along the way. "Excuse me," she said as she did.

"Why don't you sit at the bar, be quicker, lady, we'd have to clean the table before you sit down." A gangly man with a beard stuck in a net walked toward her, carrying a dirty-dish bin. His bloodshot eyes watered, and his food-splotched shirt looked like a modern-art painting. She didn't argue.

He motioned Tootsie to sit at a vacant stool at the counter. A waitress with a red-and-black-checked apron laid a place setting.

The stool's height forced Tootsie to throw her leg over its top, as if she were mounting a horse. A new red shoe on the other end of her leg momentarily shocked her. *Wow, I'll have to get used to that*, she thought and settled on her stool. While perusing the menu, someone from behind cleared their throat.

"Is this saved?" A shaggy-haired, thirty-something man in a sport coat and jeans pointed to the seat next to Tootsie. He produced an unexpected half dozen or so laugh lines around his eyes when he smiled.

"Oh, no, it's yours, no one is sitting there, no. All yours," Tootsie said, pursing her lips and primping her hair. She stiffened her back as she studied the menu, swiveling back and forth a little. Her shoes brushed against her bags underneath her stool.

"Thanks." The man—tall as he was—straddled the seat easily. With his head in the menu he said, "Now, what do I want for lunch?"

Tootsie lowered her menu and said, glancing sideways, "Well, I've ordered the half sandwich and soup deal. If you get the turkey and cheese, you get a good-sized half sandwich and if the soup is tomato, a filling meal for a good price. I think it comes with chips and a cookie, too." She returned to her menu. When she tried to cross her legs, her red shoe bumped into the man's pant leg.

"Oh, God, I'm sorry," Tootsie said. "Did I get you dirty?" She examined his pant leg. It seemed to be clean.

"Not at all, no worries." The man examined his leg then looked at Tootsie's shoes. "Wow, those kicks are snotty. So, you like the soup and sandwich deal? Maybe that's what I'll get."

"Snotty? I've never heard of shoes called snotty. What is snotty? Sounds awful." Tootsie turned toward the man, her eyes steady on his.

"Snotty, you know, hot. Sorry, no, I like your shoes." The man laughed a little, nervously. "It's a good thing, really."

"Well, that's a new one to me." Tootsie looked at her shoes. "Snotty, huh?"

"So, it's the soup and sandwich deal you like?" The man turned over the menu once and then back again.

"I'm just saying, I've enjoyed it in the past. If you're very hungry you should probably get the whole sandwich." Searching for a waitress, Tootsie closed her menu. "Warm in here, don't you think?" She said and rolled up her sleeves. "Snotty," she said under her breath.

"Better take off my coat; I'll spill on it if I don't." The man stood up and slid out of his jacket. Then he neatly placed it over the stool and sat back down. "On a lunch break?" The man shoved the menu away and turned his gaze down the counter, the opposite direction of Tootsie.

"No, hell no; I am most certainly not on a lunch break." Tootsie hesitated for a moment, then with the conviction of delivering a confession, she added, "I was fired today." Both hands pulled at her curls, and her crossed leg bounced a jitterbug.

"Fired? That sucks. Why?" He turned to Tootsie, laugh lines disappeared.

A waitress in a white shirt, with black pants about two sizes too small for her, and a large nose ring Roy Rogers' horse Trigger would have envied, interrupted their conversation by placing water glasses in front of them. She pulled out a pad of paper and pen from her checkered apron. "What are we gettin', guys?" She pointed her pen at Tootsie.

"Shoot, well I . . ." Tootsie picked up the menu again. "I was ready, but now . . ."

"If you're not ready I can come back or do him first." The waitress turned to the man and winked. "You ready?"

"Yes, I'll have the soup and sandwich deal, turkey and cheese, whole sandwich, and tomato soup. Please." The waitress grabbed his menu. She winked again.

"Ready?" She looked at Tootsie and stuck the pen in her mouth like a sucker.

"I guess I'll have the same, thank you." Tootsie handed her the menu. "Only half a sandwich for me." The waitress grabbed it. No wink.

"Coffee, either of you?"

"No, thanks," said the man.

"No, thank you," said Tootsie.

The waitress's thighs swished in her pants as she walked away. *Buy a size larger, hon. You'd be better off.* Tootsie uncrossed her legs and hooked her heels onto the bar underneath the stool. She put her napkin on her lap and straightened her silverware.

"Why'd you get fired? Steal, sleep with your boss, look at porn sites on the job?" The man smiled. He rolled up his sleeves, revealing a tree grove tattoo on his arm.

She looked away. "Very funny. I'm old, that's all. Old. Get rid of the deadwood, as they say. I am deadwood." Tootsie looked straight ahead and fidgeted with her spoon. "Bastards."

"Wow, that's harsh. I'm sorry to hear. Shit." He folded and refolded his napkin.

"Thank you. It hasn't sunk in quite yet. I left right after I was fired. I went straight to the shoe store and bought these shoes, you see, and had such fun buying them that for a little bit, I forgot." Tootsie tapped her spoon on her palm nervously, then put it down in a straight line with the other utensils. "These snotty shoes. For a moment or two, I forgot the rug had been pulled out from underneath me."

"Sorry to bring it up." The man picked up his spoon and put it next to his fork. He brushed off his lap.

"No, that's fine. Obviously, I'm going to have to think about it again." Tootsie picked up her spoon again and fiddled with it. "So, you like my shoes?" She twirled her seat around and stuck out her legs. Her shoes blazed a brighter crimson than the stools or the booths. They made her happy just to look at them.

"Yes, snotty, like I said." The man smiled. "Hot. So, what are you going to do now?" The man folded his hands in front of him. Plates clattered and people chatted over their lunches. Somewhere, someone behind her was playing a YouTube video about how to lay carpeting. "My name is Jacob, by the way." He held out his hand with the forested arm attached.

Tootsie shook it. "Hello, Jacob, my name is Tootsie, and I haven't the faintest idea what I'm going to do." She let out a high-pitched giggle. "I've never been fired before. I can't imagine what I'll do. What do you do after you've been fired? After working thirty-five years in one place. I've had a schedule for thirty-five years, the same schedule. I lived by my schedule. I'm a very scheduled person." Her heart began to pound a little faster. "What am I going to do without a schedule? Dear God, what will I do?"

The waitress returned with their lunches. After making sure they were set, she gave them each extra napkins, and their bills, and left.

Tootsie and Jacob ate in silence for a few minutes, save for a couple, "Tasty sandwich" and "The soup is delicious." Then he said, "Schedules can be overrated. Maybe you should let loose a little, don't have a schedule for a while. I don't know, seems like those shoes deserve a little fun."

"You're the second person today to tell me to have fun." Tootsie wiped her mouth with her napkin and placed it on her lap again. "Goodness." She felt flushed again and fought an impulse to cry. "Fun was going to be a Tupperware party after work today, but not now, not ever again."

"You'll find new ways to have fun—you have to keep up with those shoes." Jacob smiled. "I think my shoes are jealous." They both looked down at his brown leather loafers. "You're the fun one." They both giggled.

After his meal, Jacob reached over and grabbed Tootsie's bill. Tootsie put her spoon down and said, "Hey, what're you doing?"

"I'm buying your lunch today, Tootsie. My treat." Jacob pulled out his credit card and waved it for the waitress to see. She came over, grabbed the bills and card, squinted at Jacob, and swished off to the cash register.

"Now, Jacob, that is very kind of you, but you don't even know me." Tootsie put her hands on her hips. "You stinker."

"My privilege," Jacob said. The waitress returned and dropped his card in front of him. She shot him a final wink and left. "It's been a pleasure to share lunch with you, Tootsie. I wish you luck in your new *fun* adventures." He rolled down his sleeves, stood up, and put on his jacket to leave.

"Well, I don't quite know what to say." Tootsie jumped off the stool and without a thought, hugged Jacob. He was much taller than she, most people were, but standing on her tiptoes in her new red shoes, she managed to plant a kiss on his chin. It stirred something in her to see his neck blush pink.

"Good luck to you, Tootsie," Jacob said as he turned and weaved his way out of the restaurant.

Tootsie remounted the stool and adjusted herself. She felt light and happy. The thought of dancing around the restaurant as if she were Ginger Rogers floated into her head. *How silly. Incredible as it seems, today is one of the best days I've had in a long time.*

She finished her lunch and checked her watch. 1:07. *I suppose I better do something constructive. Go home and figure out my life. Do a t-chart. Call my insurance company, deposit the check, look for a bloody job.*

Tootsie surveyed the restaurant. People were eating pie with mounds of ice cream, drinking beers, laughing, and sharing French fries. She swung her legs back and forth under the counter.

Tootsie plucked at her curls and thought to herself, *or I'll check and see—maybe Maureen is home.*

Louise

Moss from the slick walk crept up the graying front door, the condo's former cheery yellow had morphed into a dull olive, and above the doorbell, a "No Solicitors" sign held on for dear life. Louise couldn't conceal her shock at how much her dad's place had gone to hell. She knocked on the door. Taking a deep breath, she turned the knob. The unlocked door opened easily. She yelled, "Hello, anyone home? Dad?" Stepping in from the daylight, the scent of musty wool palpable in the dank air, her eyes took a minute to adjust to the shadowy room.

"Who's there?" Her dad's voice rumbled from a dark mound on the living room couch. "What the hell're you doing here?"

"Dad, it's me, Louise. Are you awake? Remember yesterday, I told you I was coming today?" Louise fumbled for the light switch by the front door and flipped it on. Her gag reflex kicked in as she absorbed her surroundings. Stacked papers and fast-food packaging cluttered the floor. Stained carpeting—what Louise could see of it—had gone from a beautiful ocean blue to a murky sea of dark spots. Pizza boxes, bowls, and plastic utensils littered the coffee table. Unidentified liquids grew mold in mugs and glasses. Monty reclined on his black leather couch; a plaid throw barely covered up a gaping hole in its back. He rubbed his eyes.

"Who're you?" Monty gurgled more than he spoke. He pushed up his elfin round body by digging his elbows into the seat of the couch. Finally, he muscled upright to a sitting position and smoothed back white strands of hair. "Why're you here?"

"Jesus, Dad. Remember, we've been talking about this for a month. And tomorrow's the day. You have to move. Remember?" Louise said as she cleared newspapers off the single chair in the room and sat down across from her father. "You're moving to my house, with Dave and your grandson, Bryant." Her father's eyes held no light. She rose to open the front window curtains. "Let's get some sun in here for starters, that'll help. How do you know the time of day if you can't see outside?"

"The light is fine. Leave the curtains alone." Her father lay back down on the couch and shut his eyes. "Like hell I'm moving."

She dropped the curtain cord and took a deep breath—*Don't let him get to you*—she told herself and thought, *Stewart, you bastard, just because Dad and I live in the same city, you make me his caretaker. Well, guess what, I don't want the job. Not now, not ever.*

She cleared her throat. "Dad, you stopped paying your mortgage a year ago. We can't afford to help you anymore. Unfortunately, we can't. You have to move in with me because I'm the lucky one who lives in the same city as you. Just until we can find a place that takes Medicare." She loomed over her disheveled father lying with his arms crossed over his chest, eyes shut. "That's how it works."

"Bullshit." Her father tightened his knotted arms on his prone body, a defiant stance. His lips puckered emphatically. "I'm not moving anywhere."

"I'm not fighting with you." Louise put her hands on her hips. "Talk to Stewart. You can fight with him on the phone." *I don't have time for this,* she thought and pulled out her cellphone from her coat pocket. *I don't have time for YOUR bullshit, old man.* She speed-dialed her brother.

"Stewart? Louise, hi. Dad refuses to go. Says he's not moving. Talk to him. You're on speaker." *You deal with the asshole. You're his financial guy, I'm not getting into the weeds with him. Been there, done that.*

"Louise?" Stewart asked, "Dad? What's going on, Dad?"

"Say hi to Stewart, Dad." Louise's voice quivered as she thrust the phone in front of her dad. She hated how emotional she sounded. Stewart would be annoyed, and her father would just scream louder.

"Quit yelling, Ava!" Monty teetered as he struggled to sit upright. "Stewart? Which one is Stewart?"

"I'm not yelling. It's Stewart, your son, in Minneapolis. He wants to talk to you, and I'm Louise." She rolled her eyes and moved the phone closer to her dad's face. "Jesus, Dad, Ava—Mom—died forty-four years ago."

Stewart's voice boomed from the phone. "Dad, it's me, Stewart. Look, I don't have a lot of time. I'm working on a deadline. But yes, you must move in with Louise, and Dave who is 100 percent onboard, until we find a place that takes Medicare. Do you understand? We can't support you any longer. I have a new job, Louise and Dave have Bryant about to go to college and Denise is still knocking around Europe." Louise could hear the exasperation in his voice. *Good,* she thought, *Why should you be any happier than I am? You shoved me into this damn mess.*

"That's bullshit." Her father's lips sucked into his mouth.

Stewart's words sharpened. "Dad, you're out of the condo and moving in with Louise tomorrow. Seriously. You have no choice."

"What happened to my money? That's what I want to know." Monty shook his finger at Louise. "Who stole my money?"

"You spent all your money." Stewart responded more forcefully than Louise expected. Halfway across the country, she could hear his irritation. "You stopped paying your bills a long time ago, and now you don't have the money to catch up."

With a huge heave of his chest, her father's angry face sagged into one of a sorrowful clown. Unexpected sadness of her own puddled in the back of Louise's throat. She hadn't seen that look on him before.

"I've got to go, Dad. Do what Louise says." Stewart lowered his voice, "Louise, I'll call you later. Good luck." Then he hung up.

"Dad, did you hear Stewart? You have no choice; you're moving in with me. Honestly, I'm not pleased about it either." Louise watched as dejection and confusion wrinkled his forehead. She decided to let him simmer in his new reality while she looked around to assess the situation. *Honestly,* she thought, with her hands on her hips. *Always me, "Louise-in-charge," my damn job for life. Family crisis? Louise'll fix it. She'll make sure everyone's needs are met. But don't worry, Louise has no needs. She exists solely to save the day, like fucking Wonder Woman.*

Ever since her mother died, abandoning her at twelve, Stewart at ten, and Denise not yet five, her father had unceremoniously appointed Louise "in charge." She became chief mouth-wiper, meal preparer, all-around substitute parent, and relinquished any life of her own. Monty would take off, who knows where, a dad on the lam for days at a time. Just a note left on the table saying, "Louise, take care of business," punctuated by an exclamation point and a wad of money under the fruit bowl. And now, like then, without a warning or consent, she had to "take charge" of her father. True, Stewart lived a half dozen states away, and Denise had been all but AWOL in Europe for the past two years, but Louise's visceral reaction overwhelmed her. Taking care of her dad would be tough. At least she liked her siblings.

Her jaw set, she walked from his living room into the kitchen. *Disgusting,* she thought. Remnants of food and drink muddled the counters. She opened a cupboard to a network of cobwebs pinning cups and plates in their places. The drainer by the sink held varying shapes of Styrofoam packaging. Inside the refrigerator, a rotten fruit smell overwhelmed her. Fast food packets of butter, mayonnaise, and ketchup laid out like fallen soldiers. *Jesus,* she thought. *What's he been eating?*

Louise returned to the living room. "Dad, when's the last time you had a decent meal? You need more than fast food to survive." She moved closer to the couch. "Dad, are you listening?"

Monty looked up at her. He waved his hands in a grand gesture, as if he were a king showing off his kingdom. "This is my home and damn it, I'm staying. But you get out. Don't bother me with your foolishness."

"Dad, you've been evicted. You have no choice." She shook her head. *Get that through your thick head.* "What's your bedroom like?"

She walked down the dim hallway to investigate. *I hope I don't kill him before he moves in.*

The stench of unwashed old people, like every old person's home she'd ever visited, overpowered her as she entered his bedroom. A brown blanket wrapped like a turban sat centered between two yellow naked pillows. Two dresser drawers yawned open. Dingy shirts and socks hung over their edges. Her heart grew heavy. How checked out was he? He seemed his usual self only six months ago, when he'd come to dinner. A mess, an asshole, very crabby, nonetheless normal Monty. But really, the more she thought about it, was he really himself all those months ago?

It had started at dinner.

"This is my silver." He had demanded as he examined the spoon at his table setting, "I want it back. All of it."

"Dad, what are you talking about? It's my silver. Mom gave it to me for when I married. Before she died. I've had it for decades," Louise said and passed him a bowl of broccoli. The way he screwed with her, in his usual jerkoff fashion, to get a rise out of her and make her mad, infuriated her. "You're being ridiculous."

"I mean it, Louise, I want the silver back, after we eat." Monty shook a fork in her direction. "Every last piece. It's mine."

"Dad, stop. You're not taking my silver." She flicked her hand at him and shot her husband a look with raised eyebrows. Mouth full, Dave rolled his eyes.

"You think I'm kidding? The hell I am. The silver is mine. Bryant, bring me a bag for the silver," Monty said and stood up from the table. He jutted out his jaw toward a wide-eyed Bryant, who had stopped drinking his milk. He usually laughed at his grandfather's obvious pokes, but this time a tense seriousness hung in the air. Bryant looked at his parents for guidance.

Louise's voice trembled. "Ignore him, Bryant. Dad, don't be crazy. Mom gave it to me, and I'm keeping it as she intended, just as I have for the PAST FORTY-PLUS YEARS." Louise strained to sound calm. "Now, sit down and enjoy your meal."

Monty, red-faced, picked up as many knives, forks, and spoons as he could snatch, before Louise grabbed his wrists. They struggled for a moment, until Dave jumped up and seized Louise's hands tightening around her father's.

"Stop!" Dave yelled as he wrenched Louise from Monty. "Stop it!" He threw his napkin at Bryant. "Wrap up the silver!" Then to Monty, "I'm taking you home. You're being unconscionable, totally out of line." Lousie glanced around the table. They all watched as Bryant rolled up the utensils in a white linen napkin. When he finished, with downcast eyes, he gave the ungainly cloth to Dave.

Louise stared at Dave, who handed the bundle to Monty. "You're giving him the silver?" she asked, while Monty stuffed it under his arm.

"It's not worth it, Louise. Monty, let's go." Dave retrieved his keys from the kitchen counter. "Now."

Her father shuffled after Dave, out the door without a word. When he returned, Dave threw the napkin rolled with silver on their dining room table. Louise had a million questions, but the stony look on her husband's face kept her quiet. Her dad had succeeded in pissing off everyone. She gathered the pieces from the table, rinsed them, and loaded them into the dishwasher. She hadn't seen her dad since.

Louise shook her head. *Who knows with him. He's always been such a jerk, such a bully,* she thought as she sifted through her dad's dirty clothes piled on top of his dresser. *You might think your pathetic behavior will stop you from having to move, but sorry, Pops, you cooked yourself good this time.* She uncovered an old wedding picture of her parents. Tucked in the corner was a snapshot of the family at the beach not too long before her mom died. Louise must have been ten or eleven years old at the time. She remembered her dad as nicer then. Always a jokester, but not mean-spirited, just funny, making them all laugh. Even Louise, dubbed the serious one by the rest of the family. Then, after the torturous cancer took their mother, her dad disconnected from them; he ceased to be her dad. Relatives told her to be patient. Grieving takes time. But grieving or not, her job tending to Stewart and Denise eclipsed her role as a daughter. Told by others that she looked most like her mom, she imagined she'd become the special one, but he never treated her as more than domestic help. Louise dropped the photo onto a ratty t-shirt. *What I'd have given for a little kindness from you.* She left her father's bedroom feeling wretched, on so many levels. The whole situation depressed her.

Back in front of her father, she said, "Dad, your bedroom is as disastrous as the kitchen. I don't know how you sleep, and your clothes are filthy. If they can't be cleaned, I'm throwing them out."

Monty lay flat out on the couch; his eyes stared at the ceiling. He said, "I don't give a shit what you do. Throw everything out, what the hell do I care?" He lifted his head. "I'm tired; you need to go. Don't bother coming back." His head dropped back down onto the sofa, and he shut his eyes.

Louise sat down by his feet, which were tucked under a thread-bare throw pillow. The enormous specter of bad feelings she felt for her dad poked at her back. She took a deep breath. "Dad, I'm leaving, but I'll return in the morning—for the move—around 9:00. I'll bring garbage bags for the clothes you're taking. Your job is to go through your things and put what you want to take to my house on this chair. I know this is hard, but you have no choice." She stared at her dad, whose gray face twisted toward the back of the couch. "Dad, do you hear me?" He looked miserable, and even at the age of eighty-four, for someone she once thought of as a bulldog, he looked one hundred years old. *You reap what you sow, old man. Maybe if you hadn't been such an irresponsible jerk, things would be different now.* She sighed.

"Go," Monty whispered. "Now. Get out."

Louise studied her dad. "I'm going, but you better be ready to go in the morning." She stood up. "Do you understand me? Dad?" Monty didn't stir. She surveyed the mess one more time and left quietly. *He can't avoid the inevitable*, she thought. *He's so damn stubborn.* But a nagging heaviness rode her shoulders as she opened her car door. Where was his yelling and screaming, the usual theatrics? *Is he really that tired?* She tried to convince herself. And yet. She shook her head and started the engine.

The next morning, Louise arrived armed with garbage bags and a cup of coffee for herself and one for Monty. She'd move Monty and his clothes to her house, and the moving company would take everything else to a storage unit she'd rented with Stewart's guilt money. The cleaning company would come after. She stood in front of his condo, and with hands full, kicked the door with her shoe. "Open up, Dad. It's me!"

"Go away," he barked from inside. "I don't care who you are."

"Dad, we don't have time for this," she said. "It's moving day. Open up."

"Go away," Monty said. She could hear rustling behind the door.

"Dad, open up, now."

"No."

"Dad, open the goddamn door!" Louise bellowed. "I don't have time for games. I'm on a schedule."

"No," Monty croaked through the door.

"Dad, stop. You're making this worse than it has to be." Louise brought her voice down a bit. "I have coffee for you." She sipped her own latte.

"No."

"Dad, open the fucking door. The movers come in less than an hour, whether you like it or not. Let me in," Louise watched the doorknob. "Jesus, Dad. Your coffee's getting cold."

"Go away," Monty said, then paused. "What kind of coffee—a latte?"

"Yes, a latte, a big one." Louise kept her eye on the doorknob. "And it's getting cold. Open the door."

"You have coffee for me, now?" Monty asked. "Who're you?"

"Don't start with me, Dad. I'm Louise! Open the damn door." Louise rolled her eyes. *No bullshit, Monty, not now. I have too much to do.*

The doorknob turned, and the door opened. Clad in the same clothes as the day before, khaki shorts, a faded t-shirt, and socks rolled down to the ankles, her dad appeared as if he'd just woken up. Without looking up to make eye contact, he grabbed his coffee from her, waddled to the couch, sat down, and nursed it like a bottle.

"Dad, here's the deal. Listen carefully." Louise sat down on the still-empty chair. He hadn't collected any clothes. She took a deep breath. "Since you didn't get your clothes together, I'll do it. The movers will take the rest of your things to storage later today. Then you're out of here for good. Understand?" Her father didn't look at her, but instead licked the rim of the cup. *Focus,* she screamed in her head. *Focus, for fuck's sake!*

"Not much foam," Monty said. "The whole world is going to hell. No one does anything right. Everything is bullshit. Here, gimme that spoon over there." He pointed to a dirty plastic spoon on the table.

Louise wiped it off on a random napkin and handed it to him. "Enjoy your bad latte." She stood, glared at her dad, and marched down the hallway to his bedroom. *I have to do every fucking thing. He's like a child. Worse than a child. Expects me to do all the work per usual. Wonder Woman Louise to the rescue. Well, newsflash, Wonder Woman wants to quit. Stewart, you'll have to do more than throw money at me to make this right.*

She started with his dresser. Holding up a dirty, olive t-shirt from a drawer, she yelled, "Dad, these t-shirts are disgusting!" Then stuffed all of them, plus soiled pants, ripped nightshirts, and dingy underwear into one bag. *So weird,* she thought. *He used to love clothes. Mr. 100 percent cashmere from Brooks Brothers, glove leather loafers, and shearling coats. What happened to that guy?*

"Don't touch my stuff!" Monty hollered, "And stay out of my wallet!"

"You don't have a wallet!" She yelled back and quickly crammed a pair of worn slippers into another bag, along with a mixture of anger and confusion. Heaviness niggled at her again. She could handle her dad, the asshole, but what was with the money obsession? The trashed condo? And forgetting her name? She blinked back unexpected tears. She needed a drink.

After she finished packing, she dragged the bags out. "I'm dropping these at the car and coming right back for you. Be ready." When she returned, Monty remained stuck to the couch, eyes shut, the empty coffee cup in hand resting on his stomach.

"Go," he said. "I need to sleep."

"We're both going," Louise said, hovering over her father's corpse-stiff body. "Now, Dad. Up." He rolled over, facing the back of the couch. The empty coffee cup toppled to the ground. "Dad, let's go."

She clapped her hands. "Now!" She picked up the cup and threw it on the coffee table.

"No." Her dad remained still.

Louise inhaled deeply, then through clenched teeth, she said, "Listen, Dad, you either walk to my car, or I get the movers to pick you up and throw you in." She breathed out through her nose. "No more games, Dad, we have to go."

Another minute passed. He remained motionless. *Again, elder as a petulant child.* When Bryant pulled such stunts, she bribed him with ice cream. Not always healthy, but effective. "Dad, do you want ice cream? I'll get you an ice cream cone on the way to my house. Your favorite, Rocky Road."

"Now?" Monty's eyes blinked open. "Right now?"

"Yes, now, but you have to get up first." Louise grabbed her keys and jangled them over Monty's head. Slowly, he rose to a sitting position. He rubbed his head, scattering his sparse hair around his skull. From his sitting position, he slid his feet around on the floor until they found Birkenstocks to slip into. Then, with one big heave, he lifted himself up off the couch, and without a word, shuffled directly out the door. Louise squinted her eyes and watched him. He looked neither right nor left before he exited, not even a good-bye glance at his home of over twenty years.

They arrived at Louise's when the rain started, and with Monty's ice cream cone finished. She went around to open his door and watched him absorb his surroundings as if it were his first visit. Gingerly, he swung his legs out of the door. His feet tapped the driveway with the hesitation of someone who couldn't see beyond his shoes. Louise lifted the garbage bags out of her trunk while he slowly climbed out of the car. Bags in one hand, she fumbled to open the front door with the other. "OK, Dad, go in," she said pushing the door open. For the first time, she noticed he stooped, and veiny blue tributaries popped out on the top of his head. *When did he shrink into this little old man? What happened to his hair?* She forced herself to swallow the answers caught in her throat.

Inside the foyer, she brushed off the dampness from her dad's shoulders and yelled, "Bryant, Grandpa is here. Come say hi!" She moved his bags to the kitchen and threw her purse and keys on the counter.

"Where's my room?" Monty said, standing beside her. "Show me."

"Dad, don't you want to see Bryant first?" She shouted again for her surly teenager.

"I want to go to my room. I'll meet him some other time." Monty walked toward the guest room. "This is bullshit."

Louise followed Monty into his room. Bryant appeared behind them.

"Hi, Grandpa." Bryant leaned over to give his grandfather a limp hug. His grandfather patted his tall, lanky grandson's back.

"I live here now, you know," Monty said. "She moved me out of my house—not my idea." He rubbed the top of his head; wet hairs stuck to his skull and fingers. "Can you tell me what the hell's going on?"

"Um, well, yeah, I don't know, really." Bryant looked down and put his hands in his pockets. He cleared his throat. "But it sucks," he said, scratched his head, looked at the floor, turned, and left.

Louise called after him, "Lunch is soon, so don't go off some-where." Seconds later, on the floor above Louise and Monty, a door slammed, and the bass kicked in.

"Jesus, always with that obnoxious music, and no school today for some damn reason or another." Louise dumped the bag of Monty's clothes on the bed. "I don't know what I'm going to do with him." She blinked, as if to change her train of thought, and watched her dad clutch the handle of a dresser drawer to steady himself. "Dad, sit, I'll put things away." She dug out his slippers. "You want to put these on?"

"Quit monkeying with my stuff." Monty grabbed the slippers and threw them down. "How old is he?" He tottered to the edge of the daybed. "Your son?"

"Bryant is sixteen. Not sweet sixteen, however. Why?"

"Leave the poor kid alone; be glad he's around." Monty reached down in front of Louise and swept all his clothes from the bed to the floor.

"Dad!" Louise said in disbelief. "What're you doing?"

Monty stepped over the pile on the floor, laid down on the bed and pulled the comforter over him. His feet stuck out at the end like two gnarled sticks. "I need to sleep."

Louise bent down to pick up his clothes. "Jesus, Dad, couldn't you have just told me before chucking everything on the floor?" She stuffed the clothes back into their bag. "You don't make things easy, do you?" She paused and looked at her father. "By the way, I do try to be nice, but Bryant is crabby all the time. Makes it difficult."

"He's a teenager. What'd you expect?" Monty closed his eyes. "Be nicer to him. OK, that's it. I'm sleeping."

"Ha!" Louise said. "Funny, coming from you," she let loose. When I was his age, you treated me like crap." She started for the door.

"Your mother's fault." Monty exhaled a wheezy sigh. "Bless her."

"Mom's fault?" Louise turned around to face her father. "Mom was dead."

"I wish I was."

"Don't change the subject, and sometimes so do I, by the way." Louise put her hands on her hips. "How could Mom possibly have anything to do with you being so mean to me?"

"She said you'd help me. But you were just a kid." Eyes pressed shut, he rolled on his side and faced the wall. "I was mad. Furious at everyone. I couldn't be around. Sorry, but that's just the way it was. So that's it. I'm tired." Within seconds, his wheezing turned to snores.

She stood closer to him and narrowed her eyes. *Did he really just say he was sorry?* His slack-jawed face didn't move as she covered his feet with the comforter. The tenderness of her action loosened the screws in her tight shoulders and released a tiny bit of resentment from her balled-up heart. Experience taught her not to trust her dad; "proceed with caution" ruled her interactions with him. He could turn on her like a rabid dog. Yet, she heard it, and it registered within her, his virtual slip-of-the-tongue apology.

That evening, Dave worked late and neither her father nor Bryant showed up for dinner. Her dad snored in his room, and under the guise of studying for a test, Bryant burrowed upstairs with thudding music in the background. So, poking at her chicken and rice at the kitchen island, she felt sorry for herself, lonely and dejected. Her destiny loomed ahead: to be an underappreciated caretaker for the rest of her life, the woman wiping up everyone's messes, while never engaging in a carefree life.

Louise figured the doorbell had rung a few times before she heard it. The clock read 7:30. Emotionally, it felt like midnight. If the visitors were Bryant's friends, she'd send them home. If he didn't have time to eat dinner with her, he didn't have time to hang out with his buddies. As she opened the door ready to face a bunch of teenagers, she instead stood face-to-face with her sister.

"Surprise!" A beaming, diminutive woman in tapestry-woven boots and a huge scarf that swaddled her like a baby stood on the porch. "Louise, it's me, Denise!" Louise's mouth dropped open. Her baby sister stood in front of her with outstretched arms. Her blonde hair sat bunched up into a semblance of a bun and her blue eyes sparkled behind her oversized, black-framed glasses. A large tote sat by her side.

"Denise?" Louise whispered. "Denise." Her fingers scrambled around her head for errant hairs.

Denise grabbed Louise and pulled her close. Like a vise, Denise's strong bony arms enveloped Louise, and she let herself be cocooned in her sister's embrace, familiar yet awkward after so long. And extremely uncomfortable.

After they moved beyond their initial surprise at seeing each other, Denise, more animated than Louise, they situated themselves around the kitchen island. Louise poured them each a glass of wine.

"I thought you were still carousing around France or somewhere." Louise put the wine bottle on a coaster and thought, *Flitting here and there, while I saved our father from eviction and whatever else might befall him. But better you keep living your best life. That's what matters.* "It's been at least three years since I've seen you."

"Two years, and I'm a teacher! For the University of Oregon! Finally got my degree in England, masters, and PhD—amazing right? Thank God. Job starts Monday, so I thought I'd stop here first, on my way to Eugene, for the night, if it's OK with you." She winked at Louise. "I did send you postcards."

She still does that winking thing, like, aren't I the cutest ever. "Cryptic postcards I could barely read. Your writing sucks. But, wow, good for you. A toast to you." *OK, you're a college professor now. You have my attention.*

Denise blushed and cleared her throat. "More importantly, what about Dad? I talked to Stewart yesterday, and he told me a little bit." She cleaned her glasses.

"Not much to tell. He moved in with us because he's completely broke. The bastard. As per usual, I've been called to duty. Good ol' dependable Louise to the rescue. The thing is, Denise, I don't like Dad, and this time I don't want the assignment." She smiled and batted her eyelids at her sister. "Guess I don't have any choice, though, do I?"

Denise sipped her wine. "That's a little harsh, saying you don't like him. I know he's not a warm fuzzy, but he's Dad, and he loved us the best he could, considering his wife died and left him with three young kids." Denise swished her glass around then put it down. "Face it, Louise, you're the oldest and an expert at taking care of business. Hey, look what a great job you did with me." Denise gestured from head to toe with both hands, a wide smile and raised eyebrows on her face.

Louise rolled her eyes at her perky, colorful, adorable sister.

Denise puffed out her bottom lip. "I'm teasing you, Louise. Listen, after I get settled, I promise I will do whatever I can to help, whenever possible, but Stewart is in Minneapolis, so unfortunately, for the time being, you're it, dear sister. We love and appreciate you, you know." Denise bounced off her stool. "Hey, where is everyone? Dad? Dave? Bryant? How old is he now?"

"Dad is in the guest room. Dave is working late, and Bryant is upstairs, sixteen and perpetually a pill." Louise sighed and swallowed some wine. "Honestly, he drives me crazy, but whatever. Dad said to go easy on him, like he knows how to be nice. Funny, though, he did say he should have been easier on me, even said he's sorry. And blamed Mom for making me the pack mule of the family." Louise paused and looked her sister in the eye. "But Mom is dead, and we can't fact check that now, can we? Anyway, Denise, I don't want to take care of Dad. I mean it. He brutalized me." She stood and brought her dinner dish to the sink. "Are you hungry?"

"No, I'm good, thanks." Denise folded a napkin in front of her. "Dad didn't brutalize you; you and he brutalized Stewart and me. Did you know Dad told us to mind you, or there'd be trouble when he got home? We obeyed you out of fear of what would happen if we didn't." Denise's eyes glistened as she pointed her finger at Louise. "You were the golden one, and we were lowly peons. Just ask Stewart." She put down her wine glass after taking a sip. "Now, if you'll excuse me, I'm going to say hello to that sweet boy of yours," she said as she disappeared upstairs.

Louise shouted after her, "What world did you live in? I was the unpaid help, never the sister or, God forbid, a daughter." She bowed her head. *Like ripping stitches out of a wound, remembering all this shit.* Her stomach knotted as she listened to her sister tromp up the stairs. *The golden one my ass.*

A few minutes later, Denise, grinning, bounded into the kitchen. "What a doll!" she gushed. "He's looks like a male Mom—lean and lanky."

"Yeah, but Mom talked." Louise narrowed her eyes at Denise. "He just grunts."

"You crack me up, Louise. We can't all be miniature adults as teenagers, like you were." Denise sat down and winked at her. "He's more normal. He's bored at school, doesn't have a girlfriend but used to, likes designing buildings, but hates math. He wants to go out of state for college. Before he decides, I told him to visit me at U of O." Denise picked up her wine. "Just a lovely young man. Now Dad, where do you have him locked up?"

"A NORMAL teenager who doesn't speak to his mother but will have a full conversation with his aunt he hasn't seen in forever. Really." She shut her eyes for a couple of seconds. Louise pointed toward the spare-room door. "Dad will probably divulge where he buried some treasure and give it to you."

Louise watched as her pretty, younger sister entered their dad's room. People were always drawn to her, especially as a young girl, the darling of the family. Once, early after their mom died, someone gave Denise a lollipop, which she promptly dropped in the dirt. Denise started crying, and their dad found another one to give her. He was surprisingly sweet to her. So, envious, Louise thought she'd do the same. She waited an hour or so and then cried that her candy had also dropped. Inside the house, Monty looked at her through the screen door and punched at her, the screen door stopping his fist with a menacing rattle. "Wipe it off!" he'd yelled.

And now that man slept in her guest room.

"You look positively morose, sister dear," Denise said as she shut the door to their dad's room with a quiet click. "Dad's asleep. Boy, he's aged. He's almost bald. Poor guy."

"Yes, poor guy. Not. All he has to do is sleep and eat. Meanwhile, I need to find him a long-term place to live that takes Medicare." Louise knocked three times on the wooden stool. "I had to pack everything for him then actually had to bribe him with ice cream to leave, like I did with Bryant when he was a toddler. Nothing I tell him sticks. No thanks or appreciation. Nothing."

"OK, I get the picture. But really, he's probably out of his mind stressed." Denise wiped the rim of her glass with the napkin. "Hey, I wanted to share something with you." She kicked off her boots. "Something I hadn't thought of for a long time, but it hit me while driving here."

"Should I be nervous?" Louise gave her sister a sideways glance.

"I had names for you and Stewart. You were the toaster and Stewart an oven. I'd come home from school and wonder who'd be home, the oven or the toaster?" Denise swirled her wine around in the glass and grinned at Louise.

"Toaster or oven?" Louise screwed up her eyes at her sister.

Denise put down her wine glass as she spoke. "Well. You, the toaster, got the job done—in and out fast, but without emotion, tied my shoes, made lunches and off you go. Now, Stewart, he was the oven. Just a little bit older than I am but warm. He hugged. I needed them once in a while, you know. We'd lost our mom. Stewart was a teddy bear, full of affection." Denise smiled, looking at Louise. "I hadn't thought of that for a long time, the toaster and the oven. Weird what you think of as a kid."

Louise's eyes widened. "I never hugged you? Really? I mean, I did everything else for you. I brushed your hair, gave you baths, fixed your dinners. Took you to ballet practices. Everything. I sacrificed so much for you. Starting with mom's funeral. I had to take you, the baby, outside because you were crying. But I didn't hug you? Jeez, sorry." Louise avoided Denise's sharp gaze. Her words stung.

"Louise, you did do everything for me. Absolutely. You did an amazing job. But, sometimes, I craved a hug from you. Some contact. You weren't my mother, I barely knew my mother, but you were the closest thing I had to one. Sorry, sis, but that's the truth. And honestly, sometimes a hug was more important than a plate of food." Denise took a deep breath. She removed her hoop earrings and laid them on the island. "I didn't mean to hurt your feelings. I just wanted to tell you the bit about the oven and toaster. I apologize. It must have been tough to be you, at your age, to run the show for Dad, for all of us."

Louise's voice dropped to a whisper. "I'm not a hugger, Denise. I've never been, even now, ask Dave. I'm sorry. I'm just not. But I probably needed one, too, I'm sure of that, and no one gave me a hug either." She stiffened her back. *Buck up,* she told herself. *It wasn't Denise's fault Dad made me into a cold bitch.* "It's old business now, Denise. I'm good. I'm just not happy about housing Dad, that's all."

"Hello?" The sound of Dave's voice resonated from the foyer.

"We're in here!" Louise called from the kitchen.

Their conversation was tabled by Dave's entrance.

"Oh my God, Denise." Dave embraced Denise in a bear hug. "What a surprise, a great one at that!" Soon bottles of wine cluttered the table with an assortment of cheeses, crackers, and a tin of sardines. Dave remembered Denise loved sardines. Conversation digressed into telling old stories and the natural levity of old friends took over.

First thing in the morning, Louise checked in on her dad. His empty bed startled her. "Dad? Dad, where are you?" She rapped on the bathroom door. "Dad?" No answer.

She checked the family room adjacent to the kitchen. Monty sat on the couch with his two packed garbage bags flanking his feet. His hair was combed, and he wore his Birkenstocks and a different t-shirt from the day before. "No more monkey business. Give me my wallet, and take me home." He crossed his arms and looked down. "Now."

Louise sat down beside him. "Dad, listen carefully. This is your home—the condo is history." Monty clasped his hands in his lap. "Let me make you coffee."

"You don't know what the hell you're talking about."

"Right, Dad." Louise stood up. "Guess who's here? Denise. She arrived last night. Don't you want to see her?"

"Denise? The baby girl?" Monty's eyes opened wide and then squinted. "Denise?"

"Yes, Dad, the baby girl. I'll get her." Louise trudged into the office where Denise slept on the pull-out sleeper sofa.

"Denise, baby girl," Louise said to her sleeping sister, "get up, Dad's asking for you."

"Ugh, drank too much," Denise whispered as she rose from the sofa, rubbing her eyes like she did when she was young.

As Louise returned to the family room, she saw the back of Bryant's jacket as it flew down the stairs. He yelled, "I'm out. Soccer practice."

She shouted, "Bryant! Wait, you didn't eat breakfast!" But he disappeared out the front door and into a car that squealed out of the driveway before she could scream his name again. *Damn him,* she thought. *This is normal? I don't think so.*

Louise walked over to the couch and sat down at the opposite end from her father. "See what I mean with him? No breakfast, just runs out the door before I can say hello or goodbye. No matter what I do, I can't get him to stop and talk to me."

Monty didn't look at her, but stared straight ahead, glaring at the black TV screen over the fireplace. "All you do is yell at him."

"I do not," Louise said, glaring at her dad. "I certainly do not." She got up and went into the kitchen to make coffee. She grumbled, "Said the father of the year." She poured coffee grounds into the coffee maker and pushed brew. "I yell because of Bryant. He makes me."

"I never claimed I was father of the year," Her father bellowed from the couch. "I know what I was, but you don't seem to. Stop your goddamn yelling at the poor kid."

She returned to the family room while the coffee brewed, standing beneath the arch between the two rooms, and shook her head at her puzzling father.

"Daddio!" From the hallway, Denise bounced into the room and bent over to hug their dad. Then she plopped down next to him and threaded her arm through his. "Dad, have you missed me?" Denise wore the pink chenille bathrobe Louise had given her the night before. Her hair spread around her shoulders. She looked beautiful, even hungover.

"You, take me home. I want to go now. I'm very serious. Take me home," Monty said. He all but ignored his daughter's affection. Louise smirked.

Denise stuck out her bottom lip. "Dad, not even a 'Hello, how are you' after all this time? Do you remember me? Dad?"

From the kitchen, Louise fetched the freshly brewed coffee, and yelled, "It's your baby girl, Dad."

Denise scowled at Louise as she brought in a tray of steaming mugs.

"I know who the hell she is, and she's not listening either." Monty rubbed the top of his head, splaying wispy hairs across his skull. "It's all bullshit."

Louise set the tray of steaming coffee mugs on the coffee table. She handed a cup to Monty. "Careful, Dad, it's hot," Louise said as he wobbled it to his lips. "Watch him, Denise." Louise grabbed a cup for herself and sat down on the chair facing them. She took a sip and noted how remarkable it was that Denise could cuddle up to her father without a hint of resentment. Her dad's years of vanishing acts and ornery behavior didn't faze her one whit, even now when he practically ignored her. But Denise did her own vanishing, too, so maybe that made them even.

As Louise continued to watch them, a familiar emotion bubbled up in her. The feeling of being the odd man out. She'd often felt she missed the day everyone learned to bond. Like her dad and mom encoded a secret sense of belonging within everyone but forgot to include her. After her mother died, her role as family caretaker only exacerbated things. When they were younger, her siblings would share stories at the kitchen table that seemed to evade her interest or involvement, as if she had just joined the group, not like a family member at all. The feeling had never completely disappeared after her siblings aged out of the needed-to-be-taken-care-of stage. How her sister's posture could immediately devolve into a comfortable puddle around their father mystified Louise.

During breakfast, Monty provided the refrain, "take me home," and "where's my wallet," at every opportunity, even as he ate eggs and sausages and later when the two sisters cleared the dishes. Denise tried to reason with him, better than Louise, but he wouldn't capitulate. He wanted to go home and didn't understand why he couldn't.

Once the dishwasher was loaded, Denise announced she'd better get on the road to start her new life in Eugene. While she gathered her things, Louise guided their father from the kitchen back to the family room sofa. There he sat; his legs wedged between his garbage bags on the floor. Dave followed them and sat in a nearby chair.

Denise, carrying her tote into the room, said to Monty, "I'm off to Eugene, Daddio." She leaned in for a hug and kiss. "Remember, do what Louise tells you—just like you used to tell us, right?" She smiled at her dad, whose head hung low, practically in his lap. "I love you, Dad," she whispered to him. He didn't respond.

Then, Dave stood, and he and Denise hugged. Each promising to be good supports for Louise. The sisters exchanged glances, then went outside.

"Want to take Dad with you?" Louise said, half joking, as they stood in the driveway by Denise's car. "Shit, I might kill him by lunch."

"Lighten up, Louise. You'll be fine, just fine, you always are." Denise smiled and touched her sister's arm. "Thank you so much for the visit. I loved our talks. It's been too long." Then Denise pulled Louise into her arms and held her tight. Louise slowly returned her sister's gesture. "Wow, keep that up, Louise, and I'll start calling you 'oven.'" Louise smiled and backed away, but Denise grabbed her hands. "You're an amazingly strong woman. We do appreciate what you're doing for Dad, but try to like him if you can. It'll make it easier for you. He's fragile, you know."

Louise pulled her hands away from Denise and crossed her arms. "Fragile? He doesn't listen, he's bossy and a bully, but don't you worry your pretty little head about things, we'll manage. It's all good."

"Louise, seriously. You haven't noticed? He's losing it. Most likely, he has some sort of dementia. He needs evaluating." Denise climbed into her car. "He's not the same, and you know it. He needs your help and love. I'll check in, and remember, you're not alone. If you need to vent or anything, you have my number now. Use it."

"OK, OK." Louise felt her lips soften into a smile and waved as she watched her sister pull out of the driveway. She continued to smile, even after the car had disappeared. She liked the way it felt. As if her sister had sprinkled happy poppies on about everything.

Louise trotted inside and found her dad was no longer sitting in the family room. "Dad? Dad?" She called, "Dad, where are you?" From upstairs, Dave yelled down, "He went back to bed."

She wandered into his bedroom. In the dark, she could see he'd lumped himself in the chair. She observed him for a minute or two. His mouth hung open with his head back, conked out. His two garbage bags sat nestled around his legs like sleeping dogs.

Her mother had gone into an assisted living home with hospice facilities in the weeks before her death. As kids, Louise, Denise, and Stewart would run through the halls and stare at the old people in their beds. White hair topped their heads. They called them marshmallow puffs and had a good laugh. Even though they knew they shouldn't, it felt good to laugh.

She whispered to him, "Dad?" She watched him breathe shallow, interrupted breaths. Impetuously, she leaned over and kissed him on his crinkled, veiny forehead.

His eyes popped open. "You tell me, am I going crazy?" Monty's eyes searched Louise's with a clarity she hadn't seen in a while. "I can't remember a damn thing." He added breathlessly. "And, you know, I can't pay for anything."

"Dad, you're not going crazy, but you might have dementia." Her eyes stayed with his. "And you don't need money anymore."

"Dementia? Well, sonofabitch." He blinked a couple of times. "You took care of everything after your mom died. You'll take care of me, too, right, Louise?"

Louise, surprised by his gentleness, blurted, "Of course, I'll take care of you." She was just as surprised by her response.

Her dad closed his eyes again. She left the room and closed the door behind her.

Stephanie

If compartmentalizing his life were a sport, Matt would be an Olympic champion. Especially when it came to work. Skillfully, he'd tuck all other aspects of his life into cubbies where they'd remain until his workload lightened. Even though I knew this to be true, I was flabbergasted when he told me he had a business trip to Taiwan, a new product rollout, the same weekend our daughter planned to move to New York. But Heidi didn't seem to mind. Not attending her important life events because of his work didn't faze her. According to her, he always made it right with a phone call. He'd call from whatever his destination, minutes before she performed for a school recital, left for a prom, or celebrated a birthday. I wouldn't have been half as understanding if my dad hadn't shown up for me—let alone see me off to a new city and new life. But my dad did show up, for everything. Whether I played a piano solo or with the school orchestra, when I took the stage, he'd be front and center. Until he wasn't. When I was sixteen, he died from a stroke. Suddenly. After work, he got into the car to come watch me at the Christmas concert. Doctors said he didn't even get the keys into the ignition before he died. From then on, I had a tough time performing. I couldn't bear not to see his face. He and Mom smiling at me, and Dad always with a wink. Loved his wink. Matt didn't seem to understand the importance of parents showing up for their child.

I mulled this thought, his absences, as I stepped out of the shower. Heidi and I had a 10:00 a.m. flight to JFK. I wouldn't have missed setting up her apartment in New York City for the world. I reached for my towel and recoiled. Matt had hung his wet towel over my dry one. Now my dry towel would be soggy and smelly. How could he not know, not think my towel would get dank underneath his sopping wet one? I mean, after a shower, I want a dry towel. *How can he be so oblivious?* I grabbed my now-damp towel and blotted my skin the best I could. It made my flesh feel sweaty, not clean. I threw it on the floor and grabbed a fresh one out of the cupboard. After I dried off, I picked up the towel on the floor and threw it into the hamper. Now the hanging towels wouldn't match—next to Matt's seafoam green towel would be my turquoise blue one. My hands balled into fists.

I yelled from our bathroom, upstairs, "Matt, thanks for hanging your wet towel over my dry one!" I threw on my robe and tried slamming the bathroom door as I tromped into the bedroom, but his bathrobe, which hung on the back of the door, caught and instead, I heard an unsatisfying muffled bump. *Damn him*, I thought and dressed in angry yanks and tugs.

Ever since Heidi announced her move to Manhattan for her new job, Matt's behavior chafed me. He wore me down like I was the last nub of cheese on a cheese grater—what's left just before it mangles your fingers. Everything he did: leaving his shoes in front of the couch, plugging phone chargers into random sockets, hanging his coat over a kitchen chair, it all steamed me. Heidi's shoes and hair ties were everywhere, too, but he took the prize. I didn't mind Heidi's habits so much—maybe because she was my child, while he just acted like one.

After dressing, I lugged my carry-on downstairs, stopping on the landing. I called to Heidi behind her closed door, "Are you ready to go, Heidi? We have to hurry. You should eat before we leave—honey?" *Time is going to be a big issue for her without me to push her.* Tears seeped out of my eyes. What would she do without me? Who was I kidding, me without her?

I took a long breath and continued down the stairs, banging my suitcase into the walls as I did.

"Chill, Mom," Heidi yelled from behind her door. "Can you make me my usual egg and avocado toast?"

"OK, but you have less than a half hour to eat!" I parked my bag and went into the kitchen. Dirty plates sat scattered around the counter, and orange juice spills blotched the island. Matt stood frying an egg on high. Grease spit out of the pan and smoke billowed from the toaster. I wedged my arm between Matt's body and the burner and turned down the heat under his eggs.

"I dried off with a soaking wet towel, thanks to you." I grabbed a sponge, wiped up his mess, and poured myself a cup of coffee. "And I've told you, when you cook on high, it splatters."

"Really? You're upset about the towel, Steph? I'm sorry I didn't hang my towel properly." Matt flipped his egg. "Jesus." He tapped the spatula on the edge of the frying pan. Oil dripped onto the stove. "What time's your flight?"

I chewed the inside of my cheek. "At 10:00. I told you already, but you don't listen." I watched him as he scraped the fried egg from the pan, over the edge and onto his plate, dropping bits of charred egg below the gas burners. A burning smell rose in a coil of smoke.

"I forgot." With his free hand, Matt swept loose graying strands of hair from his forehead. His round, pug-nosed babyface seemed like a much younger mask in contrast to his salt and pepper hair. Over 6'3" tall, he once rocked a basketball player's body. Now ruined by years of jumping on basketball courts, his knees resembled parts of old stove pipes. He grabbed his toast from the toaster, dropped it on his plate, carried everything to the table, and sat down.

"When did you become such a slob?" I shook my head at him as he folded his egg on his piece of toast and stuffed a bite into his mouth. I walked to the fridge and pulled out the eggs for Heidi's breakfast.

"Stephanie, I feel like I'm under a microscope with you." He wiped his hands on a napkin, threw it on the table and sipped his coffee. A couple of drips rolled down the side of the cup and onto the table. "I've been eating like this for the last thirty years." He chomped another mouthful of food. Still chewing, he garbled, "Steph, Heidi is going to be fine. Just fine. Try not to take it so hard."

I shifted my eyes away from his cow-grinding-cud eating. *Has he always been a boor, and I'm just now noticing, or has his boorishness increased?* With Heidi moving, the soapy film disintegrated from my mind's eyes, revealing a clarity of my new life without my daughter. My initial denial and the sudden reality of the situation scared me, and I felt like a wobbly chair. I cut an avocado. "I just can't believe you can't come with us—that's all. It's a milestone in Heidi's life; I didn't want you to miss it. She's moving far away, for good. And she won't be back for a long time. She won't have vacations like she did in college."

Matt blotted his lips with the napkin. He swirled the last of the toast around the yolk on the plate and popped it into his mouth. "Steph, I realize that, but she's not moving to the moon, and they do have regular flights from here to New York. I have too much going on at work without you making me feel guilty."

"Always your job, your job, your job." I flipped an egg in the pan and threw a couple of avocado slices on top. "I'm only thinking how nice it would be for Heidi if we both took her." I set Heidi's breakfast down at her spot at the island. "My father couldn't be there for me. That's all I'm saying."

"I'm sorry your dad died, but you can't bring that up every time we have an event that involves Heidi—or Joel for that matter—that I can't attend. She is not you, and I'm not your dad, we've talked about this." Matt stood up and put his plate in the sink. "I'm leaving in twenty minutes, if you want me to drop you at the airport."

I looked at Matt and thought, *You'll never be like my father; you are many things but being like him isn't one of them.* "On your way upstairs, tell Heidi her breakfast is ready." I sipped my coffee.

Heidi and I said our good-byes to Matt at the departure curb. He gave Heidi a huge hug and slipped her a couple hundred dollars. He kissed me while he gripped my arm and said, "I'll see you in a week, and you, young lady, I'll see you at Christmastime. Have a safe trip. Tip for the day, find a reliable bar and bartender, and I'll call when I land in Taiwan." Heidi grabbed her dad's neck and gave him another hug. Long and lean, their bodies were cut from the same cloth. The opposite of me—I stretched to give him a kiss. His blue eyes twinkled, like my father's.

We took an Uber to her apartment from the airport, where Suzy, the roommate Heidi met online, greeted us. Dark haired and pale as the moon, she looked like she hadn't seen daylight in years. She shook each of our hands and giggled more than she talked. Over the next couple of days, the three of us whipped through a dozen houseware stores and delicatessens, and eventually the apartment looked like a home. And after tagging along with us, Suzy's cheeks glowed with a slight rosiness, which made me happy. We said our weepy goodbyes before I loaded into a cab to catch a red eye home. Matt would return a couple days after, and our new life as permanent empty nesters would begin.

I entered the house, and whether from fatigue or the emotion of entering an empty home, I felt like crying. I lugged my carry-on upstairs and went into Heidi's room. Shoes strewn on the floor, rejected shirts and pants heaped on a chair. Overwhelmed, I slumped down on the floor and used the bed as a back rest. When I peered under the bed skirt, not surprisingly, I found it packed with boxes and things I couldn't yet identify. I had a lot of clean-up to do, a perfect distraction from feeling the hole in my heart.

Two days later, Matt returned from his trip. He yelled up to me from downstairs that he was home. I heard him climb the stairs, and before I could move, he stood over me, asking if I had fallen. I looked up at him, and he looked down at me. I lay there with my arm extended under the bed.

"Welcome home," I said and rolled to my side. "How was your trip?" I sat up and dusted off my sweatpants. I smoothed down my hair, which had to be a fright. I'd been rolling around on Heidi's floor for who knew how long.

"What the hell, Steph." Matt put his hands on his hips and stood with his legs apart. His stance to make him less imposing. "This room looks worse than when Heidi left, and you, dirt on your face and your hair. How long have you been on the floor?"

"Thanks, nice to see you, too," I said and pulled a dust bunny from my sweatshirt. "How'd the big product launch go?"

"Fantastic, couldn't have gone better." Matt narrowed his eyes and surveyed the disheveled room. "Steph, really, should I be worried? Are you cleaning or what?" He sat down on the chair, after he moved some of Heidi's castaways. "What's going on?"

"I found Heidi's old Nurse Barbie. Isn't she in great shape?" I sat up and held up the Nurse Barbie I'd wrestled free from a rolled-up blanket underneath the bed. Heidi had been in love with the doll as a young girl. I always thought she'd become a nurse herself because of her.

"Wonderful. Nurse Barbie, sure. Listen, you're going to love this, Bunny and Chip were outside their house when I got out of the taxi. We haven't seen them for a long time, so I invited them over for a drink later. Thought we'd catch up." Matt crossed his arms. He flashed a dimpled smile. "Looks like you could use a break, Steph. And I'm ready for a drink."

"Bunny and Chip? I don't know, Matt . . ." I scrutinized the mess around me. "I have so much to do." I sat Nurse Barbie on my lap. "I can't possibly entertain anyone today. Look at me—I'm a mess, and there's so much to do." I started to fiddle with Barbie's bun underneath her nurse's hat and pulled out the tiny clips holding it together. I stroked the fallen tresses that tumbled halfway down her back. She had beautiful hair. Then I gathered it back into a bun and affixed her hat just the way Heidi liked it.

"Steph, listen," Matt said, eyeing the littered floor. "I'm thinking the happy hour, seeing old friends, will be good for you." Matt crouched down on his haunches in front of me. His closeness made me feel uncomfortable—like he could see into me and discover some loose wires in my head. I scooched back a bit.

"I'll unpack, put together a cheese plate, crackers, nuts, carrots if we have them. We'll have drinks, laughs. Just for an hour or so." Matt rose to full height and started to leave. He banged the doorjamb with his hand and said, "An hour and a half, Steph, not a big deal—please be ready. Be good for you, fun!" He left the room.

"I don't want to have fun," I called after him. "I want to clean Heidi's room!"

"We don't need fun do we, Barbie?" At first, I felt silly talking to the doll, but why not? Heidi did it as a kid. "We understand each other, don't we? We want our Heidi's bedroom to be perfect when she comes home." I did a high-pitched Barbie voice, "Yes, we do. That will make her happy, and us happy because we miss her a lot." Always on the same page, Nurse Barbie and I, we already missed her terribly. I pressed my lips together and fought off the flood threatening to burst from my eyes.

After showering and changing, I wandered down to a busy Matt. He sung under his breath as he loaded a platter with cheese and crackers. *Singing? Really?*

"Well, don't you look like a million bucks," Matt said. My pencil black pants were clean, at least, and my black turtleneck sweater was always a good go-to. Made of cashmere, not cheap when I bought it and now old, but timeless, and who really cared? Nice people, Bunny and Chip, but different from us. Like from a past era. If they didn't live next door and our daughters hadn't played together, I doubt we'd be friends.

"Trust me, Steph, this will be good for you." Matt came over to me, leaned down and gave me a kiss on the top of my head. "Take this to the living room, and I'll make you a drink." He handed me the cheese platter. "What sounds good, Steph? Gin and tonic? Martini? A lemon drop?" He dipped toward me into a low bow. Matt's excessively accommodating behavior irritated me.

"Maybe a martini. But I haven't had a cocktail in a while, maybe I should start with wine." I couldn't decide. *Maybe I shouldn't drink at all.* Drinking might dull my heartbreak. And, I had a feeling, make me crabby. My heart palpitated. I felt myself struggle between being nice and being bitchy. I sat on the couch.

"I'll make you a perfect martini!" Matt said. He glided over to the bar and hummed while he mixed my drink. *Oh, for the love of Pete, stop humming.* His cheeriness set my teeth on edge. I fought the urge to get up and slap him into a more normal, somber mood. He looked over at me and winked. "You're going to love this." I wanted to throttle him till he cried.

I dug a fingernail into my arm and smiled. I needed that drink now. He rattled the shaker back and forth for the longest minute ever. I half expected dice to roll out of the opening. Finally, he poured the gin into my glass, his large body hunched over the stemmed glass like a giant. How long had he been so freakishly tall?

What an unlikely couple we were. As I sat on the sofa, my shoes barely reached the floor. His would stretch beyond the table. He didn't seem the least bit depressed about Heidi. I felt like an empty shell without her. Mr. All Business from last week suddenly turned into Mr. Sunshine this week. His demeanor was the antithesis of my mood. I absorbed her loss by myself.

"Ta da!" Matt handed me my martini slowly, without spilling a drop.

"Thanks." I held the too-full delicately stemmed glass in my hand, afraid to put it down. I took a quick sip. He did make a good martini; I'd give him that. I took another sip and felt the liquid torch my throat and warm me to my toes. My body relaxed. I rolled my head. I nodded at Matt and took another swallow. What a good idea.

"Happy? Now, one for me." Matt returned to the bar just as the doorbell rang. "I'll get it. Don't move, Steph. I've got it."

Matt opened the door and greeted Bunny and Chip. I glanced at the three of them standing in the front entrance. Bunny's blonde hair piled high on her head, with as many strands loose as there were on top. Her tousled appearance channeled a blonde bombshell from old movies. At seventy, not so pretty. Her eyes resembled the mechanical unnaturally blinking eyes of a baby doll—heavily lashed and batting open and closed. Chip's Jack-Sprat thinness exaggerated her fluffiness. He wore baggy khakis and a plaid shirt. Talk about mismatched.

"Well, hello!" Bunny sang, filling the house with her shrill voice, lavender perfume, and lashes aflutter. "Oh, goodness, it's been too long!" She bounded across the room. I braced myself as she bent down to hug me. "My god, you look fabulous!"

"As do you Bunny, always," I said, as she plopped down next to me. Her violet sweater wafted fuzzy balls onto my black sweater.

"Bunny, Chip, Manhattans coming up," Matt shouted from the bar. As soon as we were all situated, drinks in hands, I wanted to be done. I wanted to be upstairs with Nurse Barbie. I wanted to grieve the loss of my best friend, my daughter, my baby who'd left the nest for good. I pulled out the toothpick Matt had stacked with an onion and two olives and munched hard on the onion.

"So," Bunny said to me, touching my arm as she spoke. "How is it with Heidi living so far away? Goodness, it's not like she can visit often, with airline tickets costing so much. I remember I missed Ginger so much when she left for college, but now she lives just up the street, bless her." She took a sip of her drink. "Yummy, you haven't lost your touch, Matt, perfect." Her tongue swabbed the perimeter of her red lips. "But when she left for college, I cried and cried and cried, didn't I, Chippy?"

"Like a goddamn leaky faucet. Shit, I couldn't turn her off." He laughed and took a big sip. "I'd have been swimming in it, if you didn't take those happy pills." He chuckled.

"True, not going to lie." Bunny glanced at me, and as much as eyes rimmed in black eyeliner and heavy lash extensions can morph into wistful eyes, hers did just that. She lowered her head and said, "Say, besides my happy pills, know what helped us get through the loneliness—cooking lessons. Ah, we had a ball, didn't we, Chippy?" She and Chip exchanged drippy glances and held their glasses up to each other as if to toast.

"Cooking lessons, for Christ's sake. Never would have guessed." He took a sip and licked his lips. "Me in an apron, Matt. Fuckety fuck fuck." He laughed and took another swallow. Then he crossed his legs, revealing voluminously hairy ankles above his sock line. *When did that happen*, I thought. *When did Chip become an ape?*

"Oh, Chippy, come on. We had fun. Remember that vegetarian meatloaf?" Bunny formed an "o" with her lips and sucked in. "Delishy," she cooed.

"Meatless meatloaf. What the fuck, right, Matt?" Chip smiled. "Not bad tasting, though, to be honest." Again, he raised his glass to his wife. She giggled.

"Chip in an apron? How adorable. Do tell, Bunny, what's in a no-meat meatloaf? Ritz crackers? Sawdust? How crazy." I chuckled, my words oozing snark. I took a larger-than-I-wanted swallow of my drink and shut my eyes. *Why aren't we talking about Heidi and how miserable our lives are without her? Barbie, I wish you could call me upstairs, and I could leave this stupid conversation. Only you and I grasp how wretched life is without our Heidi.* Then I envisioned Barbie calling me on her little pink princess phone, and I snorted a way-too-loud, ugly laugh, spraying liquid from my nose as I did. My eyes opened to everyone glaring at me. I cleared my throat. A frown formed on Matt's face.

I looked from Matt to Bunny, putting my hand on my chest. "Sorry, went down the wrong pipe." I cleared my throat. "The ingredients, Bunny, go ahead. Tell me." I downed the last of my martini, bitter tasting now, mixed with embarrassment and a little sadness.

Staring into her glass, Bunny said, "It's not that interesting, I know."

"No, go ahead." I smiled as my eyes watered. "Seriously. All ears."

"Hmmm, well it had tofu, and . . ." Bunny paused and glanced from me to Chip.

"A shitload of chopped carrots and celery." Chip sat up straight and raised his glass into the air. "And eggs, two eggs." All eyes looked his way, including mine. *Why doesn't he cover up his ankles? In twenty-plus years as neighbors, I've survived fine without knowing he's one of those super hairy guys that probably has fur on his back like some evolutionary aberration. He never does wear shorts or short-sleeved shirts, even in summer.* At that point, Chip's hairiness doused my buzz more than snorting my martini through my nose.

Bunny stole back my attention. "Cornmeal, too," she shouted. "Of all things, and cornflakes." Bunny sat up straight. She extended her pointer finger at Chip and shook it. "And . . ."

"Braised Brussels sprouts!" The two of them sang. They clapped their hands like they both discovered yeast makes bread rise.

Matt threw back his head and laughed. *Since when are Brussels sprouts funny?* His jovial response to the insipid account of a stupid cooking class nauseated me. *I have to get out of here. Barbie, save me.* I leaned back and gazed at the ceiling.

After another drink and more food talk, Bunny and Chip sighed simultaneously and said they should get going. We all hugged as if we were best friends, when really, we stopped hanging out after Ginger went to high school and Heidi still attended middle school. Now Ginger lived a minute away, and Heidi lived hours away by airplane. We watched them toddle hand-in-hand from our doorway until they disappeared inside their house. Suddenly, I felt nostalgic, like I'd never see them again after they shut their door. Punctuation to the end of an era.

Matt said nothing. He picked up the empty platter and headed to the kitchen. He seemed upset with me, so I let him be. I escaped to Heidi's room and switched on the TV. I watched a real housewife of somewhere slap another real housewife across the face for a yet unknown reason. I grabbed Nurse Barbie from the dresser, painted on smile and nurse hat intact. We both sat on the bed to see what might happen next.

When Matt came in later, Barbie and I lay snuggled under the covers. "What're you doing?" Matt asked. He stood straight, arms crossed over his chest.

"Hello, Matt." I brought the covers up to my chin. My head felt a little fuzzy. My ability to focus split between Matt looming above me, the awareness of Nurse Barbie next to me, and a screaming match blaring from the TV.

"Steph, what are you doing?"

"What do you mean what am I doing? I'm watching TV," I said and stared straight ahead. A magical anti-aging cream commercial had taken over the screen.

"I can see that. Aren't you coming to bed?" He shifted his weight from one leg to the other and scowled. He reached for Nurse Barbie, but I slapped away his hand and buried her under the covers until only the top of her nurse's hat peeped out.

Matt sighed and crossed his arms again.

"I am in bed."

"You're in Heidi's bed. Aren't you going to come to *our* bed in *our* bedroom?"

"I will in a little while. I wanted to be by myself for a minute. After the commercial," I said, looking straight ahead at the TV.

"What's going on with you, Steph?" He came over and sat on the edge of the bed.

"Nothing. I just need a minute to myself after being with those people. Hearing them go on and on about their cooking class, so damn saccharine." I avoided his eyes, and thought, *You don't understand how hard it is to be cheery with my little girl gone, and who knows when she'll be back. Maybe not even at Christmas, maybe not for months, years even. I shuddered. And the only one who can make me feel better is Barbie. Not the ape and the aging wanna-be Marilyn Monroe.*

"I thought they were great. What's wrong with being excited about a cooking class? They found something to do together, good for them. They're nice people. And for the last twenty years, you thought the same."

I exhaled loudly. "I know, but tonight they got on my nerves. I mean, when did they become so gushy? Yes-Bunny-you're-right-Chippy. Finishing each other's sentences. And did you see how hairy Chip's legs were? Oh my god, I swear he's really an ape." I looked sideways at Matt. "They've changed. And they don't seem to care about Heidi moving to New York. And frankly, I'm not sure you do either."

"What are you talking about?" Matt patted my leg underneath the covers and stood up. "Listen, our daughter left, and you're depressed. I get you two were close. So was I. We always will be, but you need to move on, Steph. Find something to do—and I don't mean going through Heidi's stuff day after day." Matt started for the door. "I'll be in our bedroom, in our bed." He glanced toward Barbie and shook his head. "I miss her, too, but I am looking forward to spending more time with you." He left the room.

"By the way, I'm CLEANING her room. Normal when your kid leaves home for good. NORMAL!" I yelled after him. I pulled Barbie out from under the covers. *You are such a rock*, I thought and adjusted her bun under her hat just like Heidi would have.

The next morning, I got up and went into Matt's and my bedroom. Matt had already left for work. Relieved that I didn't have to discuss the previous night's activities, I just wanted to get back at it in Heidi's room. I showered and changed back into my sweats from the day before. *No point in getting another pair dirty.*

From the kitchen, I grabbed a cup of coffee and a leftover bottle of wine and returned to my project upstairs. Barbie sat on the floor next to me as I plowed, dug, and sifted through Heidi's things. I lost track of time. The coffee finished, I unscrewed the bottle and poured a bit of wine into my mug. The boxes of photos I pulled from under the bed absorbed my attention. As a child, Heidi loved hearing about our family history, and I loved sharing it. We lost hours together, poring over snapshots.

"Hello there," Matt said from the doorway. I hadn't heard him come home from work. "Still at it, huh?" He sat on the bed and picked up Barbie. He fiddled with her hat.

"Don't mess with her," I said and sat up. My back ached from being hunched over for hours. "When did you get home?" I grabbed Barbie out of his hand and readjusted her hat. Her perma-grin in place. God, I loved her.

Matt followed her with his eyes and then glanced at the wine bottle. "Just now. Been at this all day?" He surveyed the room. "Making any headway?" He crossed his legs and then his arms; his limbs were so gangly they seemed to swallow the empty space in the room. "I don't see you've thought about dinner so let's screw cooking. Let's go out. Let's eat at that place we've been wanting to try, down-town, you remember?" His eyes glistened with excitement.

"I don't think so. Let's order a pizza or something. I want to keep going in here." I looked down at Barbie. *We've had such a wonderful all-things-Heidi day, haven't we?* Again, her plastic-perfect smile soothed me.

"Steph, listen, you're just wallowing in this . . . this state of mind you're in—it's not healthy. Face facts—your daughter got a great job in a great city, where she should be." Matt stood up. "You'll feel better once you're out of this room."

"I'm sorry." I tucked Barbie's loose hair back into a bun under her hat. "You go. Without me."

"Steph, I'm not talking about a cruise around the world. I'm talking about going to dinner for maybe an hour and a half, depending on traffic." He put his fingers through his hair. "Please, Steph, do it for me as much as for you, for us, let's go. Out."

"Matt, I can't. I just can't." I held my breath and pressed my eyes shut.

He stood silent for a long minute. I heard him sigh. "You pay more attention to that Barbie than you do me. You can't tell me that's healthy." Then he left the room, closing the door behind him. Not long after, I heard the front door slam. I exhaled. Barbie dropped from my hand and rolled onto the floor. I supposed I should have cried, but I didn't. I just sat there and let melancholy fill my body.

Weeks passed in a daze. Most days and nights I spent in Heidi's room. Heidi called Matt after she couldn't get ahold of me, when I forgot to charge my phone and the battery died. By that time, Matt had stopped asking me to sleep in our room or eat meals together or anything, thank God. Whether his work absorbed his time, or he couldn't deal with me, it didn't matter. I couldn't really be bothered with him. He probably ironed his own shirts and ate eggs for dinner. Throughout the passing weeks, he made several quick business trips. I didn't track when he left or came home. If I had my coffee, cream, wine, some chips or microwave popcorn, I felt fine. Sometimes I had more wine than coffee. It helped me sleep.

One day, Matt leaned into Heidi's room, as he had begun to do when he arrived home, one hand on the doorknob using a soft voice, as if I were sleeping or sick. Or touched. "Steph, good news. Heidi got a cheap ticket and is coming home tomorrow. For the weekend." Matt slowly moved inside the room as he spoke. "And she's bringing a friend with her, a male friend." I watched him wait for my reaction, and I gave him one.

I bolted upright into a sitting position from lying on the floor. "What? Heidi's coming home?" I couldn't believe it. "Tomorrow? Is she ill?" I tried to wrap my head around it. "Is she sick, Matt?"

"Steph, she wants us to meet her friend." Matt dropped to his knees in front of me. He took my hands in his and looked into my eyes. "Steph, Heidi is coming home with a boy. She wants us to meet her boyfriend. You must *really*, and I mean *really*, pull it together.

Like, get your head out of the clouds or, really, this room. I'll help you finish cleaning. But you need to snap out of it, Steph. Do you understand?" He stood up and looked around. I followed his gaze as he absorbed the surrounding chaos. Photographs spread out like a deck of cards on the floor. The unmade bed had various knick-knacks stowed in the crumpled sheets. I had moved the TV from the dresser to the end of the bed. The dresser piled high with assorted scarves, hair ties, and for some reason I couldn't think of right then, Girl Scout beads. Matt grabbed a handful of photos.

I snatched the pictures from his hand. "I can't believe it, she's coming home." Then I burst into tears. "Oh, Matt, I'm so happy, I can't stand it." I dropped the photos back onto the floor and sobbed into my hands, soaking the cuffs of my sweatshirt. Matt kneaded my shoulder with one hand and with the other picked up the photos and dumped them into an empty shoebox. I inhaled and let out a loud, "Oh, my God, tomorrow?!" A surge of energy buzzed inside me. *Her room must be immaculate.* I wiped my eyes with my wet sleeves and started stuffing clothes into loose bags. I put Barbie safely on the desk and bumped into Matt standing in the center of the room.

"Whoa, careful," Matt said, hands steadying me. "You OK? Let me help. Maybe you need to rest."

"You go." I turned him around and pushed him toward the door. "Don't worry, I'm good. Lots to do."

"Steph, you should know, I talked to your sister about you, and she was this close to coming out for a visit." He held up his pointer finger and thumb with scarce distance between them. "This close."

"Don't be ridiculous. We don't need Donna." I turned away from him and began to strip the sheets off the mattress. Just because my older sister was a retired nurse and had four kids in four different cities didn't mean she was an expert in my situation. "I'm fine."

Matt's eyebrows furrowed. "OK, but you do understand Heidi leaves again Sunday?"

"Of course. Nothing to fuss about," I said and believed it. At least she would be home, and things could be normal for a little while. We could shop, grab coffee, get a mani-pedi. My heart pumped with joy.

The next day came fast with my busyness, but after I finished cleaning, Heidi's room, the house, even Nurse Barbie's button nose, gleamed.

As I descended the stairs, I heard Matt pull into the driveway. I yanked open the door and ran outside. Heidi, Matt, and a tall, redheaded boy got out of the car. Matt slapped him on the back and grabbed luggage from the trunk. The boy took Heidi's hand as they approached me.

"Hi, Mom!" Heidi said and fell into my arms. Her body next to mine felt like heaven.

"Welcome home." I hugged her till her arms dropped. "You look wonderful." And she did, her face glowed with confidence and contentment. Thin, but not too thin, just like always, beautiful.

"Mom, meet Teran. He's from Connecticut," Heidi said and stepped closer to the rangy young man beside her. He held out his hand. "Teran, my mom. You can call her Stephanie."

"Hi, Stephanie, thanks for having me." We shook hands. A soft but strong handshake. His mass of red curls looked like a mop on a stick. *Where on earth did he get that hair?* His clear green eyes looked directly at me. "Great to meet you."

He called me Stephanie. Why didn't she introduce me as Mrs. Pile? We've just met, and he called me Stephanie. His familiarity put me off. Matt and I led the kids into the house. *At least she's home,* I thought. "Hope you guys are hungry. I made lunch."

Once inside, we paraded to the kitchen. Heidi said, "Just so you know, Mom, we made plans to meet up with Jenny and her boyfriend in about an hour. I told a few people I was coming home." She rested her hand on top of mine on the island.

"Really, so soon? I don't expect you to spend every moment with me, but I didn't think you'd leave right away." I tried not to sound disappointed. "I've made your favorite, tuna and egg without the crusts. And bought your favorite Sun Chips." I pulled away my hand.

"Mom, you're the best!" Heidi opened the refrigerator.

I rolled my eyes and thought, *You're leaving, you just got here.*

After the platters of sandwiches, chips, and fruit salad filled the island, Matt slid a plate to Teran and said, "So, Teran, what do you do in New York?"

"Thanks, Matt." Teran stood and served himself like he hadn't eaten in weeks. "I'm in marketing with Heidi. Same company. Boy, this looks fantastic, Stephanie!"

We ate and made polite conversation. Teran did most of the eating, and Matt and Heidi did most of the talking. Once we put away the food, Heidi snuggled up to me and put her arm around my shoulder. She bumped her head against mine. "We'd better get going. Jenny is waiting." She took a deep breath as she looked at me. "Mom, don't look so sad. I'm not even supposed to be here. This is a bonus trip. Come on, be happy!" She and Teran held hands as they prepared to leave, with Matt's keys in her free hand. "We'll be home for dinner," she yelled back over her shoulder.

As soon as the door shut, I said to Matt, "I don't think I like him, do you?" I didn't know why, just a gut feeling. "How about you?"

"I liked him. What's not to like? He's perfectly nice and Heidi seemed to be enthralled. I'll bring their stuff upstairs. I assume Teran's in Joel's room?" He picked up the bags before I had time to answer and carried them upstairs.

When Matt returned to the kitchen, he said, "Hey, nice job in Heidi's room. Cleaner than when she lived here, that's for sure." Then he rubbed his chin and looked at me from across the island where I sat. "Steph, I need to ask you something. On Monday, I fly to London. I want you to come with me. We can make a holiday out of it. Just you and me. I don't have to work full days, just a few meetings here and there. We could tack on extra days if we wanted. What do you say?" Matt shifted his feet. He smiled just enough for a dimple to sneak out. "Come with me?"

"I don't know, Matt." I planted my elbows on the island. My instinct was to say no. "I have so much to do here. Heidi and Teran leave on Sunday. I can't get ready by Monday. I don't think so, no." I offered up a weak grin.

"OK, don't answer me now, but promise you'll think about it. Please, think about it."

"Fine, but don't count on my answer changing." Sweat ran down my back, and my hands became clammy.

That night we ate fresh crab, and again, Teran consumed his fill. I would have ordered a couple more had I known about his voracious appetite. The conversation went a little like a *Meet the Press* interrogation. Matt asked questions. Teran answered between mouthfuls. Heidi and I injected comments as accessories. But I yearned to get Heidi alone. I wanted to whisk her away. Listening to Teran, with so many questions from Matt—I felt resentful of his monopolization of the time. After dinner, I opened the closet door where our games were stored. That's when Heidi announced she and Teran were leaving again.

"Where're you going? I thought we'd play games," I said and pulled out the Apples to Apples box from the closet.

"Mom, we're meeting back at Jenny's. We won't be late, but we said we'd drop by after dinner. Turns out she invited the gang, kind of a surprise." Heidi got up and tapped on the top of Teran's head as he bent over his pound cake and strawberries. He took another enormous bite and put down his fork.

"Yeah, right. Amazing dinner. Damn, Steph." Teran said, as he swallowed. He stood up, rubbed one hand over his stomach, then shoved both into his pockets. He smiled at Heidi and said, "Ready, babe." His wild red hair draped over his eyes.

Steph? Now I'm Steph? "I'm just surprised you're leaving again so soon." I glared at Heidi. "I thought we could have a game night. And maybe you and I could go out for a walk later."

"Mom, please don't." She huffed. I could hear her. "You cooked an out-of-the-ballpark dinner tonight. We loved it." They grabbed coats, each other's hands, Matt's keys and were gone before I had time to ask when they'd be home.

"That was fast, them leaving. Did you know they were going out again? I didn't know." I sat down at the table. "I'd liked to have known. We've barely seen her."

"Steph . . ." Matt started to respond.

"And where does he get off calling me Steph? Like we're old buddies? I mean, no one calls me Steph but my oldest friends and you." I fiddled with the leftover knives on the table. "I think that's pretty cheeky. And did you see how much he ate? Jesus!"

"Steph, let it go. They're here one more day, OK?" Matt stood up from the table and began stacking plates. "Have you given my question any more thought?"

"What question?"

"Going with me to London." Matt brought the plates to the kitchen sink.

I followed with the silverware. "No, I haven't, but like I said, don't count on it." I dumped the utensils in the sink and avoided eye contact.

"Why not, Steph?" He said as he opened the dishwasher. He placed the dishes too close together. They could easily chip. "Give me one good reason why not."

"Can we talk about this later?" I didn't have the energy to get into it, the dishes, or the London conversation. "I'm exhausted. I'm taking a bath. Don't forget to clean the tops to the pots." I left him in the kitchen, stooped over the sink, and went upstairs to our bedroom. I sat down on the chair opposite the bed. Feeling deflated, I turned on the TV. My daughter had returned home, and I'd only seen her for two meals and no time alone. I didn't really like Teran—he ate like a pig and was too familiar. And I knew it sounded bad, but the red hair? I didn't think I liked redheads. Didn't trust them. *All that cleaning in her room, and she hasn't even seen it.*

The next day, I got up early, determined to create a perfect day for Heidi. First, I made a gorgeous breakfast of waffles, sausages, and cinnamon rolls. After, I called the nail place to set up an appointment for us to get a mani-pedi. We'd eat, then she and I would go. I made the appointment for 11:00 a.m. Perfect.

While we waited for the two of them to come down for breakfast, Matt made some phone calls, and I straightened up the living room. Close to 10:30, I called the nail place and asked them to move our appointment to 12:30, just to be safe. I covered the food with foil. Then I tiptoed upstairs and listened by each bedroom door. Nothing. Not a snore or rustle from behind either. I paused in front of Heidi's door. My hand gripped the doorknob. I waited. What would happen if he were in there with her, together, all night? Did I really want to see that? *Maybe I should wait.* What if Heidi were in his room? Why not, she had been doing whatever she wanted for two months. Teran seemed to be pretty free and easy. I was sure he'd take advantage of the situation.

Matt startled me when he put his hand on my shoulder. "You scared me." My hand dropped off the knob. "What're you doing?"

"What am I doing? What're you doing?" Matt put his hands on his hips and looked down at me. His shaggy eyebrows met in the middle.

"I made a mani-pedi appointment for us and wanted to see if Heidi was awake yet." I put my ear to the door. "I guess she's still asleep."

"Obviously. Let her sleep. She probably needs it." Matt wrapped his arm around my shoulders and gave a tug, guiding me away from the door.

"Good morning, Steph, Matt!" Teran came bounding up the stairs outfitted in jogging attire. Sweat saturated his shirt and dripped down the sides of his face. He took off his hat, red hair spilling out, and wiped off his forehead. "Man, what a great spot to run. Heidi still sacked out?"

"Yes, she is," I said. "She must be tired. She probably needs it. If you'd like to shower, the towels are in the cabinet under the sink." I moved toward the stairs. "Breakfast is ready when you are."

"Breakfast sounds great, Steph. I'm starved." My jaw clenched. How did he sneak out for a run without me seeing him? *He's sneaky. That's how. Sneaky.* Not sure I liked that.

"Take your time, Teran," Matt said. "Good for you for running."

Matt smiled as we descended the stairs. He pressed on my last nerve, Mr. Friendly, the sunny diplomat.

About forty-five minutes later, both Heidi and Teran came down the stairs. She, in her bathrobe like she'd just woken up, and he, showered and dressed in fresh clothes. I'd moved the nail appointment to a 2:00 p.m. time slot. I didn't want Heidi to feel pressured while she ate.

"Well, hello, sleepyhead. Stay out late? It's almost noon. You must've been really pooped," I said to Heidi, as I removed the foil from the dishes. "Here, eat. Let me know if anything needs reheating. And I have a surprise for you, I made us mani-pedi appointments today."

"Must be jet-lagged, but I'm starved!" Heidi slid onto a stool and grabbed a plate and fork. "I can't believe I slept so late. Teran, dig in. Mom, this looks fantastic." While piling food on her plate, she said, "Mom, don't get upset, but I'm taking Teran downtown—he hasn't seen the city yet, and I want him to at least see the river front." Then to Teran, "The cinnamon rolls, OMG, they're so good." Heidi put a huge roll on Teran's already-full plate. He sat down on the stool next to her.

"Can't you go after? It's just an hour, and I'm looking forward to spending time with you. Teran wouldn't mind, would you?" I faced Teran, who shoveled food into his mouth until his cheeks puffed out.

He pointed to his mouth, indicating he couldn't talk with his mouth full. He looked at Heidi.

"Mom, we're here for such a short time, we can't. I want to show Teran around town." Heidi stood up. She came over to me and tried to give me a hug. "I'm sorry."

I stood up from my stool, breaking Heidi's hold on me. "I don't know why you bothered to come home, Heidi. All you've done is eat and run. You could have driven through Taco Bell for all the time you've given me." I didn't want to be mad, not in front of Teran, but I couldn't stop myself. "Obviously, spending time with me—or your father—isn't important." I threw Matt into the mix—strength in numbers. He sat up straight and pierced me with eye-darts. Heidi and Teran stopped chewing and watched me with bugged-out eyes. I turned and ran up the stairs to my bedroom, shutting the door behind me.

A few minutes later, there was a quiet knock on my door, followed by, "Mom? Mom, can I come in?" Heidi's voice.

"Yes," I called from the edge of the bed, my arms crossed over my pounding heart. My eyes burned.

Heidi came in and sat down next to me, like she had a million times before, for a million different reasons, on the same edge of the bed. "Mom, I know I haven't spent much time with you, but I wanted you to meet Teran this trip." She took my hand in hers. "I knew it would go fast."

"Hard to get to know a guy when he's always being dragged from one place to another." My heart slowed. "I'd hoped we'd get at least an hour together to get our nails done. That's all. I didn't realize you'd be gone the whole time you were here." I chewed the inside of my mouth. She rolled her eyes, like she was twelve.

"Mom, I planned this at the very last minute. I got a super good deal on a redeye so I could surprise you. So you could meet my boyfriend." She intwined my arm in hers.

I pulled away. "You've only been away two months, for God's sake. You call him a boyfriend?"

"I know it doesn't seem like long."

"Seem? It isn't!"

"Mom, I've barely ever had a boyfriend, ever in my life, since third grade, remember Eric Muncel? You called him weird, and we were like eight or nine years old." Heidi stood and crossed her arms; she looked just like her father. "I thought you'd be glad I met someone, someone who is nice, treats me well, is smart, likes museums, you know."

"He's a nice boy, Heidi, nothing wrong with him." I dropped my voice. "He eats like a pig and calls me Steph. That's a little weird." I fiddled with the nubs on the chenille bedspread and avoided her eyes. "Don't you think two months is a little soon to bring someone home to meet Mom and Dad?" Heidi squinted at me.

"Mom, you're impossible." Heidi exhaled. "I mean, I'm happy, Mom, really happy. I wish you could just be happy for me. Like it or not, we're going to the waterfront. We'll see you for dinner, unless you want us to eat out. I wouldn't want Teran to eat too much of your precious food." She stood and left the room, closing the door behind her.

So that's that. So much for togetherness. I exhaled from the pit of my stomach. I did notice she had a third ear piercing in her right ear and Sharpie-like painted-on eyebrows. I thought I saw a small heart tattoo on the inside of her left wrist too. My daughter had changed. She was bound to, I guessed. *Not me or Barbie, though, we're smooth sailing without a ripple.*

I opened the bedroom door and stepped into the hallway. I felt compelled to stop at the top of the staircase and listen—like a spy. Maybe I wanted to hear something I wouldn't by asking.

From below, Matt said, "How'd it go, how's your mom?"

"OK, I guess. She's so difficult sometimes. I mean, I thought she'd be glad to meet Teran. I was so excited for both of you to meet him. Dad, I don't get her, like, I thought she'd be happy for me. Boy, did I get that wrong. Like suddenly, she's so weird and possessive."

"Maybe me being here was too soon," said the redhead.

Then Matt: "She's taken your move hard, Heidi. It's been difficult for her. That's all I can say."

"Well, she needs to get over that. I mean, she had to realize, sooner or later, I would move on, out of the house. I mean, I did graduate college. It's kind of what you're supposed to do next. She's my mother, and I love her, but wow."

Teran said, "My mom cried when I left home, didn't expect that, to be honest—she's over it now, though, when I've talked to her on the phone."

"She'll come around. I'm trying to convince her to go to London with me." Matt cleared his throat.

"Dad, do you think she would?"

"I hope so. But don't worry, your mother is a tough old gal."

Weird, possessive? Tough old gal? I stormed into Heidi's room, incensed, and closed the door behind me. The shock of what I saw rocked me even more. The pristine room I had painstakingly cleaned looked like a volcano had erupted, with Heidi's suitcase at the epicenter. Clothing sat scattered around the floor in twisted clumps. *What a slap in the face.* I grabbed Nurse Barbie from the desk. My only real support in all this mess. *The only one who really understands me. Nurse Barbie, what a stalwart friend,* I thought, as I carried her to my room and placed her in my nightstand drawer. *Safer here. I don't want to raise eyebrows with our private conversations, although at this point, no one cares about what I do.* I shut the drawer.

Heidi and Teran returned an hour past when they told me they'd be home for dinner. Typical Heidi. I held in my irritation. They had a 5:00 a.m. flight the next morning, so again, no alone time for us. And no time to make a fuss.

After dinner, followed by a decadent chocolate cake—Teran had two huge pieces with ice cream—we sat in the living room. Matt stretched out on his black leather chair. Heidi and Teran sat piled on each other on the sofa. I sat in one of the club chairs in front of the fireplace. Just like old times. Except for Teran.

"Great to have met you, Teran." One leg swung up and down over the other while Matt spoke. "We appreciate you guys making the trip, right, Steph?" He looked at me and smiled.

"Marvelous," I said, staring at my daughter glued to the redhead. "As much as we saw you."

Heidi sat up and squared herself apart from Teran. "Really, Mom? You're going there now, right before we leave?" She pursed her lips. "Mom, let's plan something really special over Christmas. Whatever you want, just you and me."

"Sure," I smiled. "I'll get right on that." She rolled her eyes.

Then the carrot-top stood up and said, "Thanks so much for everything. Especially the food—everything tasted awesome, Steph." He looked at his watch. "Well, I think I'm going to hit the hay. Early morning tomorrow, right, Matt?" He arched his back in a stretch. Then he walked over to me and bent down with arms held out toward me, as if to hug me while I sat. Instead of standing, I patted him on the back while he bent awkwardly. He straightened up and exchanged smiles with Heidi. Then she came toward me and squatted to give me a kiss on the cheek. I raised my face, but I probably should have stood. We exchanged "I love yous," and I blew a kiss to her after. "I really do," I added because I really did and didn't want to lose it later because I didn't sound like I meant it the first time. She shot me a lovely Heidi grin, and they disappeared upstairs to pack or whatever.

Matt and I remained sitting in our respective seats. I felt immediately uncomfortable. Matt looked directly at me. "Steph, I want you to come with me to London." He recrossed his legs the other way. "Trust me when I say, you need it."

"I don't need anything." I shifted in the club chair. "I'm just upset I didn't get more time with her."

"Stephanie."

"I'm going to bed." I stood to go upstairs.

"We leave Monday." Matt grabbed the remote from the table next to him and turned on the TV. "It'll do you a world of good, Steph, trust me. You're not yourself."

"I am too myself." I walked up the stairs and yelled back, "Tomorrow, I'll let you know. Night."

I walked past Heidi's room. *I'm sure a big mess will be waiting for me after she leaves. Again. What a pain in the ass.* I walked into Matt's and my bedroom and shut the door. I went over to the top drawer of my nightstand and took out Nurse Barbie. I studied her. Her hat had loosened so I removed it and let her hair fall to her shoulders. "What do you think, Barbie, should I go to London or not? If I don't go, Matt will think I'm bonkers and call Donna, like she would be of any help, but if I do go, who knows. What do you think?" I twisted Barbie's hair back up into her nurse's hat, but as soon as I did, I let it down again. I liked it down, after all these years. *What do you think Barbie? Time for a change?*

Barbie answered with her ever-compassionate painted-on smile, and I flicked the hat across the room.

Lourdes

The first time she and Roger rendezvoused in the school utility closet, the cocoon of mops, brooms, and stacks of paper towel rolls titillated her. It served as the perfect backdrop for a meaningless dalliance—a disposable, gratuitous string of pleasurable moments. A foolproof formula she learned long ago. A little flirtation, a little touching here and there, and he bit like a fish-farm trout. A harmless affair for shits and giggles. He seemed no different than the others.

But boy was he.

Lourdes bolted into the first stall of the three-stall faculty bathroom. Her cross-body purse slapped at her back as she swung around and lifted a double middle-finger salute to the empty room. Resisting the urge to level the corner table of cheap perfumes and lotions, she slammed the stall door shut behind her. It bounced open. She slammed it again. "Fuck!" she yelled as, again, it ricocheted open. Flushed with rage, she stuck her finger in the hole of the metal door's slide lock, pulled it shut and secured the lock. Once sealed inside, she kicked the door with her stilettoes. No dents. She'd hoped for damage.

"Fuck you, Roger," she screamed at the door. "Fuck you to the fucking moon!"

She stepped back, smacked her butt down onto the unlidded

toilet seat and coiled her ponytail on top of her head. She pressed her fingers on her closed eyes. *What the fuck just happened?* The last fifteen minutes played out in her head. *I met Roger, like he said, before the seminar started, in the school's empty parking lot. Then, he unloaded on me from his fucking car window. "It's over. We're done. And I want you gone. Gather your things, call your union, whatever, but I want you out of here immediately." Like a punch in the face. Just like that, he not only broke up with me, but he canned me, too. What the goddamn fuck?* She opened her eyes to the ceiling. She whispered, "What now, Ma?" Lourdes's mother taught her things she never wanted to know, unwittingly, but they helped guide Lourdes through her sticky situations. The stickiness of this one, she worried, had just started.

She felt for the necklace around her neck and yanked it. A gift from Roger. The chain broke and a delicate pearl pendant slid off and fell between her legs into the toilet. She threw in the chain after it. *Fucking asshole.* Again, she shut her eyes. The motion picture of events jumped into play behind her shuttered lids. *"Go ahead, squeal. Tell who you like," he'd said. "You've been here a year. I've been here thirty. Who's going to believe you, a teacher's assistant who dresses like a street walker. You came on to me, that's my story. If I see you around here again." But his face, Jesus. From inside his car, his creepy calm face glaring at me. Threatening to call the police if I didn't leave. What a fucking dick.*

Then she'd panicked. A couple of cars turned into the parking lot. Co-workers with big mouths. They'd parked uncomfortably close to her car so to avoid being seen; she ran into the school's bathroom. The heels of her hands pounded her forehead. *I've got to get out of here.* Then, she punched the metal walls. *This is so your life, Ma.*

The bathroom door screeched open.

Her hands dropped to her sides, and she slowed her breath. Under the stall door, she saw a pair of red Dansko clogs with floral decals walk by. *Tammy,* she thought. The clogs bypassed her and entered the end stall. The door squeaked shut. *I need to leave now, before I'm noticed.* She hesitated. *Shit. The stuff in my desk. Fuck it. Go!* She stood, adjusted her purse on her shoulder, took a deep breath and reached for the lock on the stall door.

The outer door opened again, and Lourdes froze. Two sets of shoes shuffled by her stall. Lourdes slammed back down on the toilet and drew her heels back behind her. She scooped her purse into her lap. *Fuck! Stuck like a rat in a trap. Please, God. I can't do public humiliation. Please, I've got to get out of here.* She bit her nails, another habit she'd picked up from her mother.

Outside of Lourdes's drop-box-like stall, a loud voice whined, "I thought I'd pee my pants. What a worthless fifteen-minute meet and greet. Except for the free coffee and donuts. Doesn't bode well for the seminar. Jesus, look at my hair, a mess."

"Liz, shush up. You don't know who's in here," a nasally voice responded. "And your hair is fine. Hurry—we need to get back. The seminar is starting soon. The middle one is empty."

Someone in sling-backs banged on Lourdes's stall door. Lourdes inhaled. Her heart hammered. Another knock. "Hello? Anyone there? You're kidding—out of order? Two working stalls, really, for fifty women teachers? Idiots." She slammed into the stall door next to Lourdes, who watched the sling-backs walk in and face forward. Black slacks fell around her ankles.

Her eyes on the shoes under the divider, Lourdes silently prayed, *Let me sneak out of here unscathed, and I promise, God, I'll stop. I'll be good forever.* Quietly as possible, she pulled her legs up to her chest and locked her heels on the inside rim of the toilet. Purse secured in her lap, she cinched her arms around her legs into a tight ball. *Damn it, Roger, why'd you bring the drama here? You weren't my first rodeo, you know. I can handle the after. I don't talk. I'm discreet. When it's over, it's over, I get it. I wanted out, too.* The musty air was suffocating. *Like being forced to sit by a dead body while it rots,* she thought, *As if I were in a bad TV murder mystery.*

Tammy's low voice came from the end stall. "Hey, Liz, did you hear about Lourdes? The SPED TA? The one that wears stilettos like she's going clubbing."

"Yeah, like that's appropriate attire for a middle school. For God's sake." Liz's voice identified herself from the middle stall. "No, what happened?" A tinkle of liquid hit the toilet water.

Oh, shit, here we go. Lourdes scrunched her shut her eyes and tightened the grip around her legs. Her body pulsated like one big out-out-of-control beating heart.

"I heard she's having an affair with Roger," said the voice standing outside her stall.

How would you know anything about me or what I do? And that's history, baby. Ha, old news now. She sighed and blinked open her eyes back to the ceiling.

Bottles clinked from the corner table.

"You guys, check out these perfumes. I swear, who wears this stuff? Avon, Revlon, and oh my God, Jean Naté. My mother used to use Jean Naté!"

So did mine. She doused herself in it before meeting the man of the hour. To this day, the smell made Lourdes want to vomit. *OK, go on, let's hear more.*

"Is that you, Kathryn?" Tammy flushed the toilet on the end. "Please don't spray it, for God's sake, spare us. That shit stinks." Her door squeaked open. "Focus, girls, Lourdes and Roger, I think their affair is over. I heard they had a major break up this morning." The door thwacked the tile wall as she exited. "Like, Lourdes lost her shit or something."

Lourdes's arms strained around her legs. *Oh, this is rich. First off, an affair? Nope, not at all. But did I fuck him? Yes, I fucked Roger, and yes, I lost my shit. But you don't know the half of it.* Her mother's voice threaded through her thoughts. *"You have to be smarter than he is, or you'll end up holding the bag when it's over."* She rolled her head on her shoulders to ease a cramp in her neck. *You're a fucking genius, Ma.*

Kathryn's voice lowered. "What's Lourdes's deal? She seems so skittish, like nervous. She never looks you in the eyes. So weird. I can totally see her screwing around. She's sort of..." A pause and then, "skanky. I hate that word, but you know what I mean. And never friendly. Except with Roger, I suppose." She chuckled. "Awww, Avon lavender mist. I used to love this."

Lourdes swallowed Kathryn's harsh words like they were rocks. *You never gave me the time of day, Kathryn. Always giving me the up-and-down once over, you condescending cow. And skanky? Really? What a peach you are. Jesus.* She rested her head on her knees.

The water turned on and the paper towel dispenser cranked. Shoes scuffed like sandpaper on the floor. The garbage can lid swung open and shut. Lourdes prayed for their exit.

"Don't even think of spraying that," Tammy said. "But why Roger? Not only is he a dweeb, her boss, and the principal, but very much married. Is she stupid or just likes being a homewrecker? I mean pick someone better situated if you're going to fuck around with a married man."

Homewrecker? Hell to the no. They didn't like each other, he and his wife. He said so before we got into it. That home was wrecked before I showed up. Sweat dripped down her back. *Sling some shit his way, ladies. He's the real asshole. He screwed over both of us.* Her damp hands clasped together to keep her legs corralled.

"Oops," Kathryn laughed. "I sprayed." The last stall door screeched open and shut. "Ewwww, now that's skanky!" Laughter bubbled above the stall walls. The dense atmosphere of the bathroom curdled with rancid mist.

"Kathryn!" Liz yelled. More indiscriminate laughter.

A spoiled citrus odor wafted into Lourdes's dingy cell. She silently gagged, lost her balance, and leaned into the sanitary napkin bin. She pressed herself off with her shoulder. The stink in her stall triggered a memory, sitting in her mother's closet as kid. Amidst pungent smells of bottom-shelf perfumes, leftover aftershaves, and cigarettes, she'd hide while her mom entertained her friends. A smile came to her lips. *You girls would have had a hay day with my ma. When she went out, she wore fishnets and hotpants. She'd tell me, "Off to meet colleagues for drinks." Ha, drinks and what else? But I believed whatever Ma said. I wanted to, I had to. And now look at me, just like Ma. Must be true what they say, the apple doesn't fall far from the tree. Definitely a family character flaw.* Sweat blistered on her forehead. The ache of being balled into one position for so long turned torturous. *I never asked for your life, Ma. But look at me, it happened anyway, didn't it?* A sudden pounding in her head forced her eyes closed.

More women entered the lavatory. Their shoes formed a line in front of Lourdes's stall, and their voices roiled over the walls, keeping her imprisoned, cramped and crammed into her corroded dungeon.

"What's that smell, spoiled fruit?" Forced choking followed. "Hey, girls. Kathryn, I can see your shoes under there, move it." The woman banged on Lourdes's door. "Hello?" The sliding lock jiggled. Lourdes stopped breathing. Her eyes burned with tears that didn't fall.

"It's out of order," Liz said. "And Kathryn, the dummy, sprayed that awful perfume."

"It's lavender Avon, a classic!" Kathryn shouted from the end stall.

"Liz and Kathryn, I'll meet you in the hall. Too many people in here to talk," said Tammy.

"For God's sake, just finish what you started." Kathryn's voice drowned out the din of hand washing and drying. "Has anyone seen Lourdes?"

The person in the stall next to Lourdes said, "No. Why?"

Another voice quipped, "Lourdes, the one in SPED? She's cray-cray. Like clinically. I heard she has anger issues and drinks on the job."

I don't have anger issues, but I don't like to be fucked over, and I've never had a drink on the job. Lourdes took a deep breath of fetid air. *How much longer do I have to be trapped in here, for the love of God?* The walls seemed to be closing in around her. A star in her own horror movie. Her eyes scanned her box for a mental escape and latched onto a long line of marching ants crossing the chipped floor tiles. Ants made Lourdes happy.

They had ants in their kitchen. As she and her mom cleaned them from the counter one day, Ma told Lourdes that ants can carry twenty times their weight. If they were human, that would mean carrying 4,000 pounds. Her mother had flexed her arm muscles and performed a couple of deep knee bends. They both burst into laughter. Like a normal mother and daughter. Silly, but it felt good. Lourdes sighed. Now, inside the confines of her bathroom stall, every ounce of those 4,000 pounds pressed down on her shoulders, threatening to crush her. A shrill voice pulled her back into her present nightmare.

"Tammy come on—she's not in here—just tell us what happened." The red clogs shuffled back into Lourdes's view and stopped in front of a pair of denim tennis shoes.

"OK, but you guys have to swear not to say anything to anyone outside this bathroom, got it?" Lourdes saw Tammy's clogs shift under the door. Someone banged on the middle stall door.

A voice responded. "I heard you. I won't say a word to anyone, promise." The sound of pee stopped and started between sentences. "Come on, share the tea."

Lourdes's feet tingled from lack of blood flow. She readjusted her heels hooked to the toilet and repositioned her arms circling her legs. Her head nestled against her knees. *Go for it, you righteous fucks.*

They couldn't spew fast enough.

"She deserves what she gets."

"Her too-black hair and bangs—please, the worst."

"Where did she come from anyway?"

"I think LA."

"That makes sense. Her look doesn't translate from Southern California to Portland. At. All."

"Even her boots have five-inch heels."

Relentless verbal assaults filled the restroom, as Lourdes cowered inside her box. Thinking she might lose it, she pinched her calves to divert the pain pricking her heart. *None of you gave me a chance or tried to get to know me. Roger made me feel good, and I made him feel good. You don't know shit!* The irony occurred to her then: she didn't know shit either.

Lourdes recalled one of their last hook-ups. They'd just squeezed into the supply closet. He'd said, "I'm so bad, so bad, Lourdes." While she kneaded his butt cheeks, for fuck's sake. His breath reeked of coffee and breakfast burrito. "I'm a married man, I can't do this, but you're so vital." Roger's voice, his best asset, was deep but soft, like him. And the word *"vital"*—what the fuck? Old Roger, a middle-aged doughboy school principal. "This has to be it, the last time," he said. But she didn't believe him. "Smell good, stroke their ego and their ass, and they're yours." She believed Ma. She kept at him, tried to keep him on the hook, just for fun, or so she thought, but she didn't see the signs. His avoidance, the ghosting. Her obliviousness brought her down. Ma had taught her better, and yet...

"Come on, Tammy, hurry up," a voice whined. "Seminar starts in five, and someone will come looking for us."

Lourdes took a deep breath. She couldn't listen anymore. Bruised from the inside out and sickened, she wanted to throw up.

"Well, I heard Lourdes . . ." Tammy started, "but remember, not a word to anyone. And wouldn't she feel a fool if she could hear us."

Feel a fool? How about feel like my innards are being carved out like a Halloween pumpkin. Gutted. That's how I feel. Jesus.

A voice interrupted. "Wait, this is wrong. I don't think you should say anything, especially since Lourdes isn't here to defend herself." *Daisy, of course. Little Miss My-Shit-Doesn't-Stink Daisy. "Hi, Lourdes, love your outfit." Turn around and, "What the hell is she wearing?" What a piece of shit.*

"Give it up, Daisy, you trash-talk her all the time. Plus, I'm not saying anything that isn't true. You know as well as I do, she and Roger are having an affair—and yes, he's married. I ask you, what kind of woman does that?" Tammy's voice dropped to a whisper when she said, "Get off your high horse, Daisy."

He wasn't happy. He told me he was miserable. Claustrophobia gripped Lourdes. The air, like wet tissue, stuck to her skin, and the taste of soured perfume coated her mouth. She felt the collective weight of the women's bodies leaning against her door, their caustic energy pressing into her stall—at once a prison and a protective sanctuary.

A new voice offered, "I heard Roger started divorce proceedings. Do you think it's because of Lourdes?"

"I wonder," said another voice. "I know they weren't happy. Roger really is such a weasel. I'd hate to be married to him, but Lourdes made the situation worse, didn't she?"

OK, I fucked up. I get it. I suck. But he told me they were done.

"Who knows, right? But let's face it, Roger probably hasn't had any in years—his wife is a cold fish. Like him, really. You must admit, even if Lourdes is foul, he must have loved her attention."

Tapped out of patience and stuffed full of self-loathing, Lourdes's body trembled uncontrollably. *Enough. Please, stop.*

"I bet Lourdes wanted him to marry her. That's why she's so pissed," a voice spoke over a toilet flush. "Because he wouldn't."

"Lourdes makes squat for a salary—of course she wanted him to marry her. She thought he'd be her savior."

Wrong. Broke, yes. Marry Roger? Never.

Lourdes wanted to cry. She wanted tears to smear all over her face. She wanted to cry so hard that everyone would rush to hold her, comfort her, just once. But she couldn't cry. Not now. Not ever. She'd just rot from the inside out. Her head hung to her chest.

"You know what they say, men need a transition person to get out of a marriage. Lourdes is his transition person."

A voice said with authority, "Roz said he fired her right there in the parking lot, this morning, right on the spot."

A few "Oh, my gods" floated into Lourdes's stall, then fell like shards of glass around her.

"I saw his car when I parked," Liz said. "But I didn't see her. I had no idea."

"He ended it because he was afraid his wife would find out. He must have told Roz when he came in this morning. "She'd probably fuck him too. I can't stand the way she looks at him."

"Again, why Roger? Don't get the attraction. At. All."

Lourdes squeezed her eyes tight and redoubled the grip around her legs. *It wasn't serious. It meant nothing. Just a stupid game. A game taught to me by Ma.*

A hush fell over the room. Lourdes struggled to hold her grasp. *I'm going to explode on this toilet and take everyone out with me.*

"You play around with someone else's husband, you get what's coming to you, that's what I say. Lourdes should have kept her legs together," a voice boomed. "God sees all."

"Don't get religious, Jesus. More like, if you fuck someone's husband, unless you're, like, Angelina Jolie, you end up empty handed."

His marriage had ended. He told me. I believed him. I fucking believed him.

"Ladies, we need to go back to the auditorium, they're going to wonder what happened to us," a quiet voice interjected. "Well, Roger took full advantage, didn't he? She didn't have the affair by herself. If you ask me, he's creepy, and just as much to blame."

Thank you, whoever you are, Lourdes mouthed.

"I feel sad for the kids. You must admit, Lourdes has a knack with them. Remember the kid that climbed on the roof? She's the one who talked him down. And the spitter?"

"That's true, the kids love her. Kind of sad really, to lose her—if only for the SPED kids."

Another voice said, "She should have thought about that before she screwed the principal. Hey, I still have to pee—you guys go, and save me a seat. Kind of a tragic figure, Lourdes."

"And where is she now? At a bar, drinking away her sorrows wearing stilettos?" Tammy said and laughed.

"Jesus, Tammy!"

No, I'm held hostage in this disgusting tin can, forced to hear you fucking bitches shred me.

A voice bellowed from the hall door, "Ladies, let's go, seminar's starting." Shoes shuffled and scuffed their way out of the bathroom. Lourdes's eyes stung with rage, hurt, and exhaustion.

The sudden quiet of the bathroom belied the voices still reverberating in her head. One woman remained in the last stall. *Be strong, Ma would say, be stronger than anyone else.* Her ma could've written a book with all her infinite platitudes. Platitudes as solid as a soaked piece of tissue.

The toilet flushed, followed by a cough and shifting of feet. The stall door banged open, and water splashed in the sink. Then, the crank of the paper towel dispenser and the swing of the garbage can lid.

Lourdes closed her eyes.

Ma.

She had been a senior in high school, eighteen years old, when her ma disappeared for good. She claimed she'd met the real one, and he swept her off her feet to Florida. Land of sunny skies and silky white beaches. Her letter didn't give many details, only that she would be in touch soon. But she never was. Who knows what happened to her, but Lourdes survived. Part of her survival included carrying around her mother's testaments in her head. Especially after she picked up her mother's worst habit. Her ma's affirmative words about her dalliances made Lourdes feel better about hers. Like they had a special kinship in a weird way. But Lourdes didn't cry like her mom. Throughout her life, no one seemed to care when Lourdes cried, so she stopped.

Her legs unfolded and stiffly, slowly straightened out in front of her and, until she was alone, they hovered above the floor.

The last pair of shoes paused in front of Lourdes's stall. Just for a second, then they walked to the door. It opened and closed. Finally, Lourdes dropped her feet.

Her arms felt slick as she stretched them above her head. A deep fatigue weighted her bones, and her wobbly legs barely supported her. But the damage she had sustained didn't kill her. She slid the lock and pushed open the stall door; her shoes cramped her feet as she walked out. Bits of paper littered the bathroom. Someone's lipstick sat on the sink's rim. A canister of Avon perfume lay on its side, cap off. Like the dirty aftermath of a party.

Slowly opening the door to the hall, Lourdes peered out to check for people. Empty. She left the bathroom, clutching her purse to her chest and walked toward the school's main entrance. A voice from behind stopped her.

"Lourdes! We've been looking for you. Are you all right?" Tammy yelled, pulling open the auditorium door. "We've been worried."

Lourdes turned to face her, and said, "Like my mom used to say, if I'd been a snake, I would've bitten you."

"What?" Tammy shouted. "Lourdes, where are you going?"

Lourdes pivoted toward the front doors. She walked past the office windows where Roger and his secretary Roz conversed closely. Her hand on his upper arm. His hand cupped over hers.

Rain coated Lourdes's face as she left the building and rinsed away the bathroom stench from inside her head.

As she walked around the building to the back parking lot, she called Jett on her cell.

"Hey."

"Hey, yourself." Jett answered like she always did. After all their years together, she could still be counted for her consistently steady manner. Trusting and trustworthy. Lourdes promised herself, Jett would never have anything to worry about, again, and this time she meant it. Her eyes beaded with tears.

"Let's get takeout tonight."

"You're not busy?" Jett said. "Tied up with school stuff like usual?"

"No, not busy—not anymore. So, you want to get Chinese take-out, just you and me?"

"Sure. When will you be home? What time's the seminar over?" Her voice lowered.

"I didn't have to go after all. I have a few errands to run, but I'll be home soon. Hey, I love you."

"I love you, too," Jett said. Then she added, "Lourdes, you sound funny. You OK?"

"I'm OK. See you soon," Lourdes answered and ended the call.

Lourdes climbed into her SUV and reflected for a moment before she pulled down the sun visor. She removed the photo of her ma and herself from its clip. In the photo, her thirty-year-old mother stood dressed in floral bell-bottom pants and a lowcut white blouse, all smiles and bright eyes under a helmet of dark hair. Lourdes, in her teens, wore jeans and a sweatshirt. Long hair hung in her face, obscuring any details. Lourdes tore the picture into tiny pieces and let them fall into her lap. Now she had to figure out the right place to toss them. Like ashes she should have spread long ago, she wanted to get rid of them as soon as possible. No place she thought of seemed appropriate, so she stuffed the pieces into the console between the seats. She hoped, until she figured out something, her mom would get used to the confined space.

Amy

The first time we met, the three of us were vying for the same waitress position at Shirley's Diner. Turned out, each of us were looking for a little income while we searched for our post-college real jobs. We exchanged brief acknowledgments as we sat in the dining room on the only chairs not placed upside down on top of the tables. While the eyes of the other two wandered around the room, I assessed my competition. Even then, Charlene out-styled us, svelte in her matching tartan skirt and jacket. Her black hair in a razor straight bob and alabaster skin evoked images of a plastic doll, and her blue eyes were movie-star stunning. It kind of hurt me to look at her, so I chewed my nails and shifted my eyes to Nancy.

Nancy, a classic "Annie," glanced at her watch. Her mass of curly red hair sat on her head like frosting on a cupcake, while freckles spattered her face. At ease in a cherry gingham shirt, a denim skirt trimmed in lacey ruffles, and spotless white tennis shoes, you'd find her picture next to *wholesome* in the dictionary. Compared to them, I felt like a gray pebble on the beach. My homemade navy A-line dress was the only dress that fit me that morning. No bow adorned my frizzy, brown ponytail, and my glasses had a paper clip securing the arm to the frame. I outweighed them each by twenty pounds. In the looks department, I depended on my teeth to do the heavy lifting. That's my arsenal, straight teeth. Period.

Evidently, Shirley anticipated a busy summer, and we all got the job. We became fast friends, even after they fired me two weeks later for unknown reasons. At the time, I suspected my extra weight brought me down. That and my ineptness at carrying multiple plates at a time and nominal drink order retention. I brushed off the incident, per usual, by burying my disappointment and irritation deep inside me, locked away. Eventually, I'd forget about it. That's my skillset, routinely dismissing unpleasant things from my mind and being terminally fine after. A lifetime of being a chubby sister to three trim, popular brothers had taught me to be resilient and comfortable out of the spotlight. I learned to smile in the face of adversity or when simply being ignored. If a fat tree complained in a forest, would anyone hear?

Nancy and Charlene's reactions to my firing didn't surprise me.

Nancy made a droopy face my last day, and for at least the next ten times we met. She'd combine it with a consoling hand on my shoulder, then tell me how much she wished she'd been fired. The job was stupid anyway, and she would quit but needed the money too much. Secretly, I agreed. The stupid part, not that she should quit. Meanwhile, Charlene didn't so much feel sorry for me as righteous and upset with management, which, on the one hand, endeared me to her and on the other, angered me. Her excessive insistence that Shirley wronged me felt worse than being fired. "Let it go," I told her, but she was off and running—into Stan's, the shift leader's, office. I could hear her defending my honor. "She's the best, most loyal person I know. She's a hard worker, cheerful, steady," on and on. I wanted to pull her out of there and tell her I didn't need her advocacy. I didn't care about the job. I needed the money, yes, but eating the left-over French fries and the ice cream cones wasn't worth the fight. Gratefully, though, our friendships endured the drama, and together, we survived many more jobs, while inhaling the sweet perfume of nascent adulthood.

Since then, for nearly forty years, we'd met up for dinner to celebrate each other's birthdays—missing only when honeymoons, family celebrations, pregnancies, or funerals hijacked the day. Charlene always chose the restaurant. As a banker, her tax bracket topped ours, and she lived to discover the latest hot spots.

Nancy, an accountant, and me, a school secretary, didn't get out quite as often, so we happily abided by her suggestions. That didn't mean I didn't nudge Nancy under the table after I read some of the splashier menus. We balked silently at the high prices but threw caution to the wind three times a year and enjoyed ourselves. That is, until the last time.

The Italian restaurant bustled with festivity. "Charlene, you look fabulous as usual; new dress?" I cooed, walking up to the table where my consummate fashion-forward friend sat in a lemony silk dress. Her clothing budget made my children's college fund look like play money. I settled on the chair next to her. She seemed startled and turned over her phone.

"Amy, hi, darling. You silly, I've had this for ages. But look at you. You look great, always do!" Charlene stood to hug me. "You're losing weight. I can feel your bones through your sweater. You know what they say, don't get too thin; it ages you." After our embrace, I pushed the sleeves of my bulky white sweater up on my arms. I'd been the same weight, with an occasional extra ten pounds, for as many years, but Charlene flattered like no other. I loved her for it. I shoved my short hair behind my ears and felt my face flush.

Charlene sat down and swished her long, black hair off her shoulders. She unwound a scarf circling her neck and hung it on the back of the chair. "I just love this place. Best gnocchi in town. But let's get some wine first. I need some wine." She glanced at her diamond-studded watch and fiddled with the top button of her dress as she studied the wine list. "What's keeping our Nancy?" She dropped the list and began fidgeting with the corners of the menu. Exhaling loudly, almost like a pant, she mouthed the menu's meal choices. Between breaths, she chewed her bottom lip. A curious sheen shimmered on her face. She seemed uncharacteristically anxious.

"Maybe she got caught up at work. Remember, it's tax time," I said and slid on my reading glasses. "She'll be here, don't worry your pretty lil' head." I perused the menu. I wished Nancy were there to kick under the table. The prices did not disappoint—high as any place we'd ever eaten. Where was Nancy? I needed both to be present, so I could unload, process, whatever you want to call it, my shit. I needed their financial advice, both were good with money, plus, my worsening heartburn—I took prescribed medication now—scared me. And my quiet desperation to have alone time in my own home constantly niggled me, along with my new disinterest in sex. I had downloading to do with these two, my oldest friends.

"Hmmmmm," Charlene hummed. She never hummed. She tapped her menu on the table. I could feel her staring at me. She tapped louder and turned up her humming.

"Charlene? You OK?" I asked, peering over my readers, which sat low on my nose. Her eyes welled with tears. Stoic Charlene crying? She had my attention.

Charlene slammed down the menu. She took a deep breath. "OK. Amy, this is the deal. I have to share something with you, right now, before Nancy gets here. I'm divorcing John. It's over. I'm done." Charlene's chest heaved as she spoke. "I haven't told him yet, but I hate him, Amy. Hate him." She spoke in raspy whispers. I'd never seen her so upset. "After we're done with dinner, when I get home, I'm telling him."

"What? You're what? Divorcing John? But you're so happy. You're both so happy. I mean, when did this happen, you hating him? No f'ing way!" I took my glasses off and stared into Charlene's aqua eyes, each with tiny rivers poised to flood their banks. I reached for her hands spread out on the table.

"Oh, stop," Charlene said and jerked her hands away. "You'll make me cry. I don't want to cry." She took a large gulp of water, exhaled, and fanned her face with a napkin. "I want some wine. Where the fuck is our waiter?" Charlene scanned the low-lit restaurant for someone she could flag to no avail. She resumed, "For years, Amy, I haven't been happy for years. I tried. But after, you know, John lost his job, fired for opening his big asshole mouth, never did know when to shut up, and of course, it's never, ever his fault, and then me, suddenly the sole breadwinner. I didn't mind at first, but it's been almost five years, Amy. And I love my job, I do, but I thought I'd be retired by now. Amy, I'm so tired." Charlene locked her hand over mine in a firm grip. With the other hand, she threw back her hair from her shoulder.

Still reeling from the news, I half expected those at the neighboring tables to collectively put down their forks and say, "Oh, my God." At minimum, I wanted to make eye contact with someone to confirm what I'd heard. No one cooperated. "Charlene, I had no idea. You seemed so perfect together," I said in a high-pitched voice I didn't recognize as my own.

Charlene and John were the couple we wanted to be: good looking, rich and respectful of each other, like couples car shopping on TV. They never fought, that I knew of, not that Jerry and I did either, but we'd certainly had our issues after thirty years and two kids. Who didn't? But that was just it; they never seemed to have any Achilles' heels or secret seethings. Even after John lost his job, she championed him like he was a wounded soldier coming off the battlefield. And he always seemed grateful to her. He was the guy that pulled her chair out for her, helped her with her coat, and never walked ten feet in front of her like Jerry did to me. Jerry, who forgot how to be a gentleman a year or two after we married. Jerry who had to be reminded seventeen times of our anniversary and everyone's birthdays. He could diaper a baby, bandage a bloody finger, and fry chicken with his eyes closed, but chivalry was not in his wheelhouse. John and Charlene held hands while they walked.

"John is depressed. ALL. THE. TIME. He doesn't do shit. No cooking, cleaning, nada. I don't think he even looks for jobs anymore." Charlene loosened her grip on my hand a little. Her voice lowered. "I didn't want to get into this tonight because it's Nancy's birthday, and she's so damn happy being single. But I had to tell you, Amy. You're so eternally stable, but you understand, don't you—why I have to leave John?" Charlene held the napkin over her face. Her shoulders quaked. From behind the napkin, she mumbled, "I'm miserable . . ." Her words trailed off. "I can't take it anymore."

I scooted my chair closer to her. "Charlene, I'm so sorry," I said and rubbed her back. She pressed the top of the napkin into her creased forehead, leaving the rest of the dangling cloth to suck in and blow out as she breathed and whimpered. I couldn't help but think how strange it felt to comfort the imperturbable Charlene. I could only remember one other time when Charlene lost her composure, when I miscarried between JJ and Hannah. I'd been so surprised at how completely undone she became. She couldn't fix it for me, and that unnerved her. I'd ended up reassuring her that I'd be fine—just a temporary family setback. When really, I felt like she sucked the devastation out of me with her hysterics. At the time, her hijacking of my feelings pissed me off, but I'd moved beyond that now.

I was about to suggest we call Nancy and postpone our dinner, when the waiter marched up to the table in a black tux and a clean white apron. "Good evening. Something to drink before dinner?" Oblivious to the situation, the stiffly postured man directed his question to me, as Charlene's napkin draped her face. He waited, expressionless.

"No, thank you," I said. "We're fine." I gave him a limp smile and hoped he'd disappear. "Give us a minute, please." I gestured toward Charlene as if to say, "Can't you see we're having a moment?"

From behind the napkin, Charlene barked, "Wine! Bring us some wine. A bottle, your best cab, I don't care about the cost. The richest, fullest, darkest, meatiest cab, now! Please!" A garbled sob punctuated her sentence. She pressed the napkin into her eyes.

"Yes. Thank you," I said and picked up the wine list as if to order.

Before I could even make a pretense of choosing, he cleared his throat and said, "Of course, I have just the one." With the stoicism of a Buckingham Palace Guard, he turned and walked toward the kitchen. I had no doubt the wine would cost me as much as Hannah's bottom-teeth braces.

Not ten seconds after the waiter left, a radiant Nancy arrived at our table accompanied by a bald stranger. "Hi, Amy," she said to me, almost giddy. Her face dimmed as she pointed to the napkin-cloaked face of a tremoring Charlene and mouthed, "What's wrong?"

"Nancy, great to see you," I said, "Nancy, you're here." I flashed her a toothy smile and indicated tears falling from my eyes with my fingers. As my gaze shifted from Nancy to the stranger next to her, I relaxed my fingers, but not my forced smile.

Charlene dropped her napkin from her face and straightened her back. She folded a corner of the napkin and wiped off the streaks of black mascara beneath her eyes. She took a deep breath and with a plaster-of-paris smile said, "Hi, Nancy, happy birthday." To the bald stranger attached to Nancy's arm, her smirk morphed into a grimace. "Hello. I'm Charlene. You are?" She held out her hand to him, and they shook. We both glowered at him now. He towered over Nancy with a middle-age paunch bulging from underneath his orange zip-up jacket. Nancy, still slim in a purple coat, seemed tiny in comparison. He smiled, revealing deep dimples.

"This is Ted—Charlene, Amy." She pointed to each of us. "Ted is a, well, sort of a new boyfriend," Nancy said with a nervous giggle. She glanced sideways at Ted. Her cheeks burst into flames, burying her mass of freckles. "We just had a birthday drink, and I thought he could pop over to meet you before dinner." Nancy smiled at Ted. She grinned at us as if she'd just won the Nobel Prize in dating.

"I hope we didn't interrupt something here," Ted said, still holding on to Charlene's hand. "Hello, Amy, a pleasure." Not as quick as Charlene, by the time I held out my hand, he'd withdrawn his and crossed his arms. I shoved mine into my lap.

Charlene and I exchanged wide-eyed stares. An electric shock buzzed between us. Nancy had broken Rule One of birthday club: You. Never. Ever. Bring a husband, boyfriend, girlfriend, dog, NO ONE to our birthday gatherings. Ever. Birthday club was and had been sacred ground for forty years. What was she thinking? The Nancy we knew would be appalled by this Nancy. The Nancy we knew was sensitive to others, always did the right thing, and would never ever make such an enormous error in judgement. She'd be outraged at her wrongness.

The waiter returned with the wine, uncorked the bottle, and poured the deep red liquid into Charlene's glass. She swished it around and took a sip. "Perfect, thank you." She took another larger sip, leaned back, and closed her eyes for just a second.

"Shall I bring another glass?" The waiter, eyebrows rising slightly, directed his question toward Ted, as only three glasses sat on the table.

I answered with knee-jerk alacrity. "Of course," I said. "We'll need another chair, too. You'll stay for a drink, Ted, won't you?" I squished my chair closer to Charlene. Under the veil of the tablecloth, her sharpened chartreuse nails drilled into my thigh, burning as they pierced deep into my skin. I sucked my lips into my mouth and glared at Charlene to communicate my lack of choice in inviting him to stay. In response, Charlene narrowed her eyes at me.

"Oh, Amy, thank you. So sweet." Nancy's soft doe-like eyes met mine with such warmth of emotion, I momentarily forgot about the pain in my leg. I loved how Nancy made you feel as though your every act of kindness put you in the same camp as Mother Theresa. "Stay for a drink, hon?" The waiter brought Ted a chair and table-setting.

"Sure, just one. I know you gals have your special deal here." Ted smiled at me, dimples on demand it seemed. The pair sat down at the table.

After the waiter poured wine into our three glasses, he went to get a glass for Ted. Meanwhile, Ted rubbed Nancy's back and leaned over to give her a peck on her cheek. Nancy beamed. Again, Charlene dug her fingers into my thigh as we watched the couple coo and purr. This time, I flinched.

Nancy caught me, and her smile disappeared. I knew that Charlene's napkin-cloaked face when she arrived, combined with my less-than-chill self, created questions for her.

But if Nancy knew what I now knew about Charlene, she wouldn't have chosen this time to introduce us to Ted. And historically speaking, as the group mediator, I knew I'd be up to bat to douse any flare ups and, unfortunately, I felt a big one coming.

Each as stubborn as the other, they bumped heads often. We were like sisters, staunchly devoted, yet at odds too. Like the time the three of us went downtown to the Women's Protest. Charlene marched admirably for an hour, but when the rain started, she pooped out. She wanted to duck into the nearest coffee shop until it stopped. Her designer boots would get wrecked, she'd said. Nancy vowed to march till the bitter end, rain and all, and wore a rain hat, raincoat, and rubber boots in preparation. I wore flimsy rain gear, and as much as I was philosophically invested in the cause, the downpour nudged me toward a hot coffee.

We stood in the rain discussing what to do, Charlene concerned about her shoes, Nancy intent on reaching the finish line. Soaked and cold by their posturing, I suggested Charlene get coffee, Nancy should continue, and I would get the car parked near the start line. I would drive to pick up Charlene, then pick up Nancy at the finish line. Honestly, I didn't want to get any farther away from my parked car. Everyone agreed, and we marched on our merry separate ways.

Clearing my throat, with a side glance to Charlene, I took a deep breath and sallied forth. "So, how's your birthday been, Nancy?" I tucked my hair behind my ear and forced a smile.

Nancy's face relaxed. "Well, Ted took me on a wonderful walk through the Rose Gardens, then we had delicious ice cream cones. You know how I love my ice cream." She grabbed Ted's arm and leaned her head on his shoulder. He planted a kiss on the top of her head. She giggled. With a swift kick under the table, Charlene thwacked my shin.

She had a point. What happened to our Nancy? The happily-alone-never-lonely Nancy? Didn't-want-anyone-dated-here-and-there-but-never-anything-serious Nancy? She changed her own oil, cleaned her gutters, power washed her patio. Only three months before, they'd dined for Charlene's birthday, and Nancy seemed normal, solo. Ted didn't exist.

The waiter returned with the glass. He topped us off and poured some for Ted. "Are we ready to order?" He stood erect with his hands clasped on his stomach and rocked back and forth from heel to toe.

Quicker than you could say *meatball*, Ted said, "I'd love to peek at what the chefs are grilling over there—looks like an open kitchen. I love an open kitchen in a restaurant." He picked up his glass of wine, chugged the pricey liquid like a cheap beer on a hot day, and wiped his mouth with the back of his hand. A jolt struck my leg, delivered by yet another jab from Charlene's pointed fingers. I nudged her back with my leg. I prayed Nancy didn't see us. The air hung with tension—except the air Ted breathed.

Nancy smiled at Ted. "Go, check out what they're cooking, Hon. I'll stick with these two. We have catching up to do." Smiling, she nodded toward Charlene, whose usually perfectly made-up eyes were now smeared with black. I realized that I'd been biting my lower lip and quickly drank some wine.

"No worries. I'll tuck over there real fast, leave you ladies to yourselves, then swing back to say goodbye to my sweetie." He winked at Nancy, swigged what was left of his wine, and held up his glass to Charlene. "By the way, Charlene, this here is the real deal. You know how to pick 'em. I'm more of a beer guy, but this could flip me." He twirled the stem of his glass and addressed the lingering waiter. "Hey bud, can you rustle up some bread? Soaker food, you know."

"Of course, sir," the waiter said. "Anything else?" We did a communal blink at Ted. Bread? Why? After he tucked over to the chef's open kitchen, he was leaving, right? Why the bread, Ted? The waiter hesitated a few seconds, then left.

Ted stood with a quick squeeze to Nancy's shoulder. As he did, his stomach banged the table and his napkin fell to the floor. He picked it up and threw it on his chair. On legs so bowed a horse could slide through, he lumbered off toward the grill, where chefs stood chopping, slicing, and sautéing.

Nancy waited for Ted to walk out of earshot then squinted at us. "You're both acting so weird—is it Ted? It must be Ted. Listen, I wanted you to meet him. I mean I really like him." She sighed at our reticence. "You're both being so judgy. I'm very disappointed—especially in you, Amy." Her angry eyes shifted back and forth between us. We stayed mute, but I knew Charlene's fire was being stoked. Nancy addressed Charlene.

"OK, maybe it's more than Ted. Let's forget Ted for a minute. Tell me why you were wearing a frickin' napkin when we walked in." She scooched her chair closer to the table. "What is going on with you? You look a mess, and you never look a mess."

Charlene twisted the napkin in her hand and threw it down. "First off, Nancy, as much as I love you, I'm not sharing anything about my life with your new friend present." She used air quotes when she said *friend*. "I mean really, since when do we—you—bring a boyfriend, or anyone for that matter, to our birthday dinners? Even if it is your birthday." Charlene shoved her face closer to Nancy's. "Your timing sucks, Nancy, really sucks." Spittle shot from Charlene's mouth, landing on Nancy's arm. Charlene wiped it off, brushed her hair off her shoulders, leaned back and took another mouthful of wine.

The waiter appeared, as if by magic, with a heaping breadbasket. After dropping it on the table, he picked up the wine bottle and with solemn gravity, he divvied up the remaining wine into our glasses, finishing with mine, but leaving Ted out. "Another bottle, ladies?" The waiter looked at Charlene. She rotated the stem of her glass in her fingers and stared at Nancy. "Yes, please, we need it." She swallowed a large gulp and added, "Thank you." After putting down her glass, she pulled the breadbasket toward her and began buttering a piece, tearing it apart as she did.

Nancy huddled closer. "Listen, I don't know what is going on with you two, but I should be able to bring my new boyfriend to meet my oldest, dearest friends without needing anyone's OK." Her red hair dropped onto the table. She grabbed a handful and pulled it around her head to one side. "Am I right, Amy?" She watched my face as I squirmed a bit in my seat. *Sure, pull the easy-going one into the line of fire.* I understood then, the night was not mine or ours, but theirs. Did it ever occur to them that I needed to vent, be indulged? *Swallow it*, I told myself. *Stifle it because it just doesn't matter.* My mantra: *I'm fine.*

"Nancy, I'm very happy you've met someone." I dabbed my mouth with my napkin. We took a collective moment to glance across the room at Ted, who was shoving a roll from the bar counter breadbasket into his mouth. "Really, I am, but it's bad timing to introduce us, for lots of reasons." I glanced at Charlene, who rammed her finger into my thigh. "Ouch," I yelped. "Well, it's true, Charlene, you said it, the timing sucks." I stuck my finger into Charlene's side and wiggled it.

"Stop it!" Charlene glared at me. She rubbed where I'd poked her.

"You guys are driving me nuts," Nancy said as we watched her eyes follow Ted clomping back to the table with a plate of food. "Oh, God, he has food. Come on, quickly, tell me, remember, no secrets."

"Listen, Nancy, I told you, you'll get nothing with Ted here. And even if he leaves, I'm not sure I'm going to tell you anyway. You've really hurt my feelings by bringing him. I'm sorry, but that's how I feel." Charlene swigged more wine. "I'm not telling you anything." She sat back against her chair, the stem of her glass spinning between her fingers. Her teeth were turning purple, per usual when she drank too much wine.

Nancy's forehead crinkled. She rested her hand on Charlene's crossed arms. "Listen, Charlene, you can't control everything. Not everything can follow that script you have in your head. I had no idea you'd get so upset. It's my birthday, I was in a great mood and thought it wouldn't matter. I didn't bring him to piss you off. It's my birthday, for God's sake, and I'm crazy about him. There, I said it. How do you like that? Crazy about him."

"Ahem." Ted sat down with a generous portion of grilled onions and saucy mushrooms smothering a plateful of prawns. "Hey, gals, look at this, couldn't help myself. Nance, look, they have those big shrimps you love. Bon appetite—as the French say." He picked up his fork and started eating. Nancy rubbed his back, but her eyes stayed on Charlene. Ted looked up for a second and said, "Nance, girls, help me eat this. There's plenty." He slid the plate toward us but took it back when we all declined.

The waiter appeared at Charlene's side with another bottle of wine which he uncorked.

"Hey, bud, can you bring me a beer please? Coors?" Ted barely looked up as he forklifted onions, mushrooms, and prawns into his mouth.

"We don't have Coors. May I bring you a Stella Artois?" The waiter said and topped off each of our wine glasses.

"Stella? Super. Hey, man, food is good, really good." He beamed as the waiter departed.

The three of us ricocheted looks around the table. I felt a headache forming. Grabbing bread from the basket, I ripped off a hunk, buttered it and stuffed it into my mouth. Ted reached for the basket and did the same. "Good bread, huh, Amy?" he said, grinning with a mouthful.

Charlene looked at Ted, then at Nancy, then at me, and snapped, "I'm going to the bathroom." To me, "Are you coming?"

She stood up abruptly, snatching her purse from the back of the chair.

"Sure," I said and stood up next to her, chewing my bread. "We'll be right back." I shrugged at Nancy and followed Charlene as she wove her way between tables to the bathroom. The restroom was one of those luxurious types with luminous low lights, lots of products for freshening up, and a sink that sat on top of the counter and spewed water from a spigot shaped like the stem of a flower. *Nice.* I locked the door after us.

Charlene opened her mouth and pretended to scream into her hands. Then she looked me dead in the eyes and said, "What the fuck. Ted and his mouth spewing fucking food. And Nancy, fucking inviting Ted. And I'm getting fucking divorced. All I wanted was to be alone with my two besties." Tears trickled down Charlene's creamy cheeks. She slumped down onto the closed toilet seat.

I suddenly felt sorry for Charlene. "What do you want me to do? I'll do anything, just tell me. Do you want to leave, stay, should I get your wine, what do you want me to do?" I squatted in front of Charlene and put my hands on her shoulders. "Tell me, anything." My caretaker hackles fully engaged, the night was mine to save, and yes indeed, it needed saving. At the same time, my me-hackles fought for airtime. The resentment from holding in my shit flamed into a growing blaze in my gut. But I knew the drill. Different situation. Same outcome. Nancy would be all weepy when she found out about Charlene's divorce and feel bad for bringing Ted. Charlene would be pouty and angry. I'd play Dr. Phil. They'd discuss everything down to the bottom of the well and back, patch things up and, eventually, we'd all profess our love for each other. Being so different, that's how we made it work. If Charlene wore a power outfit and swept into a room, Nancy skipped in wearing flowers and bows. Me, I trudged in with sensible shoes and varying lengths of frizzy hair.

"OK, wine, bring me wine. I'm sick." Charlene's hair fell onto her face, black strands sticking to her wet cheeks. She ripped off some toilet paper from the roll and blew her nose. "You're a doll, Amy, a true-blue friend."

I stood too fast, and the blood left my head. I leaned against the wall. "OK, wine," I said, hot in my sweater. I steadied myself. On the way out, the door slammed behind me a little harder than I expected. My throat tightened. I felt a burning sensation in my chest. Heartburn. "Great night this turned out to be," I mumbled to myself. I burped. Acidic bile filled my mouth. *Focus*, I told myself. *Go to the table, get the wine, make nice with Nancy and what's his name, Ted. Who is Ted anyway?* I tucked my hair behind each ear. All I knew: no one cared about my problems. Sure, I wasn't divorcing or starting a new relationship where I had to get naked in front of a perfect stranger, but damn it, I had stuff. I was getting sick of being the Amy-who-helps-us-get-through-our-crises-patch-things-up-and-make-everything-nice-again friend. Not that I didn't love them, I just wanted a corner of the evening to share my own problems, and just because I had a husband and kids didn't mean I didn't suffer.

Braiding through the restaurant, I bumped against a chair at an empty table and sent it to the ground. "Oops, sorry," I said to no one, picking it up. When I stood, I had a perfect eye shot to our table. I watched Ted gulp beer but was startled to see Nancy staring at me. Before I could assess my situation, she came swerving around tables in my direction. I tried to smile impartially. Whatever that looked like.

"What's going on, Amy, tell me right now." Nancy grabbed my arm. "And if it's about bringing Ted, well that's nuts, just ridiculous. Charlene can be so petty sometimes. You're my friends. I wanted you to meet him. I didn't invite him to Thanksgiving dinner, and I'm not asking you to form a book club with him or share an apartment, my goodness, just a hello. Why is she so tough? I love her, but she is so hard on people sometimes." She dropped my arm and put her hands on her hips. "You understand, don't you?"

I glanced over at Ted, taking a moment before I responded. He looked intently at his beer, rolling the glass around in his hand. "Listen, Nancy, I totally get where you are coming from, but trust me, this wasn't the night to introduce us to anyone." I burped into my hand. "My mission is to fetch some wine for Charlene in the bathroom." I pointed in the direction of the restroom. "Yours is to talk to Charlene. Go to her. She needs you. Promise you, she does."

"What about Ted? I can't just leave him by himself." Nancy

looked back at Ted and waved. He returned her wave with thumbs up. "He's really sweet, Amy. You just have to get to know him. He told me he loves me already."

"I'm sure he does, but now it's more important you talk to Charlene. Tell him to order another beer or something."

"Charlene is such a pain in the ass." Nancy said and headed back to Ted. The burning sensation flared in the back of my throat as I followed her.

Once at the table, Nancy bent down to Ted's ear. "Hey, Ted, I need to talk to Charlene. It shouldn't take long. Actually, you go, and I'll meet you at your place later. Sorry, this isn't what I had in mind."

"I'm fine, Nance. You girls hash it out. I'll order another brewsky." Ted gave Nancy a thumbs up. "Don't worry about me. I'll stick around in case you need me to you drive you home." Ted and Nancy traded smiles so steamy with affection, I felt its warmth. The exchange made me surprisingly happy, but a vision of him naked followed and so did a feeling of disgust. Then, taking it to the next level—having sex with him—revulsion took over. I burped, and my head spun with a multitude of emotions. I'm sure our friend in the bathroom was furious at me for taking so long.

"OK, Nancy. I'm right behind you. I'll grab the wine, maybe some bread." I reached for the wine and glasses.

Nancy nodded and snaked her way to the bathroom.

"Good luck," Ted said, looking a little glassy eyed. He watched me, glasses and wine bottle in hand, struggle to grab the bread. "Here, let me help you." He stuffed pieces of bread in a napkin and balanced the bundle on top of the empty wine glasses.

"Thanks, Ted." I wanted water, too, but there was no way I could add that to my load.

"Butter?" He picked up a few pats of butter on the end of a knife.

"No thanks, this should do it. We won't be long." I assessed the path ahead of me and imagined crossing a demilitarized zone. "Wish me luck." Ted sent me off with a raised beer mug.

Balancing dishes wasn't my strong suit, underscored by my failed waitressing career, so why did I think drunk and a thousand years older I could do it now? Gnawing at my lips, I carefully zigzagged, around tables. Halfway there, a well-dressed man with a forehead as high as the Empire State Building leaned back too far in his chair and bumped one of my arms.

Surprised, he bolted upright. "Very sorry—hey, maybe I should follow you," he said with a laugh, flashing large yellow teeth. His three companions at the table shared in his joviality and hooted along with him. Their seventy-plus-year-old faces bloomed rosy with the myriad cocktails under their belts. Glasses decorated the table, at least a dozen I guessed. Their infectious laughter made me smile.

"Actually, looks like the fun is here," I said, nodding their way, and turned to continue my journey, accouterments teetering in my grasp. Those freeway signs that read "You'd be home now if you lived here" came to mind. The gleefulness at the table made me want to pull up a chair and laugh with them. Then, they'd tab out after dinner, go home, peck their wives on their cheeks, and sleep like babies. Perfect. But my friends and drama awaited my arrival, so I kept moving.

Finally, with three wine glasses in one hand, a stash of bread balancing on top, and a wine bottle in the other, all intact, I made it to the bathroom. I kicked the door. No one answered. I kicked again.

"You guys! Open up!" Again, I kicked. "Open UP!" I hissed as loudly as I could without drawing attention to myself. "I'm going to drop everything!"

The door burst open. Charlene, disheveled and puffy-eyed, pulled me in. Nancy sat on the toilet with hands on her cheeks. Only her hair was redder than her face. Paper towels littered the floor. I wanted to yell at them for taking so long but knew it would fall on deaf ears.

Charlene cleared a space on the counter, and I carefully unloaded my armful of fuel for our conversation. "Wonderful. And bread! You're the best." Charlene lined up the glasses and emptied the bottle equally into each. The mirror reflected her mascara-streaked face. I didn't think I'd ever seen her look so disarrayed. My surliness quieted. Charlene handed us our glasses with a fancy paper towel underneath. Nancy took hers, sniffling into a piece of toilet paper with the other hand.

"OK, girls, a toast, to Nancy's birthday! Happy birthday, Nancy!" Charlene said in a much too chirpy voice. Nancy looked at Charlene and mouthed, "Are you kidding?" Charlene ignored her, and she and I bent down to clink glasses with Nancy, who remained on the toilet. She held up her glass loosely and didn't look at us, but we all managed to touch our glasses and drink.

"So, did you two talk? Everybody OK?" I sipped my wine and leaned against the door. Nancy let out a sigh and took another sip as well. I couldn't read her expression. Mostly because her mane draped over half of her face.

Charlene hoisted herself onto the counter, barely missing the huge countertop sink. "Why do they put sinks on the counter? Such a waste of space." She adjusted her dress to cover her bare legs dangling over the counter's edge. Her blue high-heeled shoes barely held on to her toes. She slugged down more wine and put down the glass. From an elegant decanter she squirted hand cream into her hands and rubbed them together. In a low voice she said, "Well, I'll tell you, Amy. I told our dear friend, Nancy, that I'm getting divorced. Of course, like you, she found it hard to believe. I explained that it's only half the reason I'm so upset. The other half is that she brought Ted here. I've always believed in the sacredness of our birthday dinners—no strangers. Ever. So, tonight especially, I expected just you two to be here—no one else. I didn't want to deal with strangers, especially as I go through the hardest time in my life. I mean, really, is that too much to ask?" She took another swill of wine and looked at me.

Nancy exhaled loudly. "I'll repeat, Charlene. I didn't think it would be that big of a deal to introduce you to my new boyfriend on my birthday. It's not your birthday, nor is it Amy's. It's mine. I thought on my birthday I could have a little leeway to do what I wanted. And most importantly, Ted is not a stranger to me. And he wouldn't be to you either if you would've given him a chance. Secondly, I'm sorry I didn't read your mind when you were hiding behind the napkin. How was I supposed to know you're getting divorced? I said I was sorry, and I am. Honestly, I still can't believe you're divorcing. But really, Charlene, I'm tired of you being so controlling about everything. We don't work for you, you know." Nancy took a sip of wine.

"Controlling? Me? I don't think so. You're the one who broke our pact. You're the one who seems a bit controlling, changing things to accommodate you—and Tad, Ted, whatever his name is. You could have introduced us some other time." Charlene pumped her legs like she sat on a swing.

"I told you, it's my birthday and I thought, mistakenly, that you'd want to meet my new boyfriend on this, my special day. He might be my future husband, for all you know. Life is changing for us all, and maybe it's time we changed up the rules of our little group." Nancy stood and helped herself to some bread.

"Of course, things change. I'm going to be single, and now, you're part of a couple. Great time to change things up—for you. But you sprung him on us without even asking. Not giving us any respect. Liking him is beside the point. And especially you, the Queen of No-Man-Needed, good on your own, and then suddenly, poof, you walk in with a giant man on your arm. Shocking. Right, Amy? Say something."

I chugged the rest of my wine. "Frankly, you have both pulled the rug out from under me. I can't believe, Charlene, that you're divorcing and Nancy, you have a boyfriend. I get it, big stuff, but really, do you ever think I have stuff? I have stuff." I put down my empty wine glass on the counter and crossed my arms. "Plenty of stuff. Tons of stuff."

"Amy, darling. You, with your kids and your husband and dog, I love your stuff." Charlene sipped her wine and added, "I love your steadiness and predictability." Suddenly, she slapped her forehead with her hand. "Shit, I'm getting divorced!"

"Well . . ." Nancy slapped her hand on her forehead, mocking Charlene. "Gee, I have a boyfriend. And I need to check on him. And, for your information, Charlene, I'm still good on my own, even if I get frickin' married. I like a warm body sleeping next to me just like everyone else. And, little Miss-Banker-Power-Woman, you married, didn't you? For a long time, I might add. It can be done. Don't you agree, Amy? Be your own person and be married?" Nancy slugged down the last of her wine.

"I'm not saying you can't be. It's just, I feel broadsided. Right, Amy? I mean a heads up would've helped, especially tonight." Charlene jumped off the counter. "Not OK, Nancy, happy for you, yes, but not OK to bring Tad."

"It's TED, Charlene, TED, TED, TED! And I said I'm sorry." Nancy's face turned a deeper crimson. "You can be such a bitch. I'm sorry."

My last sip of wine rose back up in my mouth and soured. "STOP! Did anyone even hear me? I don't just stay locked in a closet until I see you two. I have a life, like you. Do you know or care that my acid reflux is getting worse, and I might have to take medication for the rest of my life? Or that I can't take a shit for days? How about we need a new roof to the tune of $20,000, and no idea where the money is coming from!"

I shrieked but couldn't stop myself. "Jerry and I haven't had sex in four months, and I don't care. I don't even know if I should care. And, I don't have a moment to call my own. And don't call me steady or stable ever again!" I felt sick to my stomach. Like an overfilled boiling teapot, I spewed my pent-up frustrations until the water boiled out. "I'm done," I whispered, sweating in my thick sweater.

Charlene and Nancy's eyes bugged out at each other, then at me. "Amy, honey, are you OK?" Nancy said as if talking to a small child. She reached for my hand. I slapped it away.

"I'm sorry. I've had too much to drink. I'd better go home." I remained stuck to the floor. I could feel drips of sweat sliding down the sides of my face. "I'm sorry. I'm fine."

Nancy came over and wrapped her arms around me. "Of course, we know you're alive. We're here for you anytime. Your life with Jerry and the kids seems so full, we forget that things aren't always rosy with you. And you're so good about listening to us. We're so sorry, Amy."

Tears threatened to burst like storm clouds. I took a deep breath. My heart pounded louder than my head. "Don't. Feel. Sorry for me. Nancy. And don't call me stable ever again." It came out more sharply than I intended.

"No one is feeling sorry for you, Amy. It's just, you really are our rock." Charlene moved closer to me. I felt crowded between them. "Wait, you don't want sex anymore?"

"Oh, stop. Please, both of you. I'm fine. I'm just sick of being stable or steady, reliable or anything like that. Just forget it, I'm drunk. I'm fine." Frustrated, I wanted to get out of the low-lit poor excuse for a fancy bathroom. *Why didn't they put chairs in here? Or real towels?* I needed to go home. "I'm fine," I said, but thought, *If I hear I'm stable again, I'll knock them both to the floor.*

Charlene unwrapped the bread on the counter, tore off a piece and handed me the other half. "Come on, Amy, we're all emotional wrecks. Where's your wine glass, do we have any more wine?" She scrutinized the empty bottle.

Nancy stared at the floor. "I'm not pitying you, Amy. I love your chaotic, crazy life—more exciting than my antiseptic one—except for now, I guess, with Ted and all."

"In other words, I'm living a life of a happy-go-lucky messy pig with my little piglets, and you're a fastidiously pulled together clean freak, living in a house that's impossibly spotless. And wait for it, you're absolutely spot on. No pun intended." I felt very smart.

"Oh, stop it, you know what I mean. Yes, I have an obsessively clean house. I only look after myself. You have more people to look after; you always have," Nancy said, applying lipstick she pulled from her pocket. "And if you both feel SO STRONGLY that we shouldn't bring anyone to our dinners, regardless of how important they are, even if to say hi and leave, I guess that's what we'll do. Now, I need to check on Ted, T-E-D." Nancy spelled out his name. She picked up her toilet paper clumps on the floor and threw them away. "I'm exhausted."

"Tad is probably emptying the restaurant of their food inventory," Charlene said, raising her arm against Nancy's eye daggers. "I'm kidding, lighten up. OK, that's fair. Just till I get through the next few months. I have a lot of processing to do with you girls, and I'm sorry, this might seem controlling or insensitive, but I want to do it with you guys ALONE." She added, "I say we hit the restart button and make another birthday plan for Nancy. Call this one null and void. Too late for me to make jolly. What do you say—do-over?" Charlene brushed her hair back and put on her business face as she looked in the mirror. "Shit, oh, dear," she said as she dabbed a towel in water and cleaned up her mascara. "I'm a wreck. Not a good look when you're popping divorce on your husband."

I felt like a heavy wool blanket had been thrown over my head. My fucked-up, sloppy life: lack of money, lack of sex I didn't want, and lack of my own time, gurgled in my gut. I knew sooner or later, if we continued this conversation, we'd go around and around about Ted again, and then the divorce, and eventually they'd circle back to me. They always did, but I didn't feel as patient as I used to be. At the moment, I didn't really like them very much. My cup did not runneth over.

"Group hug. We need one," Nancy said. "Love you both."

We wrapped our arms around each other and repeated our love for each other a couple of times. My eyes focused on the chandelier dangling above the sink as I waited for the first arms to let go. Charlene's dropped. "OK, enough warm fuzzies, I have a job to do, the sooner the better," she said. We gathered up our glasses and downed wine dregs that didn't exist. We threw away the rest of the bread, the paper towels, and stowed the wine bottle behind the big sink. Charlene grabbed her purse from the counter. Shuffling together in a funeral march, we filed out of the bathroom.

Me with droopy shoulders, the others straight backed, we returned to our table. Ted finished his beer and sat his glass next to the two others. When he saw us, he said, "Charlie's Angels back from the mission. How'd it go?" He stood and stretched.

Nancy slung her arm around Ted's waist. "We're good." She grinned at the two of us.

"Yes, all good, Ted." Charlene set her glass on the table and brushed her hair from her shoulders. "So, Ted, we've decided to post-pone our little Nancy birthday celebration until later. You're free to wine and dine her to your heart's content. I'll settle up." She signaled to our waiter from across the room.

"No need, Charlene, I took care of it. I intruded on your deal here, so I thought if I picked up the tab, you'd wouldn't be so hard on Nancy for bringing me."

Charlene, a formidable presence herself, especially in heels, had to look up to Ted. I thought I saw a twinge of intimidation on Charlene's face, but it passed quickly. "You didn't have to do that, Ted. I ordered very expensive wine and was fully expecting to pay. Certainly, sweet of you." Her smile didn't seem forced. She wrapped her scarf around her neck, tucked her purse under her arm, and moved closer to me. Her eyes signaled me to join her. "I do appreciate it. Now, I'd better get on with my depressing task. Ta-ta, everyone. Thanks again, Ted. Love you, girlies, mean it."

"Yes, I guess we're off. Thanks, Ted," I chimed.

"Aww, what a sweetheart." Nancy nuzzled her head into his shoulder and looked up at him. "What a guy." I swear I saw sparks when they exchanged gazes.

Their sappiness provoked another finger in my side from Charlene. I rubbed my side and shot her a scolding frown.

We traded final goodbyes with hugs for all, even Ted, then followed Nancy and Ted out of the restaurant and watched them, hand in hand, disappear around the corner. I wished Charlene good luck. She said she'd call me in the morning and let me know how things went. Before she was out of earshot, I yelled after her, "Charlene, I'm serious, don't call me stable anymore, OK?"

"What?" she yelled back.

"Don't call me stable!" I bellowed.

She gave me thumbs up and climbed into her fancy new car and roared down the road.

On the way home, I remembered a girls' trip we had made to the beach, before anyone was married. How funny it all seemed then, but now made perfect sense. Charlene had to have a bed and bathroom all to herself and had the money to pay for it. Nancy and I were good to share. We took a half hour to decide which side of the bed each would sleep on. One side had a view, and one didn't. In the end, Nancy ended up with the view side. For the next seventy-two hours of our trip, mingled with sharing our future dreams, Nancy relentlessly expressed her gratefulness to me, and Charlene routinely excused herself to change clothes. I think I drank a lot.

I pulled into my driveway to a dark house. As I walked through the kitchen door, I noticed an empty ice cream container, bowl, and spoon littering the counter. A dead beer bottle sat in the sink. As I moved toward the family room, I saw the bluish white light of the television dancing on my husband's sleeping couch-bound body.

"Next time leave a light on for me, will you?" I yelled, jarring him awake, as I turned and stomped upstairs.

A few seconds later, I heard Jerry shouting from below. "I'm sorry, I fell asleep!"

After washing my face, brushing my teeth, and putting on my favorite flannel pajamas, I crawled into bed. I thought about the evening and how tired I was from all the upheaval. I had so much to think about and cherished the few moments I had to myself. Looking at me from my nightstand, next to the heartburn medicine and glass of water Jerry set out for me, was our family photo taken last year at the beach. The four of us bracing against a strong wind, but rock solid, arm in arm, each with wilder hair than the other, and all smiling with incredibly beautiful, straight teeth.

Joy

"You've got to be kidding," Joy said through clenched teeth. Hands shaking with rage, she slammed the empty bowl on the dresser. It rolled off the edge and hit the floor, shattering into two jagged pieces. *The hell with it*, she thought, and looked at herself in the dresser mirror. Red-rimmed, watery eyes and last night's crumpled sheets embossed on her cheek reflected both her age and her mood. The bun on her head had slipped down to her neck. "I'm done, Gary, done." Her lips tightened into a scowl.

"You're getting an earful, like it or not." Joy shoved her arms into her pink bathrobe and jammed her feet into tired slippers. She kicked at a clump of her husband's dirty socks. *No more pretending what's happening isn't happening. It's showtime for that rotten brother of yours.* And like the ballerina she once was, she left the room and glided down the hallway to the living room. Forty pounds heavier and as many years older, if nothing else, her still-erect posture fueled her resolve.

Joy's eyes adjusted to the dim living room light, a combination of dusty sun particles escaping through a torn curtain, the TV and an old floor lamp tucked into the corner. Her husband's hefty feet dangled over the edge of the sofa; a crocheted blanket lay strewn on the floor. She trotted around the couch that divided their kitchen and hallway from the living room so she could look him in the eye. His scrunched face rested on a pillow stuffed into the crook of his neck. He stared at the television, droopy-eyed and oblivious of Joy. An auctioneer peddled fancy cars on a red carpet in front of a titillated audience. Joy picked up the blanket from the floor and threw it over Gary's legs. Cheers burst from the TV audience.

"Gary," Joy said, "he did it again. Roy stole my money." She looked down at her hairy-chinned husband. Unmoved, he stared at the TV. Joy tightened the belt on her robe and sucked in air through her locked teeth.

A quick-simmer minute passed. "Uhmmm." Gary's guttural voice sounded as though the pillow was over his mouth, not under it. He raised his stump, what remained of his left hand, and rubbed his unruly beard.

Joy's eyes narrowed as she looked down at Gary. "It has to be him. We both know I keep my tip money, which I'd like to remind you is really *our* money, in the bowl on the dresser. Every night I put it there. It's there when I go to bed, there when I wake up, but your brother visits like he did last night, and my money—*our* money—disappears." Her voice quavered. "Disappears by morning, Gary."

Shifting from one swollen foot to the other, Joy's hands pressed down on her broad hips. As she waited for his reaction, she studied her husband of almost forty years. His filthy black t-shirt couldn't make it over his mountainous belly, while his sweatpants rested snuggly underneath. An empty microwave container, candy wrappers, and a chip bag wedged themselves into the crevice between Gary's body and the couch. They stuck to him like burrowing puppies. The smell of old French fries and stale beer hung in the air.

Joy flicked the top of his head, his once manly mane now matted. "And it's not good for you to sleep like this every night. With all this garbage. It's not healthy, and it upsets me to see you like this." *Not to mention, you'd rather sleep here than with me in our bed. You've no interest in anything other than television. I'm sick of cleaning up your messes, and I don't even know if you love me anymore. Gary, your damn PTSD is going to be the end of us.* Joy roiled with everything she couldn't bring herself to say out loud. The truth stung like an angry wasp.

She took a deep breath, picked up a rogue beer can from the floor and slammed it on the coffee table. "So. Just so we have it straight, Gary, Roy is no longer welcome in our home. Do you understand?" Accustomed to ungainly silences, she continued, "You know this isn't his first time stealing from us, but by God, it'll be his last. I need you to take the bull by the horns on this one, Gary, and back me up. Roy is a thief, and we're his suckers."

With his good hand, Gary rummaged around for chips in the bag wedged underneath his hip. A 1967 red Trans Am slid across the TV screen: the auctioneer called first $100,000, then $120,000, then $200,000, as one bidder against another elicited whoops and hollers from the audience. "What I'd give for that," Gary mumbled as he munched his chips. Crumbs cascaded from his mouth to the couch. He brushed them to the floor with his stump. Joy stared at him for a moment longer, then she stomped back to their bedroom, her slippers slap, slap, slapping against the linoleum. "No more! He's no longer welcome here! I promise you!" she yelled as she slammed the door behind her.

Joy sat down on the unmade bed, crossing her arms and legs. She studied her bedspread. Dingy flowers covered a dull green background. She'd bought it years after Gary returned from Vietnam, but it had aged beyond its time on the bed. She'd wanted to brighten up their bedroom—cheer up the place. Now everything festered with a grayish hue. The Tiffany blue walls no longer looked blue; the white curtains hung ashen. Joy's shoulders slumped, and her arms pooled in her lap. She closed her eyes and sighed.

When they first met, she'd felt so happy. Gary had swept her off her feet at the diner. His words, when she brought him his coffee, made her blush. "Where'd you get those gorgeous blue eyes? I could lose myself in them." Who said things like that? No one she'd ever met. Finally, someone found something in her to love. Someone to fill her empty vessel of a soul, proving to the world and to herself, love belonged to her, too. After work that same day, she went home with him, he smart in his jean jacket with shearling collar, she slightly self-conscious in her uniform, and never looked back. Everyone, herself included, questioned their hastiness, but she'd walked on air. They were both happy. It seemed like enough, that happiness.

Then Gary left, to war.

He'd returned after being gone for the better part of three years. During the decades that followed, he gradually morphed into a darker shade of himself. He couldn't deal with anything. He couldn't work, pay bills, do dishes, zip. He couldn't even handle changing out the toilet paper roll. And now this thing with Roy. After they'd been so good to him. Even after Roy smashed the company truck into the warehouse wall, saying hand-to-God, faulty brakes were to blame. Everyone else swore he was on drugs, and the company fired him, but she stood by him. They both did. Then they'd let him live with them rent-free until he got back on his feet, or truth be told, until his disability checks kicked in, and he could move into his own place. She and Roy had become friends, of sorts. She could talk to him about Gary, and he understood. They were brothers, of course, but Roy knew other veterans who had issues like Gary—unable to communicate their internal nightmares, lost in their own worlds—he got it.

Of the two, Roy had always been the talker; he had opinions about everything. At least he had something to say. He'd fix up things around the house and gab and fill the void of living with a mostly mute husband. In her darkest times, Roy reassured her, Gary still loved her, even if he couldn't express it. She hung onto that notion, even if it came second-hand from Roy. It allayed her fears that Gary's inability to function somehow included his ability to love her. Eventually, though, Roy moved out.

He rented a studio apartment. Never one to hold on to friends, he spent most of his time alone, and, she knew, lonely. Probably high on who knows what too, but she overlooked that uncomfortable fact because he was family. So, they saw a lot of him, even after he'd moved out. He'd come for dinner and watch TV, make himself at home. But things changed after her money disappeared. Joy patted the bedspread. Yes, her brother-in-law had worn out his welcome. *Damn it, Roy, why'd you have to go and ruin things?* Her eyes caught a piece of the broken bowl on the floor near her dresser. Wrestling between anger and sadness, she picked up one of Gary's socks and threw it at the jagged fragment. Stealing from family—she wouldn't stand for it. She had to draw the line somewhere.

Slam! The front door. Joy's heart skipped a beat. Roy. Her chest tightened. Feeling the heaviness of her body, she hoisted herself off the bed and cinched the ties of her bathrobe. A quick glance in the mirror revealed her disheveled bun had fallen farther down her neck. She tucked a couple of strands into it and pulled back her shoulders. "OK, Roy, you've stolen your last dollar from us. As they say, the buck stops here. Pun intended." A squinty-eyed battle face, a confidence builder she gave herself before a ballet performance, a "you got this," appeared in the mirror. Her lips pressed together. She opened the door and slapped down the hall to the living room, toward her brother-in-law's grating voice. Roy's stink, rotten hard-boiled eggs, made her eyes burn before she saw him.

"Hey, bro—look at that car. Shit, that's a real fucking beauty, huh, right on, right on." Roy, wiry as a Gumby doll, stood behind the couch as a blue Mustang detailed with red flames rolled onto the carpet. "Boy, what a beast. Hey, wanna a beer?" Roy walked into the kitchen and helped himself to a beer from the refrigerator. "Hey, Gar, wanna beer?"

The TV audience gasped and whistled at the Mustang.

"No." Gary rummaged his hand around in the bag of chips.

"Right on. Well, don't mind if I do. Heh, chips." Roy grabbed the bag away from Gary as he crossed in front of the TV and plopped down into the chair flanking the couch. Dust puffed up into the air around him. "Shit, Gary, these are fucking decimated." He threw the bag on the cluttered coffee table. "But nothing like a cold one to start the day, eh, bro?" Roy air toasted his brother with the can as his legs bounced like jackhammers.

Seeing his twitchiness set Joy's teeth on edge as she walked to the end of the couch and faced the two men. Bile rose in her throat, and she fought the urge to scream at Roy—traitor, betrayer, thief. But she knew better than to engage with crazy because playing with crazy don't get you anywhere but crazier.

Walking farther into the room, she modulated her voice and said,

"Roy, you've stolen damn near $550 from Gary and me. No more, Roy. You are no longer welcome in our home, isn't that right, Gary?" Joy looked down at Gary, her lackadaisical husband, on the couch. He remained sprawled out, body inanimate with the pillow mashed to his head. Joy pressed her lips together and glared as Roy peered up at her. His legs stopped bouncing.

Joy straightened herself as much as she could. The auctioneer bellowed to the audience, "Bidding begins for this spectacle of perfection, this mighty Mustang . . . ."

But she spoke louder, "Gary, please tell Roy to leave, Gary, now please." Joy crossed her arms over her chest. She glared at her motionless husband. Her slippered foot began to tap. "You're done stealing from us, Roy. No more."

Gary remained unmoved. The bidding began. "$85,000, $85,000, do I hear $86,000 for this fine filly, $86,000, $86,000, $86,000 going once . . ." The auctioneer spoke at a racing clip, quick and determined.

Roy dropped his beer on the end table. His shoulders jerked up toward his ears, and he gawked at Joy. "You crazy bitch! Gar—you going to let your wife talk to me like that? Accuse me of stealing? You're nuts, Joy, fucking nuts!" Roy snorted and shifted his weight in the chair. He paused and swallowed a large gulp of beer and after, pointed the can at Joy. "Check yourself." His legs hopped double-time.

Roy wasn't a big man, but even on a normal day, his persistent ticks permeated any room, spreading anxiety like a virus. One or both of his legs could bounce for hours. His fingers constantly shredded through the slick strings of hair on his head. His shoulders perpetually moved—rotating and pumping like a pitcher about to toss a changeup. *He's ratcheted into high gear,* Joy thought. *He's going to blow up right in that chair.* She looked to Gary for support. His paralysis—verbal and emotional—was beyond infuriating. Gary was out-Garying himself today. There had been a time, before he fell into a pit of Post-Traumatic Stress Disorder, that if someone mistreated her, a few quick words from him would shut them down. Now Gary was dead on arrival. On a good day.

"Gary, please tell your brother to leave." Crickets. Flushed with emotion, Joy shouted, "GARY!" He remained as inert as the broken cuckoo clock on the wall. Her fists clenched until her knuckles turned white.

"I can't hear you," barked the auctioneer. "Do I hear $100,000 for this metal Madonna?"

"He robbed us, Gary." A pounding developed behind her eyes. She screamed, "Say something!" Meanwhile, Roy chugged more beer without moving his eyes away from his rock-still brother.

Joy stomped over to the TV. She didn't like to interfere with Gary's shows, his only enjoyment, but enough was enough. Sweat streamed between her pendulous breasts. She felt so alone, so defeated, so angry, her wretched circumstances gut-punched her. Between Roy twitching and gyrating, and Gary laid out like a corpse, a sour taste like expired milk coated her tongue. Tears filled her eyes.

"Gary!" She yelled again.

"Sold!" bellowed the auctioneer. Jolted by his scream, Joy clicked off the TV.

Gary closed his eyes, rolled back his head and gargled, "Joy, move." She stood firm in front of the TV, not sure what she should do. Then Gary craned his neck from the pillow until he could see Roy's face. "Roy—you take Joy's tips?" Joy slowly stepped out of the way of the television. Gary grabbed the remote and turned on the TV, then used the remote to scratch his hairy belly. Relaxing back into the pillow, he seemed oblivious to the fact that Roy didn't answer.

Joy glared at Roy. Perspiration glistened on his skin. She waited for him to start spinning a tale, his expertise. He'd weaseled out of the factory accident. He'd weasel out of this.

"I didn't take your goddamn money!" Roy's legs vibrated like a rotary tool. The beer can dented under his grip. "For fucksake."

As if an anvil pressed on her skull, Joy's headache worsened. Her eyes thinned to slits. "Roy, I'd like to point out that you are the only person that has been in this house for a long time, and I mean a long, long time. No one but you could have taken the money. And after all we did for you—gave you a home when you needed one, after you lost everything, after the accident. And that you would steal from us, well, we won't put up with it—you're not welcome here, Roy. And Gary agrees with me." Joy's voice wobbled. She sniffed and tightened her crossed arms over her damp chest. "Criminy sakes, stealing from your family." She looked down; a teardrop escaped onto her arm. "We can't afford to lose any money. To you or to anyone."

Roy's voice erupted. "Fuck! I worked my ass off when I lived here, fixed the fence, hung fucking curtains—and you call me a fucking thief? That's bullshit!" He took a swig of beer and slammed the can down hard on the arm of the chair. Liquid sloshed onto the carpet. "Family? Kiss my ass." His eyes darted between the TV and Gary and ran both hands through his greasy hair.

Suddenly, the TV audience erupted into collective boos as the engine of a brilliant white and pink Cadillac parked on the carpet failed to fire.

Joy picked up a coaster from the food-littered coffee table and slid it under Roy's dripping beer can.

"What the fuck!" Roy shifted to the opposite side of the chair.

Joy hadn't expected things to go so far south. Her body hung on her bones like wet towels, and tears rolled down her cheeks. Roy had to go, yes, but what kept slapping her in the face was how far-gone Gary was. His silence overwhelmed her.

"Bear with us, folks," The auctioneer said, "I'm sure there's still life in the ol' gal yet, patience, everyone."

"Gary." She softened her voice and bent over him, nose to nose. "Listen, I know it's hard to accept, but besides you and me, Roy is the only other person who's been here for months—except that door-to-door solar panel salesman guy, and I only let him in because I was desperate for conversation. The solar panel guy. That's it, Gary, that's the only other person that's been in this house. You didn't steal our money. I didn't. Who else?" Joy pointed at Roy. "Only him." Joy's voice cracked. "He's a thief and a user!" She stumbled back and bumped into the floor lamp behind her. The shade tilted upwards, and an oily sheen on Gary's face glowed in the light. Spooked by his appearance, Joy shook her head and righted herself. She reached down for Gary's arm and shook it. "Roy took our money! For God's sake, Gary, say something!"

Roy leapt out of his chair like a panicked cat and said, "Damnit,

Joy, don't make me come over there. I'll cut you. Sure as fuck I will." His can hit the floor and beer leaked into a halo-like puddle. He grabbed a paring knife from a block of dried-up cheese on the table and lunged towards Joy as if to attack her. She stepped back into the lamp and the lamp and Joy bounced to the floor.

"Gary!" Joy choked as she tried to scream. Her face aflame, she struggled to breathe.

"Don't you accuse me of taking things, Joy." Roy stood over her, the knife, shaking in his hand, pointed at her head.

"A collective prayer, people," said the auctioneer. Then the car turned over with a loud clank. "The power of prayer, people, she's alive!"

Gasping for breath, Joy sputtered, "Please, for the love of God, Gary! He's going to kill me!"

Gary shut his eyes and buried his face in the crook of his arm. He spoke, his voice muffled, low and gruff, "Put down the goddamn knife."

"Make her take it back." Roy held the knife higher above her. "Take it fucking back." Joy gagged, unable to catch her breath through her sobs.

"Ladies and gentlemen, a round of applause for the old dame, as she departs our stage." The audience cheered as the Cadillac crept off the red carpet.

Gary's voice resonated. "Roy. Drop. The. Knife. Now." A feverish tension filled the room.

Then, whether it was Gary's edict or Joy's will, Roy's grip weakened, and he let the knife slip out of his sweaty palm. The blade stabbed into the rug in front of Joy, just missing her outstretched leg.

Roy stepped over Joy and slumped back into his chair. His eyes fixated on the TV. A commercial touted a casino getaway. He combed back wet hair from his eyes and pulled his sweat-soaked t-shirt from his body. Leaning over the arm of the chair, he picked up the fallen beer and chugged the remnants, his cheeks inflating like bellows. Liquid trickled from the corners of his mouth. He chucked the empty can at Joy but missed and hit the fallen lamp shade instead. Then, as if someone loaded him up with change, his legs started bouncing again.

He continued to tug at his shirt, but it wouldn't stop sticking to his body. His eyes shifted from the television and squinted toward Gary.

Gary remained impassive on the couch, his breathing shallow and loud. Joy looked back and forth between the two men, waiting for whatever came next. The commercials faded back into the car show.

"Look what we have next, folks. A veritable stunner." A Bentley rolled onto the carpet to a collective gasp of appreciation.

Joy's heartbeat drummed from head to toe as she struggled up from the floor. Shaking, she tightened her belt, stiffened her back and shuffled back to the bedroom. Grasping the doorknob, she pulled the door shut behind her with a click. She propped herself up against the backside of the door, but her exhausted body gave out. She slid down the door to the floor, her legs splayed in front of her, slippers dangling off her toes. Her bun lost all control and hair fell around her shoulders. *This is not how my life was supposed to go,* Joy thought. *Everything is wrong. I was going to be a ballerina, dancing in front of thousands. Famous. Living in New York City in an apartment with all white furniture, married to a writer or an artist. Champagne and caviar every day—that's how I was supposed to live, in the lap of luxury.* "Ha," she said, laughing aloud at her outlandish dream life, while tears streamed down her flushed cheeks. "But everything went wrong," she said to no one. Joy rubbed her damp face. "Very, very wrong."

Wrong started just before her mother died. Joy had promised her on her deathbed, when all things desperate are promised, that she would care for her dad until he died. Dutifully, she did; she wasn't close to her father, but she carried out her commitment, while he lived a long and needy life. Opportunities for an aspiring ballerina with the assurance of a college scholarship dried up in no time. And with his lingering demise, so went her dreams. Then came Gary, bright as sunshine when they met, until he turned wrong too. Maybe the war did it, maybe he'd been wrong all along, but she'd been a fool for thinking he'd ever be his old self again. Always reserved, kind, and gentle, but now, well now, he barely had a pulse. Did he love her? Now? Ever? Doubt knotted her stomach.

Joy straightened her back, despair-bent, and hoisted herself up. "The worst kind of a fool is an old fool," she whispered.

She needed a plan. Shedding her sleeping ensemble, Joy threw on a sweat suit. She'd go to Sylvie's, her best friend's house. Sylvie had offered up her place before as living with Gary's PTSD grew increasingly hard. His new level of quiet felt detached to a point of being disturbing, but she'd adjusted—she stood by him like an obedient dog. *How stupid I've been,* she thought as she removed the remaining hairpins and brushed and re-pinned her hair into a bun on top of her head. "Wise up, old girl, time to cut ties—Gary ties—and move on." Her blotchy forlorn reflection nodded in agreement. Joy grabbed her purse from the chair and took a deep breath before she opened the door. She glanced back at her bedroom and spotted the two bowl halves on the floor. She returned, picked them up and pieced them back together—she loved the bowl; her mother had given it to her. At first the pieces affixed, but seconds later they fell apart. She left them on her dresser, puzzle pieces that fit each other without the ability to stick together. Joy ran a finger along their jagged edges, unloading a heavy sigh before looking away.

The living room had grown shadowy, as though black sheets draped over everything. The brave rays of sunlight from earlier had disappeared, and the turned-over lamp flickered in the corner. A dark spot on the carpet tattled where the beer had spilled.

The TV auctioneer breathlessly called out to a cheering audience as an Austin Healy rolled into the spotlight, "Do I hear $275,000, $275,000 anyone? Ladies and gentlemen, this grand dame needs a new home, please!"

Joy looked at her husband cemented to the sofa, no change in his supine position. *Of course not,* she thought. Stiffening her back, she looked from one man to the other. Then, as if making an announcement to a crowd, she said slowly, "Gary, I'm leaving you. Now. You've given me no choice. I am leaving you and not coming back." She glanced at her unresponsive husband. She felt the blood drain from her body. Her posture sagged as she sighed longer and louder than all the sighs she'd ever breathed in her life.

She turned to look at Roy. His body twitched in full vibration, a hand mixer in a dry bowl. They deserved each other. One more visual sweep around the room, and as hysterical cheers rang out from the TV, she exited.

Joy arrived at Sylvie's house a quick drive later. She peeked inside the kitchen back door before she knocked. Sylvie sat at the kitchen table decorating cupcakes for Didi, her oldest daughter, whose wedding shower was that afternoon. Joy had completely forgotten. *Bad timing*, she thought. Yet not. Sylvie and Joy loved each other unconditionally since they were little, and it was Joy who helped Sylvie through her husband's tragic death not so many years ago.

Joy knocked on the door. Greeted by Sylvie's warm hug and the fragrant baking smells made her weepy again.

"Joy, what's this?" Sylvie said, as she stepped back and wiped her hands on her apron.

"Oh, Sylvie, it's over, Gary . . . he doesn't love me anymore, it's really over."

Sylvie pulled Joy to her and hugged her again, tight. "What happened? You poor thing, you're trembling." Sylvie released her and led Joy to a kitchen chair at the table where cupcakes sat in different stages of being frosted.

"I didn't know where else to go." Joy dumped into a chair in front of the frosting bowl and held her hand over her mouth to contain her sobs.

"Oh, sweetie, of course you should've come here." Shoving a chair close to Joy's, Sylvie sat down and rubbed Joy's back in large consoling circles.

Joy caught her breath and said, "I'm so stupid. Sylvie, it's true, all true. He doesn't love me. I know now. He's changed—forever—he doesn't love me. I thought even with his issues, he'd always love me." She dropped her head into her hands. "I can't believe I'm saying it out loud: he doesn't love me."

"You poor thing." Sylvie shook her head. "Damn that Gary. For a nickel I'd tell you what I really think of him." Joy watched as both of her friend's hands fell into her lap and clenched into fists. It felt good to be defended.

"Oh, hell." Then, as if a dam broke within her, Sylvie spewed, "If you ask me, it's a long time coming. I know you don't want to hear this, but if Gary isn't going to deal with his shit, then there's nothing you can do about it. He's not the same. Never much for conversation, but now he's downright mute. Truthfully, he gives me the creeps. He's too quiet, unnervingly quiet. And don't get me started on that druggie brother of his. He's always been a freakshow. I'm sorry; I should keep my mouth shut, but if I'm really your best friend, I have to be honest with you. I'm glad you left him." Sylvie gave a little exhale and stood up. "Thrilled, actually."

Joy began to cry again, her face hot and soggy in her hands.

"You're mad at me now, aren't you?" Sylvie bit her bottom lip and laid her hand on Joy's shoulder. "Sorry, the lid fell off the kettle, kid. I couldn't hold it in any longer." She sat back down and resumed frosting cupcakes. "But it's how I feel. Bill's been dead six years, and he wasn't perfect by any means, but I know he loved me. No one could ever argue that. You, of all people, would have told me if he didn't." Sylvie held up her knife mid frost. "Say something, Joy."

Joy's hands fell to the table. "We've been married for almost four decades, for God's sake. I couldn't give up on him. I did get him in to see someone, I did Sylvie. Once. He saw a therapist, came home, and said he couldn't help him. How can that be? What else could I do?" Joy felt strange defending the man who, two seconds ago, had barely said boo when his brother threatened to shove a knife in her, let alone one who barely spoke to her. She shook her head and ran a finger underneath each eye. "I'm a mess. My life's a mess, Sylvie. Just a damn mess."

Sylvie studied Joy like a crossword puzzle clue she couldn't figure out. "What happened anyway?" She picked up a cupcake and slowly spread a knife-full of frosting across the top. "Tell me."

"It doesn't matter. Timing, I guess," Joy said, but thought, *Sylvie would kill me for Gary letting Roy try to murder me. And now I'm forced to lie to my best friend, as if there wasn't enough to be upset about. Those two losers . . . Roy especially, that son-of-a-bitch.*

"We'll drop it for now." Sylvie placed the decorated cupcake on a tray with the others. "I can't be late to the shower. I'd better ski-daddle. I'll tell Didi you're sick or something. She'll miss you, you know. When I get back, we'll fetch your stuff from your house, the necessities for right now, OK?" Standing up, Sylvie reached for Joy's hand and squeezed it. "You're just the nicest person in the whole world, and you deserve better."

Just before Sylvie left, she said, "Hon, better call the diner and let them know you're not working—say you're sick or something, but call in. They'll need to cover your shift. Back before you know it. Love you!" Sylvie blew Joy a kiss, and with a tray full of cupcakes in hand, she left.

The sudden stillness amplified Joy's hopeless thoughts. She began to shake uncontrollably. Only after a count of ten deep breaths was she able to calm herself down. "Get a grip, girl," she whispered, her dejection overwhelming her. Not since her mother died and Gary first left for war had she felt so adrift. *Pull yourself together*, she thought. *You made it through those times, you'll make it through this. First things first. Call work, get that over with. You're going to need to keep your job, that's for damn sure.*

Grabbing the phone out of her purse, it occurred to her that Gary might have called. After all, her ringer had been off. She laid the phone on the table in front of her. What would she do if he did? If he asked her to come home? She wouldn't go. He'd have to apologize first, for everything. For not giving Roy hell for stealing, not kicking his ass when he threatened her with a knife. For not getting help when he needed it. For not being the old Gary. For not loving her. *Jesus Christ, Gary.* It slapped her in the face again. He didn't love her. She could never, and would never, go back.

Slowly, Joy picked up her phone and checked her calls. Nothing. He hadn't tried to reach her. She slammed the phone on the table. After a fuming moment, she picked it back up and called the diner.

After telling her boss she had the flu, Joy rested her head on top of her hands on the table. Exhaustion covered her like a dense fog, and she fell into a slumber filled with visions of her early life with Gary. Together, on the couch when it was new, they'd watch TV with her head nestled in his lap, his hand gentling petting her hair. They'd walk in the park, holding hands, his big meaty paw, like the softest glove, would swallow up her hand, radiating his love for her throughout her body. He'd loved her; she was sure of it—at least a long time ago. She felt the faintest smile cross her face as she drifted off into a deeper sleep.

Joy awoke to Sylvie gently pushing her shoulder. "Joy, honey, it's me, Sylvie. Sorry I'm so late, sweetie. You know how wedding showers go. Didi sends her love." She sat down next to Joy.

"I must have fallen asleep." Joy felt disoriented from the nap yet comforted by her dreams. She rubbed her forehead. "What time is it?"

"It's almost 4:00. You poor thing. Are you hungry? Need a drink? Let's have a glass of wine, then we'll get your stuff." Sylvie rustled around in the fridge. She took out a bottle of white wine and poured two glasses. "Joy, tell me. Why now, why leave Gary now?"

"Sylvie, please, not yet. Nothing against you, and I promise I'll tell you later, but it's too real for me right now." Joy sipped the glass of wine Sylvie handed her. She wrinkled her nose. After another sip, she threw back her head and closed her eyes. The wine seemed to melt her organs as it traveled down from her head to her toes. She felt like mush and wanted to cry again.

"OK, I'll drop it. I'm just sorry you have to go through this mess —such a jerk. Good riddance." Sylvie clinked glasses with her. "Have a big drink, then we'll get your stuff." Sylvie gulped a large swallow, and Joy followed suit. "I'm just saying, it's time for a change. You deserve more, that's all."

"Sylvie, please. He's all I've got—or thought I had." Joy's grip on her wine glass tightened. "You have your girls, and you'll have grand-babies and . . .."

Sylvie stiffened. "Listen, you've got to start thinking about your-self—lots of people love you. You've painted yourself into a corner with your damn loyalty to Gary, and we're going to get you out. Right now, out of that damn corner with Gary and his crazy brother—let's get your things." Sylvie stood up and took another swig. "Here's to a new life!" She teetered backwards onto the refrigerator and steadied herself.

Joy stood, too. She felt lightheaded and was glad to be with Sylvie. *No one takes care of business like her*, she thought. "OK, Sylvie, lead me out of this mess, out of my corner with the ghost of former Gary."

"I'm sorry for him, sure, but you've tried. He's sick, Joy, and that's not on you." Both women grabbed their coats and purses, walked arm-in-arm down the driveway, and climbed into Sylvie's car.

As they approached Joy's house, Joy put her hand on Sylvie's arm and said, "Sylvie, I need to tell you something. Roy might be there, and he is not in a good way, so you need to ignore him, do you understand?" Joy dropped her hand and looked out her window. She tapped her fingers on her mouth. "Roy might be crazier than normal. I think he's using the hard stuff again."

"I'm not afraid of ol' Roy; he's just a punk, an old punk junkie." Sylvie glanced at Joy and squeezed the steering wheel. "I'll be fine, girl. I promise."

A couple minutes later, they pulled into Joy's driveway. She could tell through the curtains that the lights were off, and only the dim blue light of the TV bled through the worn curtains.

"Sylvie, you go. I'll wait in the car, OK? I'm not sure I can face Gary right now. I'm afraid that I might not be able to leave again." Joy knotted her hands in her lap. "Promise me you'll be careful. If it gets weird, just leave, promise?"

"Don't you worry. Roy knows better than to mess with me. I don't think he has since he tried to kiss me in the third grade." Sylvie laughed and touched Joy's damp cheek. "I'll grab your bathroom stuff, some clothes, anything else?" Sylvie opened the car door. "Don't worry. I'll be fast." Sylvie got out of the car and before she ran toward the front door, she turned and mouthed something, then gave the thumbs up to Joy. She zigged-zagged to the porch steps.

Joy watched Sylvie peer into the front window, cupping her hand over her eyes—she knew the closed curtains made it impossible to see in. Then Sylvie walked to the front door and knocked. She waited and knocked again. Turning the doorknob, Sylvie disappeared inside. Not a moment later, she ran out of the house, both hands covering her mouth. Her eyes popped out like she'd seen a ghost. Joy's stomach dropped.

As she watched Sylvie run towards the car, Joy clutched her throat and gasped for air. Now Sylvie's arms flailed above her head. She yelled. Joy cupped her hands to her ears. "I can't hear you!"

Sylvie ran to Joy's side of the car. She screamed, "Open the door, open the door!" She pounded on Joy's window. Inside the car, Joy screamed back, "What? What happened?" Together, they slammed their hands on either side of the window.

"The door!" Sylvie screamed again, still pounding the glass. "Open the door!"

Joy heaved with all her strength against her door and her friend's body pressed on the other side. A moment later, Sylvie disappeared as she slid down onto the driveway. Joy opened the door and stepped out over Sylvie's body. Joy squatted down next to her and shook her like a rag doll. "What happened? What?!"

Sylvie sat up sobbing. "It's Roy, Joy! He's dead—a knife, his stomach, and blood. Blood everywhere, walls, curtains. The rug, the chair. Gary. He has the knife. It's awful, Joy, awful!" Sylvie cried. "911, I have to call 911. I have to, Joy!"

"Gary," Joy whispered. She stood and walked slowly toward her house, eyes on Gary who had shuffled outside. His blood-spattered clothes mashed into his thick body. He sat down on the top porch step. Joy climbed up the stairs and sat down next to him.

Gary looked at Joy. "He admitted it—stealing your money. I told him, Joy, you heard me, I warned him not to fuck with me."

Joy studied the house across the street, the one she had seen every day for the past thirty-plus years. She was grateful for its shuttered darkness. From far away, the wail of a siren announced its immanent arrival. Then, Gary placed his good hand on top of Joy's hands, which rested on her lap. His large palm swallowed them, and as her body flushed with warmth, a nice blend of optimism and relief filled her heart. Certainly, Joy hadn't lived the life she dreamt of, but it wasn't all bad. Not in the least. As the ramifications of the day sunk in, she pulled her hands out from under Gary's blood-stained palm and with one hand, patted his gently. "Don't worry, Gary, you'll get help now. You'll go to a good place where people will give you the help you've needed for a long time." And she thought to herself, *I'll get a new couch, bedspread, maybe paint everything white, goodness, I'll redo my whole house. And it will stay clean.* She refixed a stray hair into her bun, as a police car pulled into the driveway. "Call me crazy, Gary, but I'm not the least bit upset anymore. Not in the least."

Meg

Richard burst through the front door with a thunderous slam. This business trip had lasted longer than the others. Lately, when he returned, Richard greeted Meg with a snarl. Friendly hellos didn't exist anymore, it seemed. She stood at the kitchen sink and watched him drop his duffel bag by the kitchen table. Next, as always, he surveyed the rooms in the house, one by one, like an army sergeant inspecting his barracks. When he finished his assessment of the house, he strode by her without so much as a grunt, through the French doors to the backyard. Sinewy and straining like a dog chained to a pole, Richard charged up and down the pathways between the plants and lawn. His mood stunk like the manure she'd spread between the flowers. She followed him outdoors noiselessly, a ghost of herself. That's how the Riesling family functioned—or didn't. While Richard had no end of affection for their daughter, Litzy, he saved all his acerbity for Meg.

"Meg, you dead-headed the roses back-ass-ward again." Richard stood with his hands on his hips, as he studied the rosebushes lining the pathway. "And you left dead petals on the ground. What a mess. You can't do anything right." He bent over and picked up the brown petals until he had a handful. "Bring me something to put these in.

Jesus. I wonder why I put up with you. You can't do the simplest shit. Un-fucking-believable, you stupid . . ." Richard's voice trailed off as he fumed, hovering over the trimmed roses. Meg couldn't hear him, but whatever came out of his mouth, she knew she didn't want to hear it. Experience taught her that.

"I'll get a bag for them." She bit down on her lip, went into the house, and returned with a paper bag. Keeping it at arm's length, she handed it to her husband, who snatched it from her. She scuffled to the patio table and sat in a chair. Fruit flies congregated above the bowl of apples she'd put there yesterday. She flicked them away. "I'll use the petals, Richard. They'll make good mulch," she said. "For the garden."

"They look a mess, like you—actually you're more like a wreck than a mess." Richard sneered at Meg. "Have you even showered today?" Richard bent back down and continued to gather plant debris, mumbling insults she could only half hear.

Meg smoothed back her short hair and brushed off gardening fragments from her well-worn denim top. Years ago, she and her mom had bought the same shirt. Her mom had died weeks later. Meg loved the shirt. Richard hated it, said it made her look dumpy. Like trash, he would say.

"Where's Litzy?" Richard glanced back at Meg as he pulled weeds from around the steppingstones leading to the vegetable garden. "Is she at school still or did she go to a friend's house? You forgot to tell her I got home today, didn't you?"

"No, Richard, I told her." Meg squirmed in her seat. "She has a painting class, remember, on Tuesday afternoons. She'll be home soon."

"God damn it, Meg! Look here, what the hell is this?" Richard pointed at something in the vegetable garden.

"I can't see from here, Richard. What is it?" Meg stood up.

"Dog shit! Dog shit, Meg. How the hell did dog shit get in my garden?" He spat his words, clenching his fists and square jawed, his anger palpable.

"How would I know, Richard? I can't monitor all the dogs in the neighborhood. I'm sorry. I'll clean it up. Please stop yelling."

"We have a fenced yard, Meg. You let in that bitch from next door, didn't you?" Even from a distance, Meg could feel Richard's rage blazing behind his glacial blue, unblinking eyes.

"I didn't let in Molly, I promise," Meg's voice pitched higher. "I didn't let in any dog."

"You know what, Meg, you're going to pick it up with your hands —no gloves, no bag. You let in the damn dog; you're picking it up." Richard smiled a thin-lipped smile. His wiry body, taut in his button-down shirt tucked into his fitted slacks, seemed like one big muscle tensing for eruption.

"I'll get a bag and shovel." Meg stood and looked toward the shovel leaning against the shed's wall.

"You'll do what I tell you." Richard pointed his stubby index finger at Meg. "You come here and pick up this dog shit." He puffed out his chest. His face burned bright red, and the veins on his neck and forehead bulged. "Now."

"I won't!" Meg heard herself scream. Then, without a moment's forethought, she picked up an apple from the bowl and threw it at him as hard as she could. The apple hit Richard between his eyebrows with a hollow thud. Before he had time to react, he grabbed his chest with his left hand and then his right. He dropped to his knees and rocked back and forth. His eyes bugged out, then they pressed shut. He shrieked at Meg, "Help me!" Then his body fell flat on the path, face down. He convulsed for a moment. Then, he ceased to move. Everything went silent.

Meg's mouth opened. She inhaled sharply and held her breath. Sweat beaded on her forehead. She blinked. Slowly, she exhaled. Lowering herself onto the chair, Meg spread out her fingers on the table. Her eyes locked onto her husband's body lying on the path. She sat still and waited. Suddenly, Richard's body jerked for a quick second, then stopped. Minutes passed. She waited and watched. More time passed. She took a deep breath and stood up. *Is he dead? Did he die?* She crept over to her husband's body until she stood above it. She nudged his shoulder with her foot. No response. She nudged it again, harder. Nothing. Walking backwards through the doors into the kitchen, her eyes remained steady on his motionless body. When she bumped into the island, she turned and picked up her phone. She held it and watched time move ahead five minutes. Then she dialed 911.

"Hello, yes, I think my husband is dead, he died. Just now." Meg spoke deliberately to the woman on the other end. "I don't know, I don't know how he died. Yes, I'll wait here." She gave her address to the operator. "No, I'm fine. I'm watching him now. He's not moving. No, I haven't tried CPR. I don't know how. OK, I'll wait."

Phone in hand, Meg walked out to the garden. She bent down and with her hand, nudged her husband again. He remained inert, like a bag of wet sand against her fingers. Satisfied, she scoured the yard for the apple she'd thrown. She found it in the dirt by a blooming red rose bush. She picked it up, brushed it off and returned it to the bowl on the patio table. She sat down in the chair and waited for people to arrive.

Tranquil, Meg thought in the stillness. She felt tranquil as she waited.

One year after Richard's death, Meg sat on the edge of her daughter's bed and watched Litzy fuss over which t-shirts she should take to college. Fall in Arizona could be hot during the days, the nights chilly and dry with little chance of an Oregon-like rain. Meg's slender fingers plucked at an eyebrow as she scrutinized the room. A dozen shirts in as many colors sat on the bed next to the open luggage. Litzy's red puffy coat and collection of jeans stacked on her bed pillows. Sneakers and sandals remained untouched and jumbled near her closet door. Digesting Litzy's chaotic piles of clothes, Meg chewed the inside of her cheek. She snatched the puffy coat, tucked the arms into its body and then gently, as if breakable, pressed it into the suitcase. She kneaded her hands. As close as mother and daughter were, Meg's anxiousness over Litzy leaving intensified as her day of departure drew nearer. Without Litzy living at home, Meg feared her internal nightmare, one that infested her like a colony of tape worms, would become increasingly more destructive.

In turn, and unaware of her mother's inner burden, Litzy's annoyance mounted as her mom's erratic behavior amped up.

"Mom, stop, please. I'll do it. I need to go at my own pace, or I'll forget what I've packed." Litzy crossed the room, pulled out the coat from the suitcase and threw it back on the bed. Then, she grabbed a cherry-colored t-shirt, turned to her dresser mirror, and held it up to her face. "Is this better on me or the light pink?"

Meg sighed and looked at her daughter posed before her. Litzy's blonde hair and blue eyes were a spitting image of Richard's, her father, whose sudden death a year prior prevented him from ever being at any occasion, ever again. Surprisingly, suddenly dead. But as Meg discovered, not gone, horribly not gone at all.

He smoldered like a dormant volcano inside Meg's brain, until he roiled to life, spewing an arsenal of expletives between her ears. Unlike his fits when he was alive, when Meg could physically exit, she couldn't escape his cerebral tirades. Meg couldn't share her silent sufferings with Litzy or anyone. Surely, even her therapist would call her nuts. But Meg knew; Richard's unpredictable mental hauntings were punishments for her crime, her secret atrocity. Breathing rapidly, Meg grabbed a nearby shirt and twisted it till it resembled a thick stick more than a piece of clothing. Then she shook it out and carefully tucked it into the suitcase.

"Mom?" said Litzy, eyes still on her reflection in the mirror, "red or pink?"

"Both are nice, pink looks good, too. Bring both?" Meg shook out the shirt again, refolded it and swaddled it into the suitcase. She performed the same ritual on another shirt she pulled from the floor. Then Meg rested her hands on her lap. She found it difficult to focus on anything for any length of time. Fear of an attack by Richard randomly gripped her. She rubbed her forehead. Meg thought, *How ironic. Litzy, at eighteen, is happily taking off for the first time alone, and at fifty-eight, I am more terrified to be on my own than my daughter.* She twisted another shirt.

"Mom!" Litzy's patience for her mother's spaciness frayed. At first, Litzy chalked up her screwy behavior to grief. But after a year, she found it harder and harder to explain away. Especially given her parents' fractured relationship. "Hello, Mom!" she yelled.

"Yes?" Meg's attention snapped back to Litzy, and she resumed folding the shirt. She laid it in the suitcase and lifted a mound of sweaters from the nightstand onto her lap. Gently, one by one, she folded and pressed each into the bag. "You have so much to do before tomorrow." Then, as gently as she packed the sweaters, Meg withdrew them to refold. "You're lucky I'm here to help." Carefully, she replaced them, one by one, back into the luggage.

Watching her mother drove Litzy over the edge. "Enough," she said, and thought, *What the heck is wrong with you?* She huffed over and plunked down next to her mom. "Forget it. I'll pack myself." Litzy shoved her long hair behind her shoulders and began thumbing through the contents of her suitcase. "Jesus, you put things in, take them out. I'm lost. You'll be the reason I have nothing to wear when I get to school, I swear." Litzy threw out one shirt and stuffed in another. Her pencil-like fingers worked through the clothes.

Meg remembered how she and Richard called them piano-playing fingers, but her daughter fought playing piano like she did basketball. Tall and athletic, they also believed she would be the next WNBA star. But Litzy had no interest in musical instruments or sports. Litzy loved art. A subject whose value Richard couldn't understand. It upset him. When they discussed it, Meg defended Litzy's interest at the risk of eventual retribution.

That night, while Meg loaded the dishwasher, Richard stood over her.

"You loaded the dishwasher wrong."

"I always load it this way, Richard."

"Well, you always load it wrong. Shall I show you how to load a dishwasher? He proceeded to throw out its contents on the floor, smashing plates and glasses into pieces. "Now clean it up, you incompetent cow." He strutted away as if he should be congratulated. She stood in disbelief for a few minutes before picking up the pieces. Then she closed it out of her mind.

Litzy watched her mother's face fall. "Mom. Mom, how many pairs of pants should I take?" Feeling uneasy, she grabbed the pile from on top of her pillows.

Meg didn't respond.

Richard kept her thoughts captive. The year before he died, his behavior, although never physically abusive, became more mentally volatile. She, his number-one target, suffered more and more. Perpetually a nervous wreck, as Richard's behavior became harder to handle, Meg barely left the house and cleaned incessantly. Sisyphus climbing the mountain with Clorox and a cleaning rag.

Meg grabbed a pair of pants from Litzy. "Take all of them." Meg's eyes glistened just a little. "All the pants."

"Mom, what's going on? What's making you so sad? Me? Dad?" Litzy suspected her dad—her mom's face displayed that intense unhappiness only he could create. She hated her father's hostility towards her mother but had felt helpless to stop it. For the most part, her school and abundance of activities kept her away from home, and she adopted an out-of-sight out-of-mind attitude when it came to her mother's life. Initially, after her father's death, a blanket of calmness covered their home. It didn't last though.

Her mom's inability to relax after her dad's passing puzzled Litzy. Sometimes, she acted like a possessed crazy woman. Dwelling on what made her so schizo took up too much head space for Litzy. So, Litzy fought between her guilt for wanting to take off for school and her dutiful need to stay and look after her mom.

"I'm sorry, what did you say? I'm just overwhelmed by everything." Meg suffered a weak smile.

"Why don't you go do something else. Really, you're making things harder for me. I'd rather do it myself." Litzy put her hand over a pile of underwear to keep Meg from grabbing them. "Mom, you'll be fine, we'll both be fine. Seriously, do something else, please." Litzy managed a half-hearted grin.

"OK, OK, I can take a hint, but packing would go much faster with me helping." Meg kept her hands on her knees until she stood. Then she stretched, placing her hands on her lower back, and arched. "I'll make dinner. Chicken soup?" Meg looked around the room. Photographs of Litzy with friends, prom dates, at art shows, pictures from her childhood to high school littered the desk and bulletin boards. Meg loved them and the display of her daughter's self-assuredness. She deserved a good life, and despite Meg's demons, she vowed to see she got one. "Soup, OK?" Meg repeated.

"Sure, soup's great," Litzy grabbed a handful of socks and stuffed them into the corners of her suitcase. She glanced up at Meg. "Fuck," she said. In an instant, her mother disappeared.

Meg had folded into herself. Her eyes dimmed and glassed over, as though she had been unplugged. Slack-faced, she stood like a wax statue by the side of Litzy's bed. She hated it when her mom did this. "Fuck," she said again, staring at her mom's empty gaze. She should have seen it coming.

Inside Meg's head, hundreds of grenades exploded all at once. Richard's voice hammered. *You poor excuse for a mother, you can't even pack for your daughter. You can't do shit.* Louder and louder, he scolded, pummeling her from within. Outside, Meg's body remained still.

At first, Meg's episodes, acting like she vacated her body, terrified Litzy, but Meg explained that Richard's sudden death brought them on, and with time, they'd go away. Not disclosing their destructive nature, she dismissed them as "silly little spells."

Litzy believed her, until lately. Instead of fading, they became more frequent. Litzy rationalized this as her mom's mourning her dad's death combined with her soon-to-be life alone. All strengthening her fear that her mom's mental instability could keep her tethered to home.

"Mom, you're scaring me, you're spacing out—can you hear me?" Litzy let a pair of socks fall to the floor. She said, "Mom? Hello, Mom, talk to me."

Meg crossed her arms over her chest, and her fingers began rubbing her elbows. The sequel to her spells, Litzy knew this behavior well. It started right after her dad's passing. Sometimes Meg rubbed her elbows until they bled.

Litzy stood and rubbed Meg's back. Meg's eyes remained glued to the wall. "Mom, you're freaking me out. You're doing that thing—spacing out—with the elbows again. It's freaking me out. Talk to me, Mom."

Meg tried to find the words she wanted to say, to reassure Litzy, but her defenselessness against Richard, his voice echoing in her head, crippled her. *You threw the apple. You can't undo that. I'm your punishment, Meg, as long as you're alive, I'm your personal hell.*

I wish you had pills, Mom, Litzy thought. She knew anti-anxiety meds had helped Meg before, but as of late, she'd sworn off them. Meg explained they'd made her feel out of it, not herself. When Litzy found out she'd quit taking them, they argued. Litzy felt her mother should have tapered, then maybe Meg's freakouts would be less intense instead of more. Meg had put her foot down. She said she didn't want to risk floating into a mindless oblivion. But Litzy needed help. At this point, with her impending departure, she felt desperate.

First thing in the morning, she'd call Meg's psychiatrist. She knew the doc would want to see Meg to get more meds, but Litzy would explain that her leaving for college had triggered her mom's relapse into bizarreness. Maybe she'd get lucky and get a prescription. Litzy continued to rub her mother's back and wished she'd thought of calling the doctor sooner. She whispered in her mom's ear, "Mom." Meg didn't break her gaze.

Then louder, "Mom!" Litzy's sharp voice cut through Richard's insult rampage like a burst of light slicing through a raging storm.

Meg blinked at Litzy and relaxed her arms. She took a deep breath and smiled. "Did I have a spell? I'm so sorry, honey. Over-tired, that's all. I'll get your soup." Just like that, Meg returned to reality. She squeezed her daughter's hand and walked toward the door.

Litzy wrinkled her forehead. She felt fed up and concerned at the same time. "Mom, are you kidding me? You disappeared, like mentally left your body. And you did that elbow thing." Litzy watched her mom wobble out of the room. "I'm so worried about you right now. Did you hear me, Mom?"

Meg sighed long and hard, then turned to smile at her daughter. She flicked her wrist. "Your job is to pack, not worry about your mother. I'm fine." Meg hated it when her daughter witnessed her breakdowns. But, once Litzy dived into college and her new life, she'd forget about them. Lines of anxiousness etched into Meg's forehead with the anticipation of her new life without Litzy, and she left the room.

The handrail steadied Meg as she crept down the steep narrow staircase. Always in a fog after Richard's heady torrents, Meg's mind wandered to when a young Litzy moved up to the attic bedroom. Meg voiced her apprehension about letting her stay a floor above them by herself, but Litzy insisted she was old enough. Richard had no issue with her move. It would strengthen her character, he'd said. In the ten years she'd slept there, Litzy never once surrendered to Meg and Richard's bedroom out of fright. She marveled at her daughter's bravery. Meg had always been so timid. Richard though, tough as nails. Take charge and show no mercy, much less weakness, that was Richard to a T.

Then: *You threw the apple, Meg. You killed me. I'll never let you forget. Ever. Litzy has a murderer for a mother, Meg. You're a murderer.* Richard returned. His vitriolic spittle spewed. Meg let go of the railing, crossed her arms, and her fingers kneaded her elbows. Slowly, eyes forward as if in a trance, she resumed her descent. Step by step, barely touching the floor. *Worthless. A fucking mess!* Sweat trickled down the sides of Meg's face.

From above: "Do we still have good bread?" Litzy shouted, leaning out her bedroom door.

Her words startled Meg, who looked up at Litzy like a frightened child. She flashed a weak grin and ran down the remaining steps, out of sight. Litzy tried to ignore the cannon ball forming in her gut, but when she heard the ice maker dispensing ice in the kitchen, the normalcy of the sound calmed her. "Jesus," Litzy said out loud, "Mom. Please. Don't go totally nuts on me. Not now." She needed to pack. If she stopped, the space for her to talk herself out of going would open and that terrified her as much as anything. More noise came from below. Litzy returned to her packing, shoving shirts and sweaters, underwear and socks, shoes and sandals, everything into her suitcase wherever they fit. *Keep going,* she told herself.

Downstairs, in the pristine starkness of her all-white kitchen, Meg took long slow breaths as she moved around. But for her, even in her bright kitchen, a miasma cast its darkness.

She counted her breaths, like the therapist had told her to do, as if not to disturb a sleeping dragon, and ladled heated soup for each of them. She set the bowls on a tray with shaking hands, then grabbed a package of saltines from the pantry, divvied up a few for each of them, and quickly wiped up the leftover crumbs on the counter. She placed the crystal glasses of ice water on the tray next to the bowls.

Then the bile returned. *Idiot, not soup! Flush it, you dumbass. You pathetic excuse for a mother.* Richard vomited into every corner of Meg's mind.

She hunched over the food tray, squeezing its handles until her knuckles turned white. She gnawed her bottom lip. "Stop, Richard, please stop. Stop torturing me," she shouted into the empty kitchen, but not loud enough to drown out Richard's voice.

Litzy thought she heard her mother and hollered downstairs to see what she needed, but without any response, reluctantly, she continued to pack.

Flush the soup, you wretched witch. Flush it! Richard screamed relentlessly.

Unblinking, Meg poured the bowls of soup down the sink and threw the crackers in the garbage. She opened the refrigerator and studied its contents: milk, eggs, lettuce, avocados, a package of cheese, some veggies in Ziplock bags and a bag of deli chicken slices. In the door, assorted condiments, and a corked bottle of white wine. *A chicken sandwich*, she thought. She grabbed the ingredients and arranged the sandwich makings in a row on the cold counter. Her trembling fingers struggled to take bread slices out of the bag. "He's in your head. Just in your head," Meg repeated loudly, but her breathing didn't slow. "All in your head."

You lowlife hag. You murdering piece of shit excuse for a human being. Litzy needs to get away from you before you ruin her life. In death, like in life, his tirades left her blurry and uncertain.

Meg never had the courage to leave or get ahead of his explosions, and now helpless as ever, he blew up unbridled within her.

"Mom?" Litzy surprised Meg as she entered the kitchen. "What're you doing—where's the soup?" Litzy stood on the opposite side of the island from her mother. Sliced chicken, bread and vegetables lay spread out in front of her. "Mom? You're as white as the walls." *Shit,* she thought.

"I thought you'd like a chicken sandwich instead." The knife shook as she picked it up. She dipped it into the mayonnaise jar, clinking inside its glass mouth, unable to grab any dressing.

"Mom, you're shaking." Litzy reached across the island and laid her hand over Meg's hand. Her stomach knotted. She couldn't leave her mother like this. "You know what, I'm going to call Dr. Crane." Litzy pulled her cell phone from her jeans pocket and started scrolling for the psychiatrist's number. She saw the panic on her mother's face as she called.

To Meg, doctors meant pills, a deep dive back into a more intense place of shapeless thoughts and disabled functioning. And Richard's voice overpowered any cocktail of happy pills. Nothing could overcome his voice in her head.

To Litzy, Dr. Crane would make her mother normal again and give Litzy hope and the peace of mind she desperately needed to leave her.

"Please don't, Litzy. I'm fine, really—just sad you're going." Meg's smile looked more like a scowl. She couldn't stop her body from shuddering and closed her eyes tightly. Richard swung a wrecking ball inside her skull, smacking its walls. *Oh, you're far from fine, Meg, far from fine. You're crazy if you think you're fine, but you are crazy, aren't you? A crazy murderer, aren't you? A pathetic weakling of a killer.*

Litzy watched her mother's face contort, as though she could hear or feel something terrible that Litzy couldn't. Oh, how she wanted to open the top of her mom's head and scrape out her demons.

Richard's voice boomed. Meg clutched at one of the glasses of water from the tray and drank. She slammed the glass down too hard on the counter, and the water sloshed out.

Litzy's call to Dr. Crane went through quickly. 6:30 p.m. The on-duty answering service receptionist answered.

Meg glared at Litzy and said, "Please no!" She crossed her arms and rubbed her elbows. *Stop listening to him*, Meg told herself. She needed to resist, be resolute, be strong, keep it together. For her daughter. Meg whispered, "Get out of my head. Please, please get out." Words that would have sent Litzy over the edge if she'd heard them. Instead, Litzy talked to the receptionist.

"My mom, I'm calling for my mom, Megan Riesling. She's a patient of Dr. Crane. You see, I'm leaving for college tomorrow, and my dad died recently, almost a year ago, and I don't know what's wrong, but she needs help."

"Thanks, it's been tough," Litzy said into the phone, and moved away from Meg. "But I'm leaving for college tomorrow, and I'm worried. She's shaking and acting weird. Can I get some medication? She used to take anti-anxiety pills."

"Stop that!" Meg said, reaching for Litzy's arm. "I mean it, no doctors, no medication!"

Litzy had only to look into Meg's wild eyes to know that medication was the only answer. She wrestled away her arm and moved completely around the kitchen's center island. She continued, "Could you please have the doctor call me back at this number? As soon as you can get ahold of her. Yes, this number is good, thanks."

Litzy hung up her phone. Meg covered her face with her hands. Litzy's heart raced. She needed her mom present and behaving like her mom. Not some freakazoid she had to take care of. Where was her old mom? The mom who would buy Litzy and her friends ice cream on the way home from school, the one who threw themed birthday parties, made cupcakes, let her throw glitter around, took her shopping. That mom. The best mom ever. The ten-year-ago mom. What happened to her?

Litzy walked over to Meg and wrapped her arms around her. "What else can I do? For the last couple of weeks, you've been totally weird again. Like Dad just died or something. Come on, Mom, I leave tomorrow. I can't leave you like this." Litzy squeezed her mom hard.

Meg couldn't quite pick up her arms to hug Litzy back, even though she wanted to. She felt paralyzed by how out of control her life had become. She couldn't escape Richard and be in the present for Litzy, she couldn't right herself the way she wanted to.

Richard's diatribe flared and Meg pressed her eyes shut.

Litzy hugged her harder. She wanted to hug her mother back to life.

Meg wished she could just stand like that forever, with her daughter's capable, confident arms around her. But inside, she knew she'd never be rid of him. Her body slid from Litzy's embrace and crumpled to the floor.

"Mom!" Litzy shouted as Meg slipped out of her grasp. Her eyelids fluttered, and her breathing became erratic. Litzy snatched an oven mitt from a hook on the island and placed it under Meg's head. She felt her face. It felt like a wet sponge. Litzy scrambled to dial Dr. Crane's office again, her eyes laser focused on Meg.

Meg's eyes flickered open. She slurred, "I must have fainted. What a silly thing to do. What a fool I am." Meg rubbed the top of her head and took another deep breath. "I must've scared you to death." Meg's arms wouldn't quite support her as she struggled to sit up, so she slumped back down.

While the phone rang, Litzy spoke to Meg in a low steady voice. "Mom, you fucking fainted, yes, of course, you scared me to death." Then she signaled stop with an upheld hand to her mother. "Hello, yes, I called a few minutes ago. This is an emergency. The doctor has to call me back. My mom just completely passed out, and I don't know what to do. Should I call 911 or what? I'm scared shitless!"

Meg could hear the voice on the other end say, "I'll call an ambulance. Is she conscious? What's her status? Let me confirm your address. Don't hang up."

"She's awake now." Litzy grabbed Meg's limp hand with her free hand and held it tight. "I'm supposed to go to college tomorrow, and I don't know what the hell I'm going to do about my mother." Litzy finished her thought in her head: *My mother is fucking freaking out. I'm driving a million miles away. I'm not packed. My freaking mother is freaking out. My dad is dead, and everything is worse than ever. Jesus!*

Meg heard the woman respond, "Is 3324 Clackamas Street still your address?"

"Yes."

"OK, an ambulance is on its way, ten to fifteen minutes max. The doctor will call momentarily. Keep your mom comfortable. Hang in there."

Interrupting the conversation, an unknown number flashed on

her phone. "I think the doctor's calling. I've got to go." Litzy clicked a button on her phone and squeezed her mother's hand.

Meg pulled her hand away and rubbed her elbows. She rolled her head around, eyes searching in corners and under counters. "Come out, Richard. Where've you slithered to? You want to fight, I can fight. You haven't won yet."

"Shit, she's talking to Dad," Litzy said and reclaimed her mom's hand. "Hello, Dr. Crane?"

"Dr. Darnell here. I'm the on-call doctor. Your mother fainted?" The man's voice sounded soft, yet firm. Litzy, still holding Meg's hand, shifted away from Meg's body. "Yes. She's confused, but awake." Meg's forehead wrinkled, and her eyes drooped. "Yes, now. Fantastic, thank you so much." She hung up.

Meg lunged for Litzy's phone, but she couldn't maneuver her leaden body. Her legs splayed out before her in an awkward adolescent posture. Her feet no longer held on to her shoes.

Litzy scooted closer to her. "An ambulance is coming, Mom. They're going to check you out and see if you need to go to the hospital. Jesus, how am I supposed to leave tomorrow?" She looked at her mom's long skinny body, so impeccably dressed. "I thought you were getting better."

Meg's brown close-cropped hair, deep green eyes the color of lily pads and full lips drew stares wherever she went. She could have been a model. The opportunities were there, but Meg didn't like being the center of attention or being touched. Never a social person, Meg stopped going out altogether after Richard's death.

As she sat on the floor with her mother, guilt niggled at Litzy. The thought of leaving weighed on her like a mountain of rocks, but still, she wouldn't let go of college. She couldn't. "Mom, you are so scaring me."

Meg sat up a little more. "Sweetie, you're being ridiculous. I'm just fatigued, really. Don't worry about me. All the doc'll do is give me pills. And I don't want any more pills. They make me loopy for days." Meg shut her eyes and clutched her daughter's hand in hers. "Please, Litzy."

"Mom, you're the one being ridiculous. You freaking fainted, and

I'm not going anywhere until you're examined by a doctor or at least the ambulance guys." Litzy stood up and gathered Meg's shoes. "Here, put these on, and let's get you up on a chair." She bent down and grabbed Meg's arm to help her up.

"I can manage myself." Meg rolled over on all fours like a dog, and with help from Litzy, she pulled herself up onto the chair next to the kitchen table. "I'm more humiliated than anything." She perused all the makings of the chicken sandwich on the island. "Oh, Litzy, I'm so sorry. I never made you dinner. At least let me clean up this mess." She stood up like she'd aged a hundred years and made her way around the island holding on to its edges. She stood in front of the food. "Let me make you a sandwich." Meg separated slices of chicken.

"Mom. Stop." Litzy snatched the chicken from Meg's hands. "Go sit down."

Meg held on to the edges of the counter and returned to the chair. An arctic blast traveled up her spine. She closed her eyes and took a deep breath. Richard's venomous rantings started again. *Take the pills, all the pills, Meg. You'll sleep, you'll be at peace.* She put her hands over her ears and squeezed. "Stop it," she shouted out loud, "stop it, stop it, stop it." She repeated the words until she drowned out his voice.

"Mom! What's wrong? What's in your head?" Litzy shook Meg's shoulders. Tears ran down her face as she watched her mom's eyes roll back in her head. "Fuck, Mom. Stop!" She shook her shoulders again. Meg seemed to refocus and patted Litzy's hands on her cheeks.

"My darling daughter."

The doorbell rang.

"Don't get that," Meg called to Litzy, already scurrying down the hall to answer the door. "Litzy, please." Her hands reached toward her disappearing daughter.

Litzy opened the door to a young man in scrubs with an EMT badge hanging from his neck. Covered by a forest of black eyebrows, his dark brown eyes radiated warmth as did his quick grin.

"Litzy Riesling? Dr. Darnell called for an ambulance for a Megan Riesling?" As he spoke, another EMT climbed out of the ambulance with a medical bag. "May we come in? Is she conscious?"

As Litzy led the EMTs down the hall, she said, "Yes, she's in the kitchen. Thanks so much for coming. I don't know what's wrong with her. She fainted—like completely out, now she's awake. She's freaking me out."

A seemingly lifeless Meg sat hunched in the chair; hands wedged between her crossed legs. Something outside held her open-eyed gaze. *She's gone again*, Litzy thought.

"Mom. Mom, these are the EMTs. They're making sure you're all right." Litzy crouched by Meg's legs and pulled her hands from her lap and held them. "Mom, OK? You OK?"

The warm-eyed EMT spoke as he took the bag from his partner, "Hello, Ms. Riesling. I need to ask you a few questions." He crouched down by Meg's side. "Let's take your vitals, see what's going on with you, sound good?" The other EMT stood by the door, arms crossed at the wrists in front of him.

Meg blinked at the man squatted by her and said, "I'm fine, really. Just tired." Richard quieted in her head, but she knew, not for long.

After a routine check, the EMT said, "Well, your heart rate is high, Ms. Riesling, but not dangerously so." With his hand on her arm, he asked, "How do you feel? Do you feel like you need to go the hospital? Do you have numbness anywhere, tingling?" He prodded Meg in different places, asked more questions and satisfied with her responses, he stood up and put away his equipment.

"Please call me Meg." Meg liked this guy. His gentleness relaxed her. "I feel fine. Like I said, just tired. I've had trouble sleeping; my daughter is leaving for college, and I can't help being a little sad." She smiled her best smile. Meg looked at Litzy. "My daughter is so beautiful. Do you know that, Litzy? Do you have any idea how beautiful you are?" Then she looked at the medics. "Don't you think my daughter is beautiful? And so completely devoted. I'm very lucky. She wants to make sure I'm all right before she leaves. She thinks I'm off my rocker, don't you?" Meg sought eye contact with Litzy, but Litzy looked down, cheeks pink with embarrassment.

Her mother sounded like a loon. Litzy wanted to run away and never come back.

Meg looked up at the EMT and repeated, "Isn't she beautiful?"

He grinned at Meg. "The on-call doctor said you have a prescription for Ambien. He suggested you take two tonight and call him in the morning. Although your heart rate is high, if you stay still and sleep, no excitement, then I can't see any reason for you to be hospitalized."

"See, Litzy, nothing to worry about." Meg inhaled and closed her eyes. "I'm just terribly weary. My brain is bruised from the turmoil. First, your dad's death, and with you leaving . . .."

Litzy blurted to the man, "She's not usually like this. My dad died almost a year ago. She took it super hard. He was my dad and sad for me, but for her, way worse. He traveled a lot, but at home, they were very close, like best friends." Litzy had no idea why she would say such an absurd thing. Maybe she could believe it to be true, if she said it, that an overdose of grief caused her mom's crazy behavior, and then she could make sense of it.

Meg looked at her daughter with watery eyes and smiled. "Of course, like best friends." She fidgeted with the zipper on her jumpsuit.

"Sorry for your loss. Grief of a loved one is very difficult," said the EMT. Then he asked Litzy to show him the Ambien bottle to confirm the dosage.

"Of course." Litzy ran into Meg's bathroom and returned with the bottle for the EMT to jot down the necessary information. Then, she handed Meg two pills with a glass of water. They watched as she dropped them into her mouth.

While Litzy walked the medics to the door, Meg took the pills out of her mouth and stuffed them under the chair cushion. She drank more water and set the glass down on the table, centering it perfectly on a coaster. She smiled at her daughter as she entered the kitchen.

What a way to leave home, Litzy thought as she mimicked her mother's smile. Litzy tried to keep it about her mother, but she fought hard not to feel sorry for herself. She knew her mom needed help, much more than a couple of sleeping pills and a good night's sleep. She knew instead of packing she should be calling University of

Arizona and postponing her semester. *But I don't want to*, she thought, *damn it, Mom*. Tears seeped out of her eyes.

She laced her fingers in front of her. "Mom, I'm glad you took the pills, even though I know you didn't want to. You'll feel better after a good night's sleep. Sleep is important, you know—to think clearly and all. I'll clean up, and then I need to finish packing." Litzy stuffed the bread slices back in the bag. "Maybe after a good night's sleep you won't be so sad."

"Of course. You're right; a good night's sleep is what I need. It's silly, but I'm a little lightheaded still," Meg said as Litzy came over to help her up. Together, they walked down the hall to Meg's bedroom. Meg had moved to the guest room downstairs after Richard's death. To distance herself from him, as if changing rooms would make a difference. "I feel so useless. You're leaving, and I haven't helped you at all. I've done nothing but make a mess of things." She kissed Litzy on her cheek as they stood in front of her bedroom door.

"Now promise me you'll sleep. No TV or reading." Litzy shut the door after she watched Meg sit on her bed. As Litzy paused outside her mom's bedroom, she couldn't help but think, *You're supposed to be the parent, not me. This is fucking ridiculous.*

Meg watched the door close. She exhaled and dropped backwards on her bed and stared at the ceiling. Her mind blanked white.

Standing in the hallway alone, a sudden kick-you-to-your-knees ache washed over Litzy. She needed her mother, the way she used to be. Tonight. Now. She had nothing to lose. She cracked open Meg's door and peered in. "Mom, this is our last night together. Maybe I could sleep with you, just one last time? I know you took sleeping pills and will be asleep soon, but maybe when I'm done packing, I can crawl into bed like I used to?"

She used to love cuddling with her mom when her dad went on his business trips. They would sprawl out in her mom's king-size bed with the high thread count sheets and the heavy down comforter. Snow White's bed in real-life, she believed. They'd watch some dumb girl movie, if Litzy finished her homework, eat ice cream, and stay up late talking. Even on school days, Meg would let Litzy sleep in. She felt like a princess. Litzy loved those times. But her father had to be gone. That's when her mom seemed happiest.

"Ah, I'd love that." Meg looked at Litzy, all grown up, but not. "Of course. Get your stuff done and come snuggle with me. That'd be wonderful, like old times." Meg prayed Richard would indulge her just this once.

Relieved, if only to hear her mother speak the words, Litzy smiled. "I'll be back. You sleep." She shut the door to Meg's room and padded down the hall to the kitchen. After eating a few slices of chicken, she put away everything and returned to her room to finish packing. *Maybe it really was exhaustion*, she thought. Meg hadn't slept well since her dad died; she said she hadn't. Whether in denial or naively, Litzy held on to that thought. A good night's rest, aided by pills, might clear Meg's head long enough for Litzy to leave, and with the doctor now on alert, her mom would be in good hands.

As she changed into her silk pajamas, Meg heard Litzy tromp upstairs. She was brushing her teeth in her bathroom when Richard returned. A chilling sweat tickled the back of her neck. Meg continued to brush, trying to ignore him and the frigid feeling. She closed her eyes in front of the mirror while she spit out her toothpaste. Avoiding her reflection when she turned out the light, she left the bathroom. Her body began to tremble as she slipped under the bedcovers. She turned off the lamp next to her on the nightstand. Her eyes popped open wide. She listened.

Meg. The pills under the chair cushion. You better get them; you won't sleep without them. Take them all, Meg, get the bottle, and take them all.

"Shut up! Shut up, Richard! Shut up!" Meg sprang up to a sitting position and pressed her hands on either side of her head. "Shut up!"

Get the pills Meg, the pills, take all the pills. Richard's voice rumbled through her body.

Wet with perspiration, Meg's pajamas stuck to her body like plastic wrap. Her breaths shallow, tears rolled down her cheeks. "Go away, Richard, please go away!"

Remember Meg, I'm here because of you. We're together forever. Richard's ravings devolved into snorting laughter. *Litzy is leaving, but you'll always have me. Take the pills, all the pills, then you'll have peace. Take the pills and you'll be rid of me forever.*

Meg's head rolled around on her shoulders, as if her neck was unable to hold its weight. She thought, *If not for Litzy, I'd do it again.* "I'd do it again and again and again," she said out loud, laid her head on the pillow, and pinched her eyes shut.

Outside the bedroom door, Litzy stood for a half minute, her eyes closed, too. Then, quiet as a cat, she tiptoed into the room and slid into her mom's bed, under the heavy down quilt. She waited to hear her mother's deep breathing but didn't hear anything, so she raised herself up on one elbow and looked at Meg.

"Mom!" Litzy said. Her mother's open eyes were the last thing she expected to see. "You're awake? How can you be awake?"

"I'm sorry, Litzy, I couldn't sleep." Meg blinked up at her daughter.

"What do you mean, you couldn't sleep? You took pills. They should have knocked you out for hours! Jesus!" Litzy collapsed back onto the bed.

"Litzy, I have a confession," Meg spoke softly, staring at the ceiling. "I didn't take the pills."

"What? You didn't take the pills?" Litzy propped herself back up on her elbow and bent over to look at her mom. "Yes, you did. I saw you take them."

"After I put them in my mouth, I took them out and hid them under the chair cushion. I'm not taking pills, ever again, Litzy."

"But Mom, you're a wreck. You're still upset over Dad's death, and me leaving hasn't helped, plus you admitted you don't sleep. And you act like a crazy person. Folding and unfolding my clothes? Half the time you look like you're lost in outer space. Mom, you're not yourself, and I don't think I should leave you." Litzy's eyes watered as she continued, "You're a mess. Honestly, he was my father, I loved him. He treated me fine. But to you, he was a bastard. For as long as I can remember. Honestly, I don't get it, what's making you this way? His death, my leaving for college, both? You're out of control. I shouldn't go. I can't go. Not with you like this."

Meg sat up in bed and turned on the nightstand lamp. She crossed her arms and rested her head on the quilted headboard. "First of all, you're going to college tomorrow. That's nonnegotiable. Next, I need to tell you something I never wanted to tell you, I thought I never would tell you." Meg took a deep breath. "But I need to tell you now." Meg looked at her daughter. She pulled Litzy's hand out of her lap and into her own. "This is going to sound horrid, unforgiveable even, but you must know." Meg took another deep breath. "I killed your father."

"What? What the fuck are you saying?" Litzy pulled her hand away. "Dad died from a heart attack, Mom. You didn't kill Dad. That's nuts. See, you're losing it." She covered her face with her hands, cheeks wet with tears and shook her head. "Don't do this, Mom, please. Don't go any crazier tonight, please."

"I've never been saner, Litzy." With Meg's next breath, her whole body heaved up and down. "Listen to me. I'm only saying this once. Your father stood out in the garden. He wanted me to pick up dog poop, dog shit, with my fingers, my bare hands." Meg splayed her fingers in front of Litzy. "But I refused. He got more and more angry. Then I threw an apple at him. It hit his forehead. He went down. Then, he had the heart attack." Meg rested her hands on her lap. "He died."

"That's right, Mom, he had a heart attack, you didn't kill him—with what, a stupid apple?" Litzy sat up. "Mom, stop."

"He went down, and I did nothing. I saw him twitch once, maybe twice, but I didn't go to him. I sat there until he lay completely still. I think I knew he was dead, but I waited to call 911, Litzy. I waited and waited. I could have tried to save him, but I didn't. I am so sorry. I'm so sorry I killed your father." Meg's arms clamped down the comforter on either side of her body. Facing forward, she continued. "The thing is, Litzy, I detested him and would do it all over again. I killed your father, and I wouldn't blame you if you never forgave me."

Wiping off the dampness from her cheeks, Litzy took a deep breath. She said quietly, "This is what I know. I came home from painting lessons. A policewoman met me at the door and guided me to this bedroom. She told me my dad had a heart attack and died. She didn't want me to see his body in a body bag, so she asked me to stay in the bedroom while the coroner took him away. She hugged me while I cried. Then, I heard a conversation through the door. I heard you ask somebody, I couldn't see who, how Dad died. The person answered that dad died almost instantly from a heart attack. That, Mom, is how I am going to remember how my father died. If you want to feel guilty for the rest of your life because you threw some stupid apple at him, then you really are nuts. And that's all I've got to say about it."

"Litzy. He had the heart attack after I hit him."

"Mom, one more time. Dad died of a bad heart. He had a massive heart attack and died almost instantly. Not one person mentioned that he died any other way. That's it, end of story." Litzy reached over Meg to turn off the light. "Instantly, Mom, end of story."

Side by side, mother and daughter slid under the covers in reverential silence. After a few minutes, Meg pulled Litzy to her, wrapping her long arms around her grown daughter. The compounded emotional exhaustion of the past eight hours eventually buried them in a sleep reserved for the dead.

Meg woke early. She looked over at her slumbering daughter curled on her side in a tight ball. Her long blonde hair covered her face. Meg smiled at her and slid out of bed. She threw on her bathrobe dangling from the hook on the back of her bathroom door and walked down the hall to the kitchen. She paused by the island. The morning light spilled through the French doors and onto the gleaming tile floor, making it impossibly bright. The lightness saturated Meg's body, and she felt a surge of airiness—an anti-gravitational pull upward, like the weight of a boulder had dropped from her shoulders, causing her to momentarily levitate. She put her hand over her heart and surveyed the room for any darkness, from the ceiling to its corners to the baseboards. She cinched her bathrobe belt tighter. Her heart raced, anticipating a chill. But the chill didn't come.

She started a pot of coffee, spilling some coffee grounds on the counter as she did. All quiet. Wiping them up, she felt the deliciously deafening silence. She sat down on a chair. Meg looked around. Nothing but serene brightness. She felt underneath the chair's cushion for the pills. She grabbed them, walked to the sink, and dropped them down the drain. Then she opened the French doors. A warm breeze blew through her hair. Did she trust he was gone? She wouldn't know for a while, she supposed, but somehow, she felt different. As if all the windows in her brain had opened like the French doors, letting in sweet fresh air and blowing away the noxious cloud that had inhabited her for so long. Her daughter was leaving. Meg would be overwhelmed and scared and lonely, but now, quite possibly, she would also be marvelously alone. Absolutely, singularly, and peacefully alone. She laughed to herself and then out loud, she slowly recited the ingredients she pulled from the fridge to make an omelet. Litzy would love it.

Meg didn't know how long Litzy had been watching her from the hallway, but she surprised her. "Litzy, good morning! I'm making breakfast for you. Come and sit."

"Mom, you seem so happy, like really happy, like you're a different person." Litzy put both hands over her heart. She'd heard her mom laugh for goodness' sake.

"I am happy. Like an enormous dark cloud has been lifted." She smiled as she chopped mushrooms for the omelet. "I'm so grateful for our talk last night, Litzy, thank you." Meg pressed her lips together to hold back tears. "I am so relieved you don't blame me for your dad, his death. So relieved."

"Mom. Seriously, you should have told me all that a long time ago." Litzy walked over to her mom and hugged her from behind. "Jesus, Mom. Carrying that guilt around, no wonder you were crazy." Then she walked and stood in front of the French doors.

"I'm just so relieved." Meg threw the mushrooms in the skillet and started to cut an onion. "Thanks to you, Litzy."

"You have no idea how relieved *I* am, Mom, no idea." Litzy reached for the handles on the fastened doors. "Let's get some fresh air in here."

Meg put down her knife, and looked at her daughter, then she glared at the closed doors. "But I did open them, Litzy, I swear I just opened them..."

"The wind must have blown them shut. I'll just open them again, no big deal." Litzy pushed them open again.

Meg moved to the end of the kitchen island where she looked out into the backyard. The breeze coming through the open doors gave her goosebumps. Without thinking, she walked outside and picked up a handful of errant rose petals from beneath the bushes, gathering them in her apron as she did.

Litzy watched her from inside the kitchen. "Mom, you know petals make good mulch. Why don't you leave them?" Her mother laughed and gathered a few more just to be sure.

Millicent

Summer 2016 • Seattle

Dear Millicent,

How do I write this? How do I acknowledge to you, in the space of this simple notecard, how much you mean to me—how much you have meant to me for the past thirty-five years, when I haven't even begun to accept the unthinkable, the inconceivable, the unconscionable. How do I convey the magnitude of this time, the grandness of you and the precious-ness of our friendship in so little space?

Fall 1982 • San Fransisco

We started drinking early. Dollar drinks at Carol Doda's, the North Beach strip club, flowed like water, and we took advantage. Like any broke twenty-four-year-olds, quantity took precedent—wherever we could get it. And, as always, after we downed a few stiff G & Ts, we were hungry. Little Joe's, a been-around-forever dive served mediocre Italian food across the street. Convenience shared top billing with quantity, so Millicent and I locked arms, a la Dorothy and the Scarecrow, and set off to the restaurant's enticing garlic aromas.

When tipsy, Millicent spoke fluent French, belying her English origins from across the channel. After living in the U.S. for five-plus years, a cozy still covered her teapot and tea was served in china rather than in ceramic mugs. Thanks to years of boarding school, she had ballerina-straight posture and rarely used contractions when speaking. She ate using a knife and fork together and never skipped a please or thank you. Her sensible shoes complemented her demure attire, and an ever-present wide-brimmed hat shielded her freckles from the sun. She said "lovely" instead of "pretty" and "brilliant" over "awesome." Aloof in demeanor, a straight-lip line on her face indicated perturbance, if upturned at the ends, happiness. If intoxicated, however, Millicent opened like a bottle of champagne, and out poured the French. With nary a slurred syllable, she spoke with remarkable fluency and clarity—even drunk—she had a gift. Guys loved it, and after drinking and eating, guys ranked next on our list of priorities. In particular, the pursuit of meeting our future husbands. Millicent's French kicked in as we crossed the road. Each step sprouted a *"oui, oui"* and *"pardon moi"* to angry drivers as they slammed on their brakes to avoid hitting us.

Inside Little Joe's, the fluorescent lights dangling from the ceiling and chartreuse walls tinted everything a sickly green. I put on my sunglasses to help offset the ghastly ocular effect. Millicent, unaffected, giggled at me. I picked up my menu and held it next to the candle flickering on our table.

Millicent picked up her menu. "How can you see with those glasses on?" She shook her head. "Ah, *j'aime* their pesto. I will have pesto and a glass of cabernet." She put down the menu and leaned her head back on the booth. "I think I might have the spins," she chuckled. *"Vah, vivre pleinement"*

"Try dark glasses. They help." My eyes shifted around the restaurant. Tables of people sat engaged over plates of food or lost in conversations. Clattering dishes competed with piped-in opera music. Two guys at the bar swiveled around in their stools and checked us out. I returned their stares behind my shades. *Hmmm,* I thought and turned to my menu. *Cute. Be cool. Don't look. Focus on ordering.* "Protein. Protein. Ah, roasted chicken on a bed of vegetables, sort of like a salad, perfect. And bread, lots of bread." I glanced up. The guys were still staring. I reached over and shook Millicent's hand, which rested on the table, to jolt her up. "Don't look now, but two guys at the bar are scoping us out." Slowly, I lowered my glasses and looked at them. *Very cute.*

Before she could comment, a grizzly-faced waiter approached our table. "What'll it be? More time?" He seemed annoyed at our presence.

"No, we're ready." I pushed up my glasses on my nose and brushed my bangs from my forehead. "Mill, go first."

We ordered, she the pasta and me the chicken-and-veggies like salad. Wine and bread, of course. The waiter disappeared quicker than you could say spaghetti.

"No personality," I said. "I hope he hurries with the bread. I'm out-of-control starving to death."

Safe behind my sunglasses, my eyes drifted back to the guys. A mirror behind the bar reflected their faces. Because Millicent's back faced them, she wasn't able to see. Like twins, the guys wore leather jackets and black jeans and sat with their legs crossed the same way. One had shaggy, shoulder-length hair, longer than the other. Suddenly, they swiveled around and outright gawked at us.

I shook Millicent's hand again. "Don't look. Guys are looking at us. Oh, look. They turned away. Wait, don't look. Wait, OK, no wait, stop. OK, now look. No stop."

"What? Do I look or not?" Then, without waiting for my answer, Millicent twisted her entire body toward them, as if welcoming old friends. The guy I liked most, whom I determined to be my guy, waved and then turned back to the bar. They nudged each other with their elbows.

I covered my glasses with my hands. "Millicent! Why'd you do that? I can't believe it! God, I can't believe you!" I hissed. "Now they know we're looking at them."

"Do not worry, Dotty. *Tout ira bien,*" she said. The waiter interrupted my embarrassment by delivering our food. Millicent took a sip of wine and dove into her mountain of green pasta. *"J'ai tellement faim que je pourrais manger un cheval."*

"Oui, oui, whatever. You're so fricking obvious sometimes." My dinner was more like a stew than a salad, but my stomach didn't care, and I dug in.

Millicent's next bite was huge. Too huge. Somehow this triggered her, with a full mouth, into a bout of body-quivering giggles.

Like catching a yawn, I followed suit and burst into hysterics. I dropped down onto the booth's fake leather bench to catch my breath. The coolness of the material on my cheek felt good. I removed my glasses to the soothing blackness of the table's underbelly, glad that it was too dark to identify the number of gum wads barnacled to its surface.

"Dotty, oh, Dotty, we have company," Millicent sang from above. I rose to a sitting position. The bar guys stood in front of our booth—drinks in hand.

"Oh, hello," I said as I straightened my blouse, coat, and hair. I laid my glasses on the table.

My guy spoke first. "Hi. You both OK? Looked like you choked or something." He towered adorably over the other guy, long hair dusting his broad shoulders. His gorgeous brown eyes complemented his cute piggish nose.

"Oh, we're fine," I said. Millicent and I exchanged a restrained snicker.

"OK, cool," my guy said as he brushed his hair back from his forehead.

"Yeah, that's good," Millicent's guy said. He had bushy eyebrows and a mole above his upper lip. Like a movie star. Not as cute as my guy, though.

"Would you care to join us?" Millicent said, casually. She dropped her hand to the bench beside her and slid over to the far end. In solidarity, I swept to the end of my bench and dropped my hand too. We kicked each other under the table. *"J'ais de vie."*

"Huh?" My guy said.

"My friend speaks French, like fluently, when she's been drinking."

"Cool. Sure. So, I'm Stephen, pronounced with a 'ph' like with an 'f', and this is Kevin," said Stephen, my guy, who scooted in next to Millicent—closely, touching shoulders. His leather jacket zipped up to his throat and fit tightly around his arms and chest. He smiled across the table at Kevin, who teetered on the far opposite end of my bench.

"I'm Dotty, and that's Millicent," I said to Stephen, who stared at Millicent.

For the next hour, we threw back several drinks a piece, and Millicent powered up into full French mode. Short of throwing myself on the table, I couldn't sustain Stephen's attention. Evidently, he loved French. For my part, if Millicent said *"Tres bien"* one more time, I was going to smack her. Kevin chewed his ice compulsively while fixating on his glass.

Eventually, we decided to move to a different bar, split the bill, and stumbled out of the restaurant. Stephen hailed a cab. Kevin made some excuse to leave and took off. We watched him make his way down the bustling street, thoughtlessly unbalancing our foursome. Millicent, now 100 percent French and Stephen 100 percent ensnared, I made one last attempt to flirt. I spoke in broken Spanish. No one noticed. For all the attention they paid me, I might as well have been in Spain.

As the cab pulled up to the curb, the three of us climbed in. Then, suddenly and without warning, Millicent threw up. Spewed all over the cab and Stephen, while I avoided any direct hits. Remarkably, Stephen remained calm. In the front seat, however, the cab driver screamed at us in a language I'd never heard before. Stephen told him we'd clean up everything. The cab driver turned his back to us, clutched the steering wheel at 2:00 and 10:00, and banged his head against it. As Stephen helped a dazed Millicent from the car, I ran into the restaurant and grabbed a wad of napkins from the bar. Stephen used them to clean up a very compliant Millicent and the cab. Once finished, the driver peeled off like Mario Andretti. Stephen hailed another cab and told Millicent to call him when she got home. Maybe they could get together tomorrow if she felt better. I was flummoxed. *She threw up on him, for God's sake! Damn it!* I thought. *Like a magic spell, speaking French always works.*

Our boldness shielded us in those days—stupidly bold and full of adventure. And the best part of our adventures happened the next day at one of our kitchen tables. We sipped strong coffee and, with a coroner's precision, dissected our previous night—as much as we could remember, anyway.

Fall 2015 • San Francisco

Millicent clutched at her lower back and winced as she climbed the narrow stairs to her apartment. The cool fog from San Francisco Bay beaded up on her hair and jacket.

"What's wrong?" I asked from the top of the landing. I watched her grab the rail with her hand. Her pace slowed to that of my eighty-nine-year-old mother. Condensation glistened on her forehead.

"Nothing. I think I pulled a muscle yesterday in exercise class." She smiled up at me, but I saw veins pop out around her temples. "I will be fine." Her breath labored with every step. She used the railing to drag herself up, as she put one foot in front of the other.

Once at my side, she put her hands on her hips, took a deep breath with surprising assurance. Her translucent green eyes stared steadily into mine. She smoothed back her dyed-red hair, which stuck out like the working end of a broom. Her cheeks shone like shiny ripe plums. "I am good," she said.

"Millicent, I want you to get checked out," I said, mimicking her stance. She smiled. I didn't smile back. In the two days I'd been visiting her, I'd seen her much too calculating with her physical movements. She walked with measured steps, not with her normal stalwart pace. And at random, her reliably sunny face would crinkle into that of a suffering old woman.

Fifteen years earlier, Millicent had suffered through breast cancer. It not only knocked her to her knees—as a survivor, it also never left her mind. And for that matter, mine. Whenever I visited her—every six months or so—she'd have an odd ache or pain that needled her, but ultimately, they never amounted to anything. She didn't complain much, but I knew her too well. Her lined forehead and tight lips signaled distress. I didn't expect her health to be an issue this trip. Instead, taking center stage would be her upcoming nasty divorce and stabilizing the worlds of her college-aged son and daughter. Those issues alone would take a toll on anyone's health.

"Oh, Dotty, you are such a worrier. I promise to see the doctor when my new insurance kicks in, in a day or two," Millicent said as she led me into her apartment. Following her, as always, I admired her erect posture and her calves, muscled apple shapes tapering down to thin ankles. Thirty-plus years after moving from England, she was still the epitome of a female sheepherder: a combination of ruddy, freckled skin, warm red hair—even if now dyed—flying all around, and naturally flushed lips. "Come now," she said. "Let us have a cup of tea. You must be on the road soon."

Millicent had moved to San Francisco from Menlo Park after her separation from Jim, her second husband. Her little duplex had a lovely view of the ocean. And even if a heavy fog blanketed the scenery, the scent of the thick wet air wouldn't let you forget your proximity to the beach. She loved living in the city. Her small living room opened into the kitchen where a wall-to-wall window and sliding glass door showcased the undulant weather patterns. I sat in my designated sitting spot on the couch opposite her favorite orange leather chair. From our perches over the rooftops of six or seven rows of houses, the ocean view waved in the distance.

I watched her futz in the kitchen, setting down two china cups and saucers on the counter. She clicked on the electric kettle and draped a tea bag into each cup. With a tiny spoon, she dropped two sugar cubes in her cup. It never ceased to amaze me that she still used sugar cubes. After the water boiled, she filled the two cups and said, "You must not worry so much, Dot." Her lips rested in a thin line upturned at the corners, while she stood, arms crossed over her breast-less chest, in front of the steeping tea.

"You're right, probably nothing at all," I said. My gut churned in protest. In a couple of hours, I'd be leaving, going back to Portland, and I knew I didn't have time to argue or best-case scenario, convince her to call a doctor first thing in the morning. We sipped our tea and laughed about our devil-may-care exploits and tried to recall names of people we should have remembered. The time flew by. I felt marginally better about everything as I gathered my things from the back bedroom and brought them to the front door. She slipped on the shoes she'd pulled from the foyer's shoe cubby. We trudged down the stairway, banging the bags against the walls as we went.

As I loaded my stuff into the trunk of the rental car, I said, "Thanks for everything, Mill. Remember, get your back checked, and keep me updated." I could feel tears forming. "I love you, Millicent," I said. We hugged.

Millicent stepped up from the street, onto her apartment's front steps. "Do not worry. I will be in touch, I promise. Thank you for coming. OK, bye-bye." She waved as I climbed into the car and did a quick U-turn to get me headed toward the airport. As I turned, I saw Millicent clutch her lower back with both hands and bend forward as she disappeared into the stairwell.

Summer 2016 • Seattle

You are a friend's friend. When we're together, we're like two perfectly matched Legos. I never have to explain anything to you. Like when we would sit in the backyard of your garden apartment and talk about our dreams. You'd declare yours, and I'd declare mine, then we'd hang them up on a proverbial clothesline and examine them, as if they were schematics for the rest of our lives. We believed in each other uncondi-tionally. I was going to write a book. You were going to produce an Emmy-winning TV show. Our worlds were ours to shape. We had unwavering faith, and all the time in the world to make things happen.

. . .

Spring 1987 • San Francisco

"So, Dotty, let's go whale watching today. I have always wanted to, and you have never been, so let's go, shall we?" Millicent called early one Sunday morning. "I will pick you up in an hour. We board near Petaluma—a three-hour excursion. It's not that expensive either. What do you say?"

"I just woke up, Mill. I need sleep. It's Sunday. So early." The clock on my nightstand read 7:00 a.m., way too early for a weekend. My head flopped on the pillow. "I just went to bed. I drank too much."

"Now come on, get up. You will be fine. I'll bring you coffee. Pick you up at 8:00. Cannot waste the day in bed, you know." And with that, she hung up.

I rolled away from the clock and closed my eyes. They blinked open. *An hour, really? Whales? OK, Mill, you win. We'll see whales.* In the ten years I'd lived in San Francisco, it was true: I'd never seen a whale.

Punctually, at 8:00, Millicent honked her horn outside my apartment. I stumbled out the door, eating a piece of dry toast. "Boy, right on time," I said as I slipped into the passenger seat. Crumbs fell from my sweatshirt as I stuffed the remaining bit into my mouth.

"Good morning, Dotty," Millicent said and handed me a cup of coffee in a Styrofoam cup. "Drink your coffee, you will feel better."

"Where'd you get this?" I asked, taking a sip out of the steaming cup.

"Judy's, the restaurant down the street. They sell to-go coffees now. Lots of restaurants do, you know. I think the next thing we do is open a coffee stand and sell coffee to go. We'd be rich."

"Yes, great, put it on our to-do list," I said and sipped my hot coffee. "So much to do, so little time." I closed my eyes.

"I want to talk to you about something, Dot." Millicent spoke in her serious I-just-discovered-how-to-make-a-million voice. "Firstly, I was laid off on Friday, but I have a plan. I want to start my own production company. What do you think?"

"What? You were laid off from KRON? They love you." I nearly choked on my coffee. "What did they say? I'm shocked." I sat up in my seat.

"Well, the station sold, and the new owners wanted their own people." She looked at me sideways. "They fired my boss and most of my department, too." Her calm expression remained, but she tightened her grip on the steering wheel and tapped the gas a little harder. "Heart wrenching."

"Unbelievable," I said and slumped back into my seat as we crossed the Golden Gate. I watched sailboats float below in the deep blue bay. A ferry chugged by, creating waves for the boats to navigate. *Boats make me seasick*, I thought and took a deep breath. "Mill, if anyone can bounce back, you can. Did they give you a decent severance package?"

Millicent glanced at me. "Not much—three months, wages, but I have six months' rent in savings," she said and focused back on the road. "I think I could launch my production business in that time."

"Six months saved? How'd you do that? When did you do that?" I took a sip and stared at Millicent. "Impressive. I could never do that."

"I have been saving for a long time, and you party more." She stared ahead with a grin. "You know I've always wanted to start my own company, so, I put away money each month. Time to use it."

"Well, again, if anyone can run a successful business, it's you. You won an Emmy at KRON for goodness' sake. How awesome is that. You're so talented. I'd be scared to start my own business."

"But you have." She side-eyed me. "You're a freelance graphic designer. You pay your bills with that income, don't you?"

"Yes, but if I focused more, didn't party so much, I'd have more money." I watched the people jogging on the bridge as we drove past. They looked so healthy and ridiculously awake. "I should have tried harder at school, too, but having fun was always my priority."

"Why?" Millicent asked.

No one had asked me that before. I had to think a minute. "I guess, for one thing, if I remember correctly, every time I left the house, my mother sent me off with a too chipper, 'Have fun.' School, work, a date, anywhere, it was 'Have fun,' not work hard or do your best, just 'Have fun.' Always." I sighed. "I admit, I've perfected it. I'm usually broke, haven't advanced my career, and I'm not married, but damn it, I know how to have a good time."

Millicent shot me a quick sideways glance. I could tell she was on the precipice of imparting some sage wisdom, counteracting all I knew to be true. "Well, Dot, if for my entire existence my mother had told me to have fun, that's what I would try and do. Such a strong message to receive all your life."

I blinked at Millicent then studied the outside view. The bridge had disappeared behind us, and the mountains emerged ahead. The words "Just have fun" written in cursive neon and lit up in the front of my brain flickered and dimmed. I felt a shift, like a dissolvement of bedrock supporting my core beliefs, a tectonic movement forever casting an altered view of my horizon. "Wow, Mill, amazing." A razor-thin smile stretched out across Millicent's face. All this time, I'd been fulfilling the expectations laid out by my mother—effective programming on her part—not just me being a hapless flake. At least not 100 percent.

We didn't see whales on that trip. In fact, if a school of a hundred whales had been visible in the ocean, we would have missed them. We spent our time with our bodies heavy and bent at the middle—our shoes anchored to the deck, our arms and heads flopped over the boat's railing. Occasionally, we rose to eat a soda cracker, then we'd fling ourselves back over and make deposits into the ocean.

After the eternal three-hour cruise ended, we drove home in a comfortable quiet, both of us feeling much better about everything.

Winter 2015 • Portland

I was preparing salmon for my neighbor's sixtieth birthday party when I got the call.

"Hello, Dotty, this is Millicent. How are you?" It was a beautiful day, almost three months after my last visit to see her in San Francisco. Her voice continued, "I went to the doctor."

"Well?" I said, scared for her to continue. I wiped my hands with a dish cloth. "Tell me everything." I sat down on my kitchen chair.

"It's returned, in my back and a couple of tumors in my lungs. I know it sounds bad, but they have better treatments. Everyone is very upbeat about the success rates." Her voice never faltered.

"Oh, my God, Millicent, I'm so sorry." I didn't want to become hysterical, but my mind went immediately to my late mother. A year after a surgeon removed a malignant tumor from her gall bladder, her cancer returned. Cancer had metastasized in her back and bones. We lost her fewer than two months later. I took a deep breath. "So, what's the next step?"

"I have a doctor's appointment Friday. They have new chemo treatments, more precise—they zero in on the cancer-infected areas—like targeting the tumors in my lungs. The chemo attacks them, like bombs hitting a bull's eye. Afterwards, I will get a PET scan to determine if it is working." She spoke matter-of-factly. "But everyone is being very positive. OK, I better go, but I wanted you to know. I'll be in touch after the treatments."

"But what about your back?" I asked and stood up. A lump grew in my throat.

"I will take a different kind of chemo for that, but not until the lungs are treated. OK—all good with you and your family? Sorry to rush, but I must be going."

"Yes, we're fine. Millicent, please keep me updated. Also, can I have Sarah and Ian's numbers, just in case I want to get ahold of them? I assume they'll be with you." I'd always been so impressed with the maturity of Millicent's children, and I knew they'd step up now. They'd been through her first bout with cancer as little kids. They'd been a part of the continual battle with Jim, their father and Millicent's horrible ex-to-be, and they'd be her biggest supporters now. But, making things worse, a contentious battle over college financing loomed in the future. Jim threatened to stop paying for anything connected with the children, beating down Millicent any way he could. Her cancer couldn't have returned at a worse time.

"Yes, of course, I will text you their numbers," Millicent said. "I really must go, Dotty. Sarah leaves for Seattle University at the end of this month, and we are off to do some shopping."

"Mill, when can I visit again?"

"Anytime. Always good to see you. Love you." Millicent hung up so fast, I didn't realize she'd gone until I didn't get a response to my next question—was she keeping ahead of her pain?

Summer 2016 • Seattle

Your zest for life is inspirational. Your overwhelming optimism is cult-like, your belief that everything is possible and reasonable is palatable. You can sit in a postage-stamp-size apartment, unemployed and broke, and be certain your next iteration will deliver you success. Even in your current vortex, living with a killer disease, you don't descend into a bleak cave of despair. No sitting on hands, or crying into your soup, you tweak and regroup, and you never stop charging forward. Your refusal to accept defeat transcends all aspects of your life, and I'm 100 percent charging ahead with you.

Summer 2013 • San Francisco

We set off from San Francisco to the Sonoma wine country early to beat the traffic, although SF traffic is unbeatable, even when I had lived there twenty years before. Our destination: Francis Ford Coppola's Winery restaurant to celebrate Millicent's decision to leave her husband. Get the ball rolling as she would say, and the last day of my visit.

"I made a lunch reservation. You will love this place." She winked at me like Santa Claus at Christmastime. I pushed my seat back and hooked my heels on the dashboard. The return of twinkly-eyed Millicent filled me with happiness.

"So, bet you'll love moving back to San Francisco?" I asked, looking at her. I still marveled at how anyone could sit up so straight while driving a car—her English heritage at work. "Will you ever miss Menlo Park?" Her red hair set off her olive-green jacket.

"I will miss nothing about Menlo Park. I cannot get far enough away. Jim is such a miserable person." Millicent looked straight ahead, both hands grasping the wheel, lip line straight. "But let's not talk about this now." She turned on classical music.

"Of course, sorry." I scanned Millicent's stoic face and then watched the eucalyptus trees shimmering past my window. "I forget how pretty the wine country is." I felt awkward and confused. We hadn't discussed her decision to divorce much in the last few days, and I had imagined that's all we'd talk about. I didn't know if I should applaud her impending split or grieve the end of a failed marriage. She didn't share her feelings often. Business or life plans always, but typically, emotions dripped out slower than water from a used tea bag. Perhaps her Englishness keep her stoic, but that part of her drove me crazy. The whole of Beethoven's Fifth played without us speaking. I opened the window to smell the eucalyptus trees. I needed patience, but my visit was almost over. Her reticence made me feel helpless as a friend.

Finally, she cleared her throat. "Nice to be here with you, Dotty. You understand me."

Do I? I thought. I rolled up the window.

She continued, "You know how hard things have been. How horrible Jim has been, how he tied me up as a person. I think you are one of the few people that does. I appreciate that in you."

"Well, you've been unhappy for years, I know that much. You needed to get away from him—the sooner, the better." When I remembered the things she did share about him, a protective rage filled me. She, always at fault and he, relentlessly mean to her. He gave their son a black eye for some stupid reason and kicked their daughter out of the house for coming home late. I wondered at how she stayed in the marriage for as long as she did.

"Things are going to get better. I know they are." Millicent's crescent-mooned smile, lips pressed together, reflected a woman on a mission. Her eyes narrowed in concentration, like she was plowing through fields of painful thoughts, tilling them with those of renewal and restoration. Not once did she degrade into bitterness or self-reproach. And just like that, the conversation ended. Her steadfast demeanor demanded it.

After arriving at the winery restaurant, the maître d' led us to a white tableclothed table where we sat in front of the menus, hardbound three-ring binders. I peeked over mine, and seeing Millicent's calm face made me feel wonderful. With the worst behind her, she looked downright robust.

She leaned back against the chair and said, "This place reminds me of all the places we used to wine taste when you lived here. We would have just enough money for wine tasting but never enough to eat. We owe it to ourselves now."

"Yes, and I am going to eat. A. Lot. And drink a lot. On this my last day of vacation with you," I said, opening the menu between us. "This looks amazing!"

"Now, Dotty, you are not going to order a salad, are you?" Millicent looked at me over her menu. "You must order something else."

"I always order a salad. I love salads. You know that, and they look delicious here." I read the salad section of the menu. Their descriptions were like any other restaurant's I'd ever read, but I always ordered a salad. That's how I rolled.

The waiter came over, recited the specials for the day and left to get the cabernet Millicent ordered.

"I want to tell you about my new idea, Dot," Millicent said as she leaned in. "I think this is it. I want to produce an internet TV show. Like a network TV show, only it streams on the internet." She paused with the return of our waiter.

"Your wine, Miss." He showed Millicent the bottle of wine. She nodded, and he poured her a small amount to taste.

"Delicious, thank you." Millicent smiled up at him as he topped off her glass and poured mine.

He asked for our orders.

"I'm looking at the Shrimp Louie. Looks fantastic, with egg and avocados."

Millicent frowned. "Come on. Order something you would never make at home. How about the fish? The special crusted trout?"

"What's better," I asked the waiter, ignoring Millicent, "the Shrimp Louie or the Chicken Cobb?"

"Dotty, come on, get something you never eat. How is the fish?" She asked the waiter. "I don't want her to order salad. I want her to get something special. Life is short, right?"

"The fish is wonderful. We cook it in parchment paper with a dozen spices, and it comes out with a crispy skin and so tender inside. One of my favorites." He smiled at Millicent and asked me, "Do you like fish?"

"Yes, I love fish, but I order salads." I sighed, knowing that I would not win this battle today. I inhaled loudly and said, "OK, the fish." I handed the waiter the menu.

Millicent's lips spread into a long-upturned line across her face, with parentheses punctuating the ends. She said, "I would like the Shrimp Alfredo and a small Caesar salad, please."

"Excellent choices. Neither of which you'll regret," the waiter said and left the table.

"Happy, Millicent? Do you realize how hard that was for me? The Louis came with avocados for God's sake. OK, finish telling me about your streaming TV show." I sipped my wine.

"Well, you know when you get commercials on Facebook? I would develop a fifteen-minute show that works almost like a commercial but would present as a sitcom, only on Facebook or a similar platform. People would see the first show and want to see the next and the next. They would pop up randomly like a commercial, but each day, the storyline would advance. What do you think?" Millicent's eyes sparkled as she sipped her wine.

"OK, like a sitcom? It would just flash on the screen while I'm searching for a friend or something," I said, trying to envision it.

"Yes, like a little window would pop up. Day one, a fifteen-minute story about something appears, the next day a story that builds on the first and so on and on—but randomly—you wouldn't know when they would pop up." Millicent swirled her wine in her glass. "Now here's a question for you. As long as I've known you, you've only ordered salads. Why?"

I thought for a moment and said, "Probably because I think they're less fattening than anything else." *Pretty simple*, I thought. At that point, ordering salads was reflexive. Leave it to Millicent to ask.

"And I was a fat kid." In truth, throughout my life, any event could trigger my unhealthy childhood relationship with food and teeter-tottering weight. I credited my dear mother. But I didn't want to go deep into it at that moment and hoped she'd drop the subject. For the most part, I'd made peace with myself enough to at least order something other than a salad. "So, how do you make your idea come to fruition?"

"Network with people in the business." She paused and with a ruler-straight mouth said, "I have never known you to be fat."

"Ask my mom. Or my dad, too. They'll tell you differently." I switched the subject back to her. "Sounds so doable. You're amazing, you know. You're embarking on this huge divorce drama and, at the same time, you're planning your next business venture."

"Why waste the energy being negative? Like you. You are an adult. Why should your parents' childhood judgements of you impact you now? It's plain silliness. Let go, Dot. Look at you, you're fine."

Millicent shook her head and held up her glass. "Let's toast. To you saying *au revoir* to childhood negativity that doesn't serve you anymore. And me for my new project and the freedom to pursue it. To stepping outside of our respective boxes." We clinked glasses and swigged. "Life is just opening up for us, *ma cheri*." She winked. "This is truly our time." I heartily agreed.

Full and content, Millicent drove us back to San Francisco, listening to Mozart in a satiated silence. Soon I'd say my goodbyes in front of her apartment, satisfied that Millicent's future dreams could be realized, knowing soon, she'd be free from Jim's shackles.

We hugged our final time in front of my rental car.

We vowed to be in touch soon. I left her waving the queen's wave, standing pencil straight and pink cheeked. Her observation of my own food-and-weight-shackled self felt like a kick in the pants to oust my parents' version of what's best for me as my younger self, for a "you're not the boss of me anymore" healthier, adult self. Time would tell how well the kick worked, but I was grateful to hear from Millicent how obsolete my behavior sounded. Regardless of how long we'd go without seeing each other, her caring and perspective stated parsimoniously, always enlightened me in the most positive way.

. . .

Summer 2016 • Seattle

I arrived at Millicent's apartment around 4:00. My drive to Seattle had been tediously slow, stop and go traffic the whole way. I felt tired and irritable. And scared. I rang the entrance bell. Millicent buzzed me in.

"Hello, come on up!" Millicent's lilting voice surprised me. I trudged down the hall into the elevator, slamming into the narrow walls with my suitcase and oversized handbag. I set down my bags once I arrived outside her door and rang the doorbell.

"It's open!" Again, with the cheery voice.

I pushed the door ajar, dropped my bags, and a nose-full of stale medicinal air, a mixture of Ben Gay and spiced tea, enveloped me. My friend toddled toward me in a kelly-green turtleneck with a moss-colored scarf twisted around her neck. She wore the fuzzy socks I'd sent her a few months prior, stretched up over the bottoms of her sweatpants. A horizontal smile stretched across her face—her translucent skin creased with wrinkles I hadn't noticed on my last trip.

"Mill!" I said, "Hi there, old friend. How are you?" Besides her wrinkles and pale skin, I thought she looked better than I'd been cautioned to expect. In a conversation the night before, her daughter, Sarah, had warned me how much weight Millicent had lost since I'd last seen her. She went so far as to say I'd be shocked. But thankfully, I wasn't. Her thick, bristly red hair and her round cheeks seemed intact.

"I am fine, really fine," Millicent said, holding out her arms for a hug. When we embraced, I felt the change. Her undiminished head belied the body I felt: her bones had no meat and her bulky sweater sleeves masked her skeletal arms wrapped around me. "Here, come sit." Millicent dropped her arms and shuffled me into her living room. A blanket spilled onto the floor from the couch, and a bed pillow sat propped up on the couch's arm. A small table held a teacup, spoon, a tiny bowl of sugar cubes, and in her handwriting, a grocery list on a piece of paper. I sat down in the chair opposite.

"Well," I said. "You look great, Millicent." The lie stuck in my throat like a lemon wedge. My eyes involuntarily welled with tears, and I was sure my smile was upside down. My urge to rush to her overwhelmed me. I wanted to hold her and sob uncontrollably, but instead took a deep breath and looked at the brilliant sunlight outside her window. I took another breath.

"How was your drive? Much traffic?" Millicent asked as she wrapped the blanket around her. "I get cold easily. I hate it."

"Can I get you anything, Mill?" I said and moved to the edge of the couch. "Tell me, really, how are you?"

"No, thank you, and I will tell you everything, but not now, I am too tired. I get so tired. Sarah will be home soon, and I thought you two could shop for dinner together. I thought chicken would be good." She pulled the blanket tighter around her shoulders.

After my long drive, the last thing I wanted to do was get back in a car and go shopping. I needed a drink, that's what I needed. "Of course, when she gets home, we'll go," I said. I wanted Millicent to offer me a glass of wine, anything to normalize the moment. "Where's Ian?"

"He's got his own apartment now, near the college. Not too far from here." She pointed to my bags. "Do you want to put your things in the bedroom? I told Sarah to put clean towels in your bathroom."

"Perfect, yes, of course." Relieved to leave the room for a moment, I carried my bags to my room. I heard the front door open.

"Hello, Mummy!" Sarah called from the entryway. "Is Dotty here yet?"

In an instant, I joined her in the entry. "Sarah! Hi! Wonderful to see you." I gave Millicent's twenty-three-year-old daughter a hug. Once again, I had to swallow a lump in my throat. "I just arrived." I stood back and looked at beautiful Sarah. She had the face of her father, down to his dimples and the space between his teeth, but the heart and soul of her mother.

"You two, come in here," Millicent called from the living room. We exchanged looks and hurried to join her.

Sarah took a spot by her mother on the couch. "How was your day, Sarah?" Millicent held Sarah's hands in her lap.

"Great, how are you?" She looked at her mother. "Are you warm enough?"

"Yes, I am fine. I hoped you and Dotty could go to the store and pick up things for dinner. How does that sound?"

"Mum, Dotty just drove here from Portland. I bet she'd like a glass of wine first. Glass of wine before we go, Dotty?" Sarah said as she got up from the couch and walked into the small kitchen which adjoined the living room. She poured wine into two glasses.

"Love one, thanks, Sarah. Perfect," I said, taking the glass from her. "What store?"

"We can walk to Trader Joe's. It's just up the street." And with wine in hand, she sat back down next to her mother.

"Perfect," I said. "Mill, can I get you a glass?"

"No, I cannot drink anymore. Makes me nauseous," Millicent said. "Could you please put the kettle on? I'd like a cup of tea, though." She lifted her teacup from the table for me to take. I took it to the kitchen and turned on the electric teakettle. Next to the kettle, a tray crammed with assorted pill containers and liquid prescription bottles sat by a notebook logged with her prescription drug use. Stacked spoons rested in an overflowing spoon rest and a pile of tea bags filled a little dish nearby. The kettle whistled. "I would like Smooth Move, please." Millicent called from the couch. "I get constipated with all the meds. Just leave the bag in water in the cup, and please bring it to me."

Sarah came over to me in the kitchen. "I can do it, Dotty. Please, you sit down. You must be tired, and Mummy is already making you work." Her dimpled smile invited me to relax and get used to my surroundings.

But I couldn't.

"Thanks, Sarah, I've got it." I dipped the tea bag into the china cup. I needed a task to help me adjust to the current situation. The stifling heat in the apartment, or maybe the effects of the wine, made me feel sweaty. "Do you have any crackers?" I needed something to soak up the wine.

"Sarah, get Dotty something to eat." Her voice strained as she sat cocooned in her blanket, reclining on the couch. "Crackers in the cupboard in front of you, and cheese in the fridge."

I grabbed a couple of crackers from a Wheat Thins box. I felt anxious. My heart raced. I needed fresh air. "Maybe we should go shopping and get it over with. Then we can eat. Are you hungry, Mill?" I asked. Sarah handed me a slice of cheese to top my cracker. I popped both into my mouth. Then, I poured hot water into Millicent's teacup.

Sarah put down her wine and said, "Yes, let's go now. Will you be OK, Mummy? Do you need anything besides the tea before we leave?" She bent over her mother and pulled the blanket up on her shoulder. "Do you want any cheese and crackers?"

"I will be fine. You go." Millicent pointed to the table, directing me where to put her tea. I dutifully placed it where she instructed. "I can nap, and when you get back, you can make dinner," she said. Her body took up less than half the width of the couch, but her wild hair splayed all over the pillow. "Sarah, don't forget my list and the credit card."

I grabbed the list from the table. Standing over her as she lay on the couch, I felt huge and in the way, like I took up too much space and breathed too much air.

Sarah grabbed the credit card from the counter. We both said goodbye as we slipped out.

After Sarah closed the door behind us, I stopped. "Oh, my God! You warned me, but I had no idea. I had absolutely no idea." I wanted to cry. Sarah hugged me. I hugged her back.

"Tell me everything, Sarah. I mean, four or five months ago the treatments were working, the tumors were shrinking. Fuck! What happened?"

We spent the next half hour catching me up on Millicent's condition. She'd responded well to the treatments at first, but then the cancer metastasized. At one point, she scheduled a hip replacement to alleviate her hip pain, but it would have increased the risk of the cancer spreading. Then a PET scan revealed tumors in her brain. So, all treatments stopped, setting palliative care in motion. No one used the word hospice. Not yet. She no longer fought her death; she'd accepted it. I, however, had not.

Sarah and I walked around Trader Joe's, picking up Millicent's very particular requests. Everything had to be organic. The irony was not lost on Sarah that her mother would never reap the benefits of any organic foods. "Why spend the extra money now?" she asked. We picked out a good bottle of wine—non-organic. We'd need it.

Carrying our bags of groceries down the apartment-building hall, we stopped before Millicent's door. Both of us inhaled deeply, and after Sarah turned the doorknob, we entered. The dusky outdoors seemed bright compared to her murky apartment. We could barely see Millicent's silhouette lying down on the couch. Her sudden, very chirpy "Hello" broke up the shadows with a burst of light.

"You're awake?" Sarah asked as she turned on the lights. Millicent laid in the same position as when we had left. Her head stuck out of her blanket wrap, hair standing up all over. The half-full teacup sat on the table.

"I am. Did you get everything?"

"Yes, and then some," I said. "I got some really good cookies." I unpacked the food.

"Wonderful." She poked up her head a bit. "So, let us get started on dinner, shall we? Bake the chicken—Sarah will show you where the pans are, Dotty, and we can have broccoli and some potatoes. Sarah, please show Dotty where things are." Millicent laid back down and propped up her head with her arm behind it, so she could see us.

"I'm on it, Mill." As my stay for the weekend unfolded, I became the cook, the cleaner, and the shopper, for which both Sarah and Millicent expressed their eternal gratitude.

I learned Millicent didn't like too much food on her plate, even if you told her not to worry about finishing it or to eat as much as she liked. She made me remove half or more of every portion I gave her. She only ate a few bites of anything. I scrambled eggs one morning and she, and Sarah for that matter, vetoed them and Millicent scrambled another batch, the only thing she still cooked. Millicent always had been and remained the best scrambled-egg maker I'd ever known. Don't ask me why or how, but she was, and I never made an egg without thinking of her.

She didn't like too many pillows behind her head, just one or two because her neck would crick and cause her pain. She needed help putting on her socks because she could no longer bend forward—back spasms. The same went for shoes. Slip-ons were better, but she still needed help. She took her morning and afternoon naps at the same time every day, but I didn't have to be quiet. Most days she took a short walk of a half a block or so, but the pace was akin to my ninety-four-year-old father's shuffle.

The day before I was set to leave, Millicent and I took such a stroll. That's when she told me about her plan to rent a cabin on Orcas Island for a couple of weeks in July.

"It is a beautiful house with a great view of the water. Even my bedroom has a view of the water." Millicent's eyes shone more clearly than I'd seen in a long time. "I was thinking of asking for a doctor's help, you know. While I am there."

"You mean like have a doctor visit you there for treatment? Great idea. The place sounds ideal, Mill. You'll do well with a vacation," I said. "You always feel so much better by the water."

"Dotty, I am not going to feel better. I am possibly getting dying assistance, or I will just pass the rest of my time. I want to die there," Millicent said without emotion and a linear serious mouth.

"What? Why don't you just go there for a vacation? Why do you have to go there and die? What happens if you feel better or something comes up—a new drug or something?" I stuttered. My ability to fully accept what my friend said escaped me.

"You see, Dotty, it is really OK with me now. I have provided for the children. They will be able to have this apartment through the end of the year. My brother will continue to take care of all the financials for them from Australia." Millicent stopped walking and looked at me. "You see, I am ready, Dotty, whatever happens, however it happens, I am fine."

"But I don't get it, Millicent, are you so ready you want to do it yourself?" I asked, looking at a crawling rose bush reaching out for me from behind a fence. I pulled at a branch. "I'm just so surprised. Although I shouldn't be—I know logically what's happening to you —but I guess I'm in denial, Millicent. Way in denial." I yanked at another reaching rose.

"I know. I know, Dot." She patted me on the back. "But it is a wish of mine that since cancer has controlled my life, I want to control my death. Sarah and Ian will be with me and so will Jean." Her dear friend, Jean, now living in Seattle, had worked with Millicent in San Francisco when I lived there.

"So, you've thought this through." I tugged at the stem of another errant rose. "I applaud you for having such presence of mind. July, huh? Less than a month away." I nicked off a rosebud and threw it down the street.

"Yes, Dotty, July. Let's go back now, shall we? I'm tired." She took my arm with her bony fingers, and we turned back toward her apartment. We'd gone a block and a half. I felt like I'd walked a hundred miles, and a brick had smacked me in the chest along the way. My eyes rimmed with tears.

The next morning, while I packed my bag to leave, Sarah came into the bedroom to say goodbye. "I am meeting up with some friends —a birthday breakfast—but I wanted you to know how much you mean to me and Ian, and of course to Mum. To come up here, be so much help and well, everything, Dotty. We love you so much."

"I don't know what I would have done without you, Sarah. You're a gift to your mother and to me. And so is Ian," I said, wiping back tears that had begun to pour. "Stay in touch, please." She assured me she would, smiling her dimpled smile. We hugged, our faces tucked into each other's necks as we exchanged damp goodbyes. Then she left, yelling a final goodbye to her mom.

"Well, that was sad, Mill," I said as I entered the living room to Millicent lying on the couch swathed in her blanket. "Saying goodbye to Sarah. Hard. Boy, is she wonderful. Your kids are amazing. Considering everything they've been through, absolutely amazing."

"I know they are, thank you," Millicent said. "They have really been my rocks through everything."

I sat down on the chair opposite Millicent. "I'm curious, and I must ask. Was Jim a good father when the kids were babies?"

"Yes, yes. He was a good father back then. I think things became different after my first bout with cancer. After that, he changed. Resentful maybe, and it grew into something bigger and uglier."

"Makes sense, I guess. He couldn't sustain acting like an adult when times got rough, but I am glad he did when the kids were young." I watched Millicent's face fall a little. *Shut up, Dotty,* I told myself. *No more Jim talk.* "So, Mill, I want to wrap the graduation present I bought for Sarah before I go. Do you have any wrapping paper or tissue I could use?"

"No, you'll have to go and get some. Down the street by Trader Joe's is a lovely stationery store," Millicent said. "Will not take you long."

I was taken aback. Instead of wanting to spend the last hours of my visit together, forever, she was sending me away. "You don't have any tissue I could use? It's just a small locket to wrap."

"No. Go to the stationery store by Trader Joe's. You will love it." She pulled the blanket over her shoulders. "I'll have a lie down while you're gone."

"Of course. Down the street to the stationery store, it is. Get some rest." I left her apartment a little bewildered, a little hurt, but aware enough that she needed her rest regardless of my feelings.

I walked down the street lined with cute little boutiques, coffee houses and restaurants. The stationery shop Millicent sent me to offered luxurious handmade cards and envelopes artfully displayed, a feast for my eyes. Tissue and giftwrap were no different, all sumptuously and uniquely designed. Eventually, I chose a floral-patterned gift bag. Then I perused the cards. *I should buy Millicent a card,* I thought. For the second time that day, tears filled my eyes. How do I pick a card for a friend that's dying? At last, I chose a small card with a fancifully drawn heart on the cover. Probably for lovers, but it suited my purpose perfectly.

I walked out of the store with my emotionally wrought package and into the neighborhood coffee shop. My latte order came up fast, preventing me from dawdling before the task ahead. I sat down at an outside table. I slid the card out of the bag and out of its plastic sleeve. The paper felt soft but substantial. I took a sip of coffee and set it down. I looked around at all the happy morning coffee drinkers. Then, without notice, teardrops landed on the envelope of the card. *Stupid me, get it together,* I said to myself. *Write. Write. Write.*

Summer 2016 • Seattle

What do I say to you, Millicent? What words can possibly bear the weight of my heavy heart? Tell me, dear friend, how do I leave you, this final time?

Perhaps like I always do. Regardless of how far apart we are, you are ever by my side. And so it goes, I will love you as I always have, and as I always will.

Acknowledgments

This book would not be written without the help of some very important people in my life. Not unlike sitting in a car propelled through a carwash, I kept the car on the tracks, but without the steady pull of a conveyor belt of encouragement, expertise, and kicks in the pants, I think I'd still be sitting in the car waiting for the soap brushes. Thanks to the following:

My husband Dan Cunha and sons Jake and Ben Cunha, whose relentless support of my writing never wavered even as my computer screen remained blank for long periods of time.

Ann Perrins, with whom I've shared a mutual love of reading and writing since the eighth grade. Her suggestion of taking a writing class activated the creative juices for this book.

Cece Hall, who I'm sure if she saw another year with "write a book" on my list of New Year's resolutions would scream or throw one at me. Yet, she always believed in me.

Without the separate yet consistent nudging from Noel Hanlon and Claudia Johnson, over countless lunches reminding me of my passion for writing, I might have thought it impossible to write a book.

Laurie and Don Scott. Laurie helped me decipher the bird's-nest processes of query letters, and with Don's help, became proofreaders, consultants, and excellent restorers of wine in my glass throughout the sometime painful writing experience.

The moral support of my Book Group, who volunteered to read my finished stories, meant the world to me. A hair scrunch in your direction. Thank you for being my first larger-than-one-person audience. And such a positive one at that.

My dad for instilling the love of reading in me at a very young age by handing me at nine years old *The Count of Monte Cristo*. I never looked back.

My Beta Readers: Eric Stromquist, Anne Laufe, Mark Plumlee, and Lori Stromquist for whose invaluable editing I will forever be indebted. Lori, the French translation! How did you do that?

And most of all and as big as I can make a thank you, to Jenny Bates. My mentor, my coach, my confidant, my editor, my champion, the best dog not-liker putting up with Penny, and the biggest cheerleader in the world. You told me years ago that I had "it" and although I didn't know what 'it' was then, and maybe still don't, I know with you walking the walk with me for these past eight years we made "it" happen. Thank you, thank you, a million additional commas more.

About the Author

Judy Savinar studied creative writing at the University of Colorado and worked as an advertising copywriter before becoming a frazzled middle school librarian. She lives in Portland, Oregon, where she enjoys writing, reading, running, visiting sons on opposite coastlines, and spending time with her husband, Dan, and tranquil dog, Penny.